SALSA IN THE SUBURBS

First published in 2025
Published by Puncher and Wattmann
PO Box 279
Waratah NSW 2298
www.puncherandwattmann.com
web@puncherandwattmann.com

Text design and typesetting: Miranda Douglas
Editing: Ed Wright
Proofreading: Claudia King
Printed by Ingram Spark

ISBN 978-1-923099-63-0

A catalogue record for this book
is available from the National Library of Australia

NATIONAL
LIBRARY OF AUSTRALIA

SALSA IN THE SUBURBS

Alejandra Martinez

PUNCHER & WATTMANN

For my family

I am a good-looking gentleman in my early seventies. I like to garden. I like to walk, and I like to dance, especially the tango, although I don't mind a little salsa. I have been a widower for seven years. I would like to meet a friendly lady to share conversations and outings with.

Soy un apuesto caballero de unos setenta años. Me gusta la jardineria. Me gusta caminar, y tambien bailar, sobre todo el tango, aunque no me importa un poco de salsa. Soy viudo desde hace siete años. Me gustaria conocer una dama con quien compartir conversaciones y salidas.

LOLA

9 March 2012: Lewisham

I can't believe she wrote that fucking ad. Just like that she thinks Papá's grief and loneliness will be over. That's how Betty operates, when there is a problem, you need to find a solution. No respect for what the person is going through or if it's culturally appropriate. The crazy thing is that Papá is okay with it. He was more surprised that she wrote the ad in English and the paper translated it into Spanish at no extra cost. I'm still trying to understand how it happened.

I put the pen down, close my journal and pour myself a glass of wine. Then I flop onto the couch in the living room. Tonight, I have the house to myself. Leo is out practicing with his band and the boys are at friends' houses. Soon Kerry will be here. Maybe she will understand. I tried to talk to Leo about it before he left. He said I was overreacting. It would be good for the *viejo* to find a woman. Then maybe I could stop worrying about him so much.

The ring of the doorbell jolts me from my thoughts. I walk over to the door and nearly trip over a set of bongo drums. Leo and all his bloody instruments.

I open the door to Kerry's familiar smile. As she wraps her arms around me, my face is buried in her shoulder and the collar of her shirt presses against my cheek. I let out a sigh and feel my shoulders sag. Kerry rubs my back before she releases me from her embrace.

'How are you Lols?'

'Come and sit down and I'll tell you.'

'Oh, it's that bad hey?'

We wander through to the kitchen. I take out the last clean wine glass from the cupboard and pour Kerry a glass of sav blanc. I move the unpaid electricity bill and Leo's notebook, open to a page of unintelligible scribbles, from the kitchen table to make room for the bottle of wine.

Daniel's school bag is on one of the chairs and Alex's jumper hangs off the back of the chair nearest the back door where Kerry usually sits. I grab it quickly before she sits down and put it on top of Daniel's bag.

'So, what's happened?' Kerry asks, after we have clinked glasses and sipped.

'It's Betty. She's gone and put an ad in the Spanish paper for Papá to find a woman to go out with. Can you believe it?' I can feel the anger rising up from the bottom of my stomach to my face as the words pour out.

Betty, who lives eight hundred kilometers away and hardly sees Papá. My sister is so selfish, she didn't even return from India until Mum was on her deathbed. Now she comes swooping in to fix Papá's life. I'm the one who's with him every day and she doesn't tell me what she's doing or ask me how I feel about it first.

Kerry looks at me like she doesn't understand.

She takes my hand. 'Lola, this doesn't need to be a bad thing you know.'

Why doesn't anyone get it?

Kerry looks over at the photo of my parents, on the shelf, next to the cookbooks.

'She didn't ask him, that's it! You know your dad would never have agreed to it if Betty had asked him,' Kerry says.

'Exactly my point, you can't just do that without asking the person if they are okay with it.'

'I think now you have to go with it and see what happens.'

'And Betty gets her way as always.' Since we were children, Betty had been sure of herself. She didn't doubt herself like I did. She was able to tackle things head on, whether it was the mean girls at school or disagreeing with our parents about a decision they made for us.

Kerry takes a sip of her wine and looks at me.

'I'm going to tell you this because I care about you. You cannot control what Betty does and, clearly, it's hurting you more than her. You can't control everything Lola and that's okay.'

I'm suddenly aware of the overpowering smell of dog. Coco. I get up and light the candle on the kitchen bench. It was Betty who had also come up with the idea of a dog for Papá, to keep him active, she said, and get him out more. That was how Papá ended up with Coco the golden retriever.

The vanilla candle seems to shroud Coco's smell. I get up again and open the back door slightly. When Coco was a puppy he pooped everywhere, chewed everything, and dug Papá's plants. Papá couldn't train him. He couldn't leave Coco alone as the dog barked and whimpered and annoyed the neighbours. Now he takes Coco everywhere, including here, that's why the carpets smell of dog, which I dislike, but I do love Coco. When I'm having a difficult time and Coco comes around, it's like he knows something is wrong and he stays close to me, while I stroke him.

I'm angry but Kerry has disarmed me, and I start to cry. She tops my wine glass and crouches next to my chair and takes my hand again.

'How does your dad feel about it?'

I look at Kerry. She is still the same strong woman I met at university, just over twenty years ago. The first time I saw her, she had bright red spiky hair and wore denim overalls. She looked different to the other girls at uni. Most wore tidy pastel-coloured clothes, ribbons in their hair and had private school accents. I was fresh out of the school with the highest migrant population in the state and felt so out of place.

Kerry and I were in the same psychology tutorial. I loved the way she would argue with the tutor about Freud. He was a misogynist, she would say. Back then I had never even heard of the word misogynist. I hadn't even heard of feminism.

Kerry was a feminist and explained to me about the various types of feminists. The radical ones, who believed that men were the oppressors, they were mostly lesbians. Kerry was one of the socialist ones, who believed the capitalist economy was the oppressor, she told me shortly after we met. I wondered if I was a feminist.

Kerry lived with her boyfriend Gary, a law student. Whenever I wasn't at lectures or the library, I hung out at their house. Sometimes I think I learned more there than I did at uni. I grew up in a very political household, but one that was alienated from Australian politics. My parents had little English. They fled a dictatorship in Uruguay and landed in the Western suburbs of Sydney. Western Sydney in the seventies was a long way from Uruguay.

They found themselves without words in a slow, bland world still in its adolescence. My mother lost her youthful laughter and never regained it. My sisters and I learnt to interpret our new world and we became the ears and voices of our parents too.

I take a tissue from the box on the kitchen table and wipe my tears.

'The thing is that my dad seems to be okay with it. He might even be a bit excited about it.' I heard it in his voice when he told me on the phone.

Kerry's green eyes light up as she smiles, making the lines around them more apparent.

'Wow, Betty has really opened up a can of worms and who knows where this will take you all?' Kerry knows the fear of change is making me anxious. She was there the year it all spilled out into the ocean of anxiety I continue to float in. Some days I can swim and get places, mostly I float, and thank fucking Christ I'm no longer drowning.

'Betty is a cow. Sometimes I hate her.' I've stopped crying and a spread of dirty tissues sit on my lap.

Kerry knows my sisters well. When we were at uni, sometimes she made the journey from Newtown to Fairfield, by train with me, and we had dinner with my family. Betty was still living at home, she'd started her nursing course and was going out with a medical student from the Eastern suburbs she met at uni. Malena had nearly finished her law degree and was also still at home. After dinner, Kerry, my sisters, and I would clean up so that Mum could put her feet up and watch the news on SBS. Betty told us stories about smoking dope with her boyfriend and how free it made her feel. I can still see it now, Betty, dancing around the kitchen, pretending to be stoned. Malena telling her how stupid she was and that she was wasting her life away. Kerry explaining the theory of Jung and the collective unconscious and surely, he must have smoked pot. Papá shouting out from the lounge room for his coffee.

Kerry is right I can't control this situation. Betty has put us on this journey, and I have to see where it goes. Maybe I'm angry at myself, for been a scared spectator yet again.

JUAN

Fairfield

Lejana tierra mía
Distant land of mine
Bajo tu cielo, bajo tu cielo
Under your sky, under your sky
Quiero morirme un día
I want to die one day
Con tu consuelo, con tu consuelo
With your solace, with your solace
    '*Lejana Tierra Mia*', Carlos Gardel y Alfredo le Pera

My daughter is mad. She is always having ideas to fix my life. I know she wants to help but she really needs to look at her own life. I'm okay.

As I open the cupboard underneath the sink to take out the dishwashing liquid, a block of pink soap falls out. It's one that Betty brought the last time she was here. I have never used it.

Betty gave up a good career as a nurse to make soaps and oils. Not cooking oils. No, the ones used for massage. Where a stranger rubs a person. I don't like that. That type of touching should be something between a man and his wife. The soaps they take a long time to make. It's quicker to go to the supermarket and buy ten packets of soap in the time it takes to make one of Betty's soaps. I put the block of soap back in the cupboard and take out the Palmolive dishwashing liquid. I squeeze some of it into the warm water. I take a plate and put it in the soapy water. The water instantly warms my cold hands, but it is the citrus smell of Betty's soap that lingers in the air not the Palmolive.

Betty means well and maybe she is right. It would be nice to have someone to go out with, to talk to. But what did she mean; Lola needs some time for herself? That girl can't be left alone, she can't cope. When Leo is away, there are days when she doesn't even get out of bed. She needs me to check on her every day; to make sure she is alright.

Leo is a friendly, *sympatico* man, but a hopeless husband. He needs to get a proper job. One he can go to everyday, so Lola doesn't have to work in that supermarket.

I wash the last of the dishes and dry my hands on the old tea towel with the faded kangaroo. Lola is very upset. It was a mistake to tell her on the phone. I knew I should have told her in person. Sometimes my mouth starts and my head is behind trying to catch up. I put water in the jug and turn it on. I'll drink a few *mates* before I go out into the garden.

Part of me is a bit excited about what this ad may bring. Of course, I cannot tell Lola that. I'm an old man but I think I don't look too bad for my age. My hair is thick and white and I still have plenty of it. A few wrinkles around my eyes, but not too many elsewhere. My skin is good. I'm not fat. I am lucky. I can eat anything, and I don't put on weight. Lola is like me, but poor Malena is like her mother. Whatever she eats makes her fat. And now that she is in Italy and eating pasta every day, she must be getting very fat. That is why she is not in any of the photos she sends me. Only my grandsons and the *Italiano*.

The whistling jug shakes me from my thoughts. I pour the hot water into the *termo* and fill the *mate* with *yerba*. I'm using the small round gourd we bought from a street seller in Montevideo the last time Carmen and I went to Uruguay. I put in a bit of lukewarm water into the gourd and let it sit so the *yerba* absorbs the water. Coco comes up and sits beside me. He knows there will be something to eat with this. I walk over to the pantry and take out a packet of Sao biscuits. This has to go with cheese. I open the fridge and take out the cheese. Coco is standing beside me, waiting.

I pour myself a *mate* and sit at the table for my morning picnic. Coco rests his head on my lap, his begging eyes looking up at me. I give him a Sao biscuit and he takes it gently from my hand with his dribbling mouth.

My health is quite good for an old man. Of course, I have some arthritis and high blood pressure, so I take the fish pills and don't eat too much salt. I can't eat olives anymore. But that is okay, I've eaten olives for more than fifty years. But no more salami. I miss the salami. What I do sometimes is,

I take a bottle of wine and a good salami over to Lola's house. We share the salami, I don't eat too much.

Betty asked me about my diet today when she rang. I say very good. I don't like to talk about food with Betty. Eating is something you enjoy with family and friends, you give them the best. Food is for savouring. You can't do that with Betty. She eats beans and spinach with no taste. Her poor children have never tried meat. In a rich country and she doesn't give them meat.

I cut a piece of cheese and put it on a biscuit. Coco has finished his and his head is back resting on my lap. 'You want more, cheeky dog. No shame for you.'

The problem with Betty is she has never been to South America, unlike Lola and Malena. They understand. Betty was too young when she came here. The culture absorbed her.

My beautiful Carmen said we need to take the girls to Uruguay. I was scared. I never tell her. I say I need to work, we have too many bills to pay, we cannot pay for a holiday. The horror that the *milicos* made was too big. That was not the country I loved. Pain on the streets, silent stares, that is what we would see. The girls did not need to see this. I put the pain in a box inside myself and closed it very hard. If we went back the box would open and the pain would spread everywhere and what if I could not pick it up and put it back in the box? Uruguay was my life before, now I had a new life, I had to keep going.

Carmen always wanted to go back one day. She didn't feel her real Carmen in Australia. She left part of herself there among our scattered belongings, family, and those places so familiar to us. But I knew I could not open that door again.

Now Carmen is gone, and I am here. Juan Sanchez, with an ad in the Spanish paper. Carmen what would you say? Please forgive me. I am an old man. I always thought we would be two old people, together, watching television with the blanket you knitted covering our laps. We would be eating *buñuelos*, banana ones, they are my favourite. Drinking *mate*, both of us very old but happy. Oh, my Carmen, I miss you so much. You will be laughing to think of me with my ad in the paper looking for a woman.

I look down at Coco, his head still on my lap. I pat him gently.

'Time to go out into the garden *amigo*.'

BETTY

Mullumbimby

Lemon Myrtle Soap
Ingredients:
- olive oil
- coconut oil
- shea butter
- sunflower oil
- water
- sodium lactate
- lemon myrtle essential oil
- poppy seeds

I unscrew the lid of the lemon myrtle oil and bring it up to my nose. It has a sweet camphorous scent. I made this oil last year from the red myrtle and the camphor is much stronger. It's this strong citrusy fragrance that always takes me back to the first time I met Chris at Eden Nursery, where he was working.

I had only been in Mullum for about three months, and I was in awe of the place and the people. It was so different to everything I knew. It was fresh and vibrant, lush and green. I grew up in Fairfield in Sydney's west among a community, heavy with loss; imported sorrow seeping into the next generation. I saw it in both my sisters. Stories frozen in time, like the photos my mother kept in an old shoebox. That was my parent's story in that old shoebox. They had no story in the streets of this new country, and they were fearful of merging the old with the new. They clung to the old, afraid that without it they did not exist. I needed to escape and create my own stories.

I was staying in a community up in the hills and had become interested in growing food. Eden's was the closest nursery. I went there to buy organic seedlings. I was standing among the lemon myrtle, when a man in his late twenties came up to me and asked if I needed any help. He was tall and I had to look up to meet his blue eyes. His bare arms, the colour of golden honey, holding a pot of lavender.

'What's this plant used for?' I asked as I pointed to the lemon myrtle.

He explained it was a bush tucker plant used for flavouring foods, like you would use lemon verbena, except that lemon myrtle was a native. I remembered Mum had shown me a lemon verbena plant at her friend Alba's house. She said her mother made tea with the leaves when they had stomach aches.

I didn't know what bush tucker was but was too embarrassed to ask. He put the lavender pot down, picked a lemon myrtle leaf, rubbed it slightly between his fingers and held it up for me to smell. His hand almost touched my nose as I took in the citrusy smell.

'I'm Chris, by the way.'

From that day I visited regularly, following Chris around the nursery as he explained the various plants and what they could be used for and the best spots to grow them. He had a lightness about him, an optimism that drew me close.

I add the sodium lactate to the lye solution and set it aside to cool down. While I wait, I weigh the coconut oil and shea butter and melt it over the stove top on the old camping stove I have in my work shed.

I smile as I think of the time Chris invited me to dinner at his house. He told me he was going to cook me a vegan meal.

'I love vegan food,' I answered.

When I got home, I asked Maggie, one of the women in the community, where I was living, what a vegan was. She explained that they didn't eat animals or any animal products.

I became a vegan. My parents came from cattle country, where cows are stewed, roasted, barbequed. Every part of the cow is eaten, even the intestines, *chinchulines*.

I can't talk to my family about veganism; they refuse to see my point of view.

'It's a luxury only people living in rich countries have,' Lola and Papá tell me. 'When you're poor, you eat everything. You don't have a choice.'

I know that, but I do have a choice.

Chris became my anchor and I settled in Mullumbimby. Some weekends I would stay at his house, and he walked around naked in the garden. At first it unnerved me and then I too became comfortable walking around in my bare skin, feeling the softness of the breeze on my breasts and belly.

I add the olive and sunflower oils to the melted coconut and shea butter. It looks gooey and wonderful. I pour forty-five drops of the lemon myrtle oil into the soap mixture and stir the thick yellow liquid gently with a wooden spoon.

When I first moved to Mullumbimby, I worked at the local hospital, but I knew I no longer wanted to work as a nurse. At this small hospital, doctors didn't refer to their patients by their injury or illness, like in the big city hospitals, where it was the broken leg in bed four, or the gall bladder in bed seven. However, it was still western medicine, and I wanted more than that. I enrolled in an herbal medicine course. It had to be better than western medicine, it was based on ancient cultures that had been around for thousands of years. During this time, I thought of Mum. On the rare occasions where she sat in the backyard, after cleaning on a Saturday afternoon, and looked out over our suburban backyard. 'That is called *diente de leon*,' she said, pointing at a weed. Her mother made a tea with it when anyone had an upset stomach. The leaves could also be eaten in a salad. Some of the women in her town said it could prevent cancer.

One time she came up to my place and, on a walk, we came across lantana. She stopped to look at it, picking one of the orange and yellow flowers. She held it in her hand, twirling it and then examining it.

'It's lantana Mamá, a weed. The flower is pretty, but it's not good in the Australian bush.'

'Lantana, I know *mija*. My mother boiled the leaves and gave it to us to prevent worms. She would mix the flowers and leaves, beat and grind them in a wooden bowl with a pestle, then add oil to them. She put the mixture in a jar and after a few weeks it was ready. She would use it for ulcers, or muscular pain.'

Although Mum never said it, my grandmother was a healer. Maybe that's why I'm attracted to healing. It's in my genes. Mum said you had to make do with what you had. Medicine was too expensive to buy. Smiling to myself, I pour the fragrant mixture into the soap, softly remove the bubbles, and sprinkle the poppy seeds on top.

As I make my way to the house I can hear the phone ringing. I walk in the door as Lola is leaving a voice message.

'Hi, it's me. What the hell were you thinking? Papá is not ready for this. Ring me.'

LOLA

Saturday 11 March 2012

It's been three days since the ad was published. When Papá comes over today, I'll ask him more about it. I can't stop thinking about this. Last night I dreamt about Papá, arm in arm with an old grey-haired woman, with too much make up, high heels and tight blue skirt. It made me want to vomit. What was Betty thinking?

When I walk past the train station at Newtown, I see two buskers playing Andean pan pipes. The sound of 'El Condor Pasa', floats above me as I walk up King Street.

I cross the road and walk towards Vinnies. Outside the IGA an older woman sits on the ground, an old blanket wrapped around her. She is eating a pie.

I see Kerry and wave at her. She walks towards me, and we embrace.

'How are you, Lola? Are you feeling better?'

'I'm alright. And you?'

'Good. Now come on let's see what we can find you. Jeans you wanted, wasn't it?'

We wander past the racks until we find the jeans.

'Hey Lola, try these.'

Kerry passes me a pair of Wrangler jeans. I hold them up.

'They're low rise.'

'Try them on anyway, see what they look like.'

I wait for a change room to become available.

A young woman, with short purple hair and a nose ring walks out of a change room and I slip into it.

'Lola, how do they look?' Kerry asks me from outside the change room.

Her voice is loud, and it pierces through my thoughts of this morning's dream. I can't let it go. The whole place is noisy and buzzing. Vinnies in

15

Newtown on a Saturday morning, what did I expect.

'Too tight and way too low, my undies show when I bend down.'

The change room feels stuffy, and I want to get out of there. I look at myself in the mirror, pulling my top up. The jeans sit just below my belly button and a small layer of flab hangs above it. Yuk.

'Let me have a look?' I can hear the impatience in Kerry's voice.

'No, I'm taking them off.' As I say this Kerry rips the curtain open and practically falls into the change room.

'Let me see.' Her eyes examine me. 'You look good Lola, you've got the body for it, flaunt it.'

Usually, I can count on Kerry to give me an honest answer. This time, however, I don't believe her. When I look at myself again in the mirror, I bend down just to check if my undies show. They do. I try and pull the jeans up higher.

'Stop it Lola, that's how they are. It looks sexy', Kerry tells me. She is now standing so close to me, I can smell the coffee she had for breakfast on her breath. The change room is closing in on me. I want Kerry to get out.

I look at her, unbelievingly. This is the Kerry that argued with every male lecturer at university, telling them they were sexist, and were presenting a patriarchal view of the world. Now she's telling me to flaunt my body.

'You sound like Leo, Kerry. Whatever happened to women looking at themselves through the male gaze, instead of their own? Now go, get out and let me get changed.' I push her out, harder than I meant to and she almost falls over.

'Shit Lola. What is wrong with you today?'

I'm irritable and everything is bothering me.

Kerry steadies herself and continues talking through the closed curtain.

'Lola seduction, flirting is part of the fun of a relationship, that's probably what Leo means.'

I stick my head out from the change room to answer her and as I do an elderly woman in the next change room walks out and grins at us. I can feel myself blushing. I close the curtain and continue trying to pull the jeans up higher. Why would anyone make jeans cut this low?

'Lola stop being so self-righteous. We're not in a women's studies course at uni any longer, just let go, relax a bit.' Kerry barks at me from outside the change room.

'Kerry, to me sex is a political issue.' I shout back at her.

'I know but also keeping your husband happy in bed is a political issue, it's what keeps a marriage together.'

I can't believe I'm having this conversation with Kerry and here of all places. My face is feeling hot and flushed.

'Is that what you do Kerry?' I pull the jeans off and throw them on the floor.

Kerry continues talking through the curtain. 'I know it's necessary to keep it all together. It got us there in the first place. You need to think of it as an investment. The more you invest, the happier he will be and more likely to do the things you want.'

Where is Kerry? Some sort of Stepford wife has invaded her body and brain. I pull my old jeans back on, relieved that they come up to my waist, tucking my roll of flab away neatly. I pull the curtain across and look at Kerry.

'You might be happy to compromise, or invest as you call it, but I don't want to. I am not showing my undies so that Leo will watch less television or stop playing his guitar and talk to his son. I can't do it, it's not me.'

I walk outside the change room and put the low-cut jeans back on the five-dollar rack. Kerry walks behind me. The shop is now much busier than when we came in. It's mostly women. What I love about op shops is that you never know what you might find. It's often nothing that you're looking for but when you find a piece of clothing or an item for the house, you feel like you've won something. There's this burst of happiness that I get that I found this before anyone else. It's this thrill that keeps you going back. It's hip to go to op shops now. In Fairfield in the late seventies, everyone went to op shops, out of necessity not hipness. We were looking for a cheap pair of shoes, jeans, or a dress. Malena felt the shame. She was in the midst of a fragile adolescence, every emotion permeating through each layer of protection. Mamá didn't understand, she told her to stop being ridiculous, there's no shame in being poor. In fact, if it wasn't for the working class the world would come to a stop. Malena didn't respond. She would keep her head down and try to become as small as possible. She never argued with Mamá or Papá. I think this compliance paved her way to depression. Betty and I laughed as we tried on clothes that were too big, too colourful, failed fashion.

'Let's go grab a coffee,' Kerry suggests.

'I can't, Dad's coming over, come and have coffee at my place.'

After I say this, I realise that I'm angry at Kerry. But I want my friend back and the Stepford wife to die. Almost as if she can sense what I'm thinking Kerry puts her arm around me, and I lean in and put my head against her shoulder.

'You need to relax Lola; the stress is going to make you sick again. Let's get out of here.'

Papá said he would come over today at 11.30am. It is now 11.15am. He is never late. I know that if he arrived and I wasn't there he would start panicking. He doesn't think *she's running late*, or *she's stuck in traffic*. It's always *a disaster has occurred!*

He has a key to my house, so he can let himself in, but I'm still anxious about being late. The boys and Leo are at soccer, so there's no one home.

I run two red lights. Kerry is driving behind me. She stops for the light, and I lose sight of her for the rest of the drive home.

When I finally open the door to the old terrace on Newington Road, I can hear Papá talking to Coco.

'*Hola*, Papá, it's me and Kerry's just behind me,' I shout out.

Papá comes towards me, with Coco close behind him.

I kiss Papá on the cheek, and he gives me a hug. Coco is excited to see me and wags his tail madly as he pushes his head between my legs. I bend down to pat him. 'Good boy.'

'How are you, Papá?'

'*Bien mija*. My knees are bad. It's the weather. The cold is no good for my arthritis.'

Since Mamá died Papá is always complaining about pain. His right knee has been giving him trouble for over a year and his doctor has suggested a knee replacement. He doesn't want to do it; he can't go back inside a hospital. It reminds him of Mamá and all the suffering she went through. We walk through to the kitchen, Coco close behind us.

'Kerry's coming over soon.'

I take the percolator and empty what is left of this morning's coffee into the sink. I give it a quick wash and fill it with water. The coffee is still on the bench, and I ask Papá to pass it to me.

'Why you buy Harris coffee? It is cheap and bad.'

'I know Papá, I know. Alex got it when I sent him up to buy coffee.'

There's a knock on the front door. Coco barks loudly and runs to the door.

'Here's Kerry.' I shout out for my friend to come in. Papá walks down the hallway calling Coco back.

'Kerry, how are you?' I can hear him say between Coco's barking.

'*Bien* Juan and you?'

'Very good. Your Spanish improving.'

'I hope so.'

Kerry likes Papá. She knows he's a good man and how lonely he is. He's usually here when she visits. He always finds something to keep himself busy like fixing dripping taps, screwing the loose handles on the kitchen cupboards, checking the oil in my old Toyota.

They come into the kitchen and sit down. 'How is Coco? He looks happy.' Kerry tells Papá, as she pats Coco's head.

'Coco cheeky as always. You know what he do? I go to bed and then he softly softly goes to sofa and sleeps there.'

Kerry laughs. She catches me rolling my eyes as my father imitates the dog quietly climbing up onto the sofa.

'You spoil him, Juan.'

'What you mean spoil? I look after him very well. Cook him rice and pork, give him little chicken wings.'

'That's what spoilt is Juan, you treat him like a king.'

'Oh, I think you mean spoil like food that is no good.'

Kerry laughs and I roll my eyes again. Coco is lying at her feet.

'You want a coffee, Papá?'

'No, I don't like the Harris. I finish fixing the door in the back room for you. I know Leo has not fixed it.'

Why did he have to say this? Of course, Leo hasn't fixed the door. To Leo it's not even a problem, it still opens and closes.

Kerry and I watch him as he picks up the toolbox and walks away. The dog following close behind.

'Your Dad just cracks me up.'

'That's because he's not *your* dad. He drives me around the bend. He rings me three times a day and he's here every second day.'

'Well maybe the ad might fix that.'

I pour a coffee for Kerry and one for myself and sit down opposite her.

The unpaid electricity bill is still on the table. I asked Leo to pay it last week.

'I doubt it. He'll never get over losing Mum. The women I know that are widows, do things. They see their friends, go to groups. When I suggested to Papá to join a group, he said why I would want to hang around with a group of old people?'

Kerry's mobile rings. It's Ella, her daughter.

'Yep, I'm at Lola's. I'll be there in fifteen minutes.'

'Better go, duty calls. I'll see you at yoga on Friday. And stop frowning, you're doing fine Lola. You're lucky to have such a nice Dad. By the way I think he's right about the coffee. It's pretty bad.'

I walk her to the door and give her hug.

In one way she's right, my father doesn't shout, he's not rude. It's just that he's here, here all the time.

The ringing of the phone interrupts my thoughts.

'Hello?'

'Malena, so good to hear from you.'

'Yes, he's here.'

Do I tell her about the ad? Betty should be the one to tell her.

'Not much, working. What about you?'

'That's great, it will be good for you to be working again.'

'Hmm, I'm sure you're ready. An au pair? What's wrong with after school care?'

'I know you can afford it.'

'Yes, you're right, it will help with the kids' English.'

'She's from USA? You know the kids will end up with American accents. Papá will hate that. Do you want to talk to him?'

'Okay, I'll tell him. Love you too. Kisses for the kids and love to Gian-Carlo.'

I hear a drill coming from the back of the house and I go out to see what Papá is doing.

'Papá why are you drilling holes?'

'The door needs new hinges.'

'The landlord can fix that.'

'When? He never fix anything for you.'

He's right; the old Macedonian, who owns the house, rarely fixes anything. This house is his retirement, and he doesn't want to give any of it away.

'Leo can fix it.'

'That is very funny Lola. The only thing your husband can fix is a broken guitar.'

I know he is right. Leo will not fix it. He can change the strings on his guitar or the skin on a *bombo* drum, but he never fixes anything we actually need.

'Malena rang. She said hello and she'll ring you tomorrow.'

'Did you tell her about the ad for the lady?'

'Of course not. You or Betty can tell her.'

He bends down to pick up a screw, not wanting to look at me.

'Kerry go home?'

'Yes she had to get Ella. Do you want to stay for dinner? We can take Coco for a walk this afternoon before I cook.'

'What are you cooking?'

Why did he always ask that, it wasn't as if he had a better offer? 'Roast lamb, with potatoes.'

'Lolita, I buy frozen potatoes now. I found at the supermarket. You put in the oven for ten minutes and they taste very good.'

'That's great Papá. But really, it's not that hard to make baked potatoes.'

'Yes, but your potatoes are never crispy outside and soft inside, like your Mamá make them.'

I wonder if he ever says anything to Betty about her potatoes.

'Mamá used to boil them first. I don't have time.'

'What you mean no time? You having coffee with Kerry.'

He puts the screw on the drill and begins to drill into the door hinge. The noise drowns out my voice as I try to answer him.

JUAN

Sus ojos se cerraron y el mundo sigue andando
Her eyes have closed and the world goes on
Su boca, que era mia, ya no me besa mas
Her mouth, which was mine, no longer kisses me
Se apagaron los ecos de su reír sonoro
The echoes of her sonorous laugh have gone
Y es cruel este silencio que me hace tanto mal.
And this silence is cruel, it hurts me so bad
    '*Sus Ojos se Cerraron*', Carlos Gardel y Alfredo Le Pera

I look over at Lola standing among the tomato plants, by the shed. Her long dark hair blowing with the wind, hands on her hips as she looks at the plants. She bends down to smell the tomatoes. I know the sweetness will delight her. I watch her as she takes one and puts it in her mouth. The juice spills down her chin.

This year I have grown some spectacular Roma tomatoes.

Lola looks over at me. 'Wow, this tastes amazing.' Coco has walked over to her and is sitting beside her, looking up at her as she eats the tomato. Food makes people happy. If only this was enough for Lola.

My tomatoes are always good, not like those tasteless things you buy in the supermarket. I have been growing tomatoes for many many years.

'Can I pick the ripe ones?' Lola asks.

'Yes of course.'

I go inside and get a bowl for her to put them in. Coco follows me in and back out. I walk over to Lola and hold the bowl as she bends down and picks the dark red fruit. While she is crouching down, she takes an elastic band from her wrist and ties her hair into a ponytail. Coco lies down beside us, enjoying the sun.

Three years ago, I grow cucumbers. They turned out bitter, so I never plant cucumbers again.

One year I had a beautiful pumpkin crop. Betty was visiting and she cooked huge pots of pumpkin soup for all of us. I had pumpkin soup in my freezer for three months. After that I don't grow pumpkins again.

I like tomatoes. I try different varieties, and I don't use snail baits; I just pick the snails and squash them with my boot. I don't use chemicals. My tomatoes are natural.

'Not that one, it's too green.' It's too late Lola has pulled it off the vine. I like them to ripen on the vine, it makes them juicier.

Growing vegetables is like a meditation. It slows the thoughts. The focus is on preparing the soil, planting the seedling, or watering the plants. When I worked as an electrician it was the same. I concentrated on the job, and nothing could get in. When I was a boy, I do this too. I walked around Montevideo, looking at the *platano* trees and the sky. I watched the leaves dance in the wind, on those cold grey Montevideo days. Some days their dance was hypnotic, and it erased the gnawing of hunger in my belly.

'I think you should stick to growing these tomatoes all the time Papá. They are so tasty.'

I walk over and pick two that have fallen onto the ground and put them in the bowl.

'You think? The ones in 2006 were a good crop. Remember you made the pizza sauces, the best you ever made.'

'Yeah, they were good. But the Roma are just so delicious in salads. Remember how Mamá made us eat tomatoes when we were kids? She cut them in half and sprinkled a little salt and a drizzling of olive oil and we devoured them.'

'She was a clever woman your Mamá.' I smile to myself, thinking of Carmen in the kitchen and the wonderful food she cooked. How she could make something out of practically nothing and make it taste delicious.

'Papá, what did you want to tell me the other day? You left before we had a chance to talk.' Lola has stopped picking tomatoes and is looking at me, her arms crossed.

'Ok let's go inside, make some coffee and I tell you.' I give her the bowl of tomatoes to hold.

I take off my gardening boots and leave them at the door, next to Coco's water bowl, before we go inside. Coco follows us.

I wash my hands in the laundry with one of Betty's soaps. It is yellow and smells like lemon. This one I like.

Lola is already sitting at the kitchen table, she has put the bowl of tomatoes on the table, as if they were a vase of flowers. She is flicking through the local paper. She is sitting with her legs crossed tightly, wrapped into one long trunk, you can almost feel the tightness by looking at her. Coco is lying at her feet.

I pour the coffee beans into the grinder. Making coffee is a ritual. I grind the beans, so that the coffee is fresh, smells delicious and tastes good. I buy the beans from Joe, the Italian who owns the delicatessen. I like the mix of Colombian and espresso. While I wait for the coffee to brew, I boil the water to put in the cups to make the cups hot. This is very important because if the cups are not hot, your coffee will get cold and who wants to sit down and drink a cold cup of coffee? I tell this to Lola. She never does it, she's too lazy. She does everything quickly. She cooks quickly, makes the coffee quickly, and washes the dishes quickly. In this country everything is like this, fast, fast. Everyone is in a hurry. They hurry for what? Get quicker to their coffin?

Lola puts milk in her coffee so I must warm up the milk for her, and make sure it doesn't boil. If the milk boils the taste is bad. I tell Lola, you don't need milk in coffee, you can't taste the coffee. But she always has the milk.

Because of the high blood pressure, I must make decaffeinated coffee most of the time. I still like to have one cup of good strong coffee a day, so usually I wait for Lola for the good coffee.

'You want a biscuit, Lolita?'

'No, Papá.'

'Why not? You're not fat. Have a biscuit. I have Tim Tams.'

'No, Papá, I don't want a biscuit.' She closes the paper and looks at me.

'I'm going to have one.' I take out the packet of Tim Tams from the cupboard. On hearing the noise, Coco opens his eyes, gets up, gives himself a little shake and walks towards me.

'Just tell me what you were going to tell me.' She uncrosses her legs and taps her foot.

I sit down at the kitchen table, opposite Lola. Coco is waiting to see if I will give him a biscuit. I break off a piece and give it to him. Lola shakes her head.

'You can't give him sugar. It's like poison for dogs.'

'He likes it, besides it's only a little bit.' I watch Coco eat the biscuit in one bite. 'Do you want me to tell you about the ladies?'

'Yes, of course I do.'

'You know I miss your Mamá very much. She was the first woman I go out with.'

'I know Papá.'

I watch Lola, she is fidgeting, impatient for me to tell her. She has taken the elastic band out of her hair and is playing with it.

'When I met her, she was so young, so beautiful. She looked like a movie star. Elegant. Her dark hair tied up, she was tall and thin. I had to ask her father's permission to take her out.'

I remember how nervous I was, walking to Carmen's house. It was a blue house with a yellow door. It had a porch, where Carmen's father, Don Manuel, would sit to smoke his pipe. That day luckily, he was not on the porch. I stood outside the door and took a few deep breaths. I could feel my heart was very fast, ba boom, ba boom, like a parade of *candombe* drummers were playing inside my chest.

I looked up at the red bougainvillea, climbing up the porch posts. I took one last deep breath and I knocked on the door, ta, ta, ta. My knuckles were burning.

Carmen's sister, Gladys, opened the door and asked me in. I asked her if her father was at home. She called out to him, and Don Manuel came out, holding a hammer. He looked at me and told me to come with him. I followed him out to the backyard, where he was fixing a chicken coop. He handed me a box of nails to hold for him, while he stepped onto a ladder to get to the roof of the coop. We talked as I passed him nails to hammer a new piece of wood to replace the broken one. When there was a break in the conversation, I asked him if I could take his beautiful daughter, Carmen, for a walk in the park tomorrow afternoon.

'I was so nervous Lola, and her father looked at me, very serious and asked. "Do you want to marry her?" I was very surprised, so I say to him, "Don Manuel I don't want to get ahead of myself." He looked at me, even more sternly and said, "If you don't want to marry her don't bother; she can go for a walk with her sister". I replied, "Of course, I want to marry her." Don Manuel then said to me; "Tomorrow you go for a walk and in two months you marry." Then you know what Don Manuel say next Lola?'

'I think I do Papá; I've heard this story a few times.'

'He knew I was an electrician, but he asked me to make sure. When I replied I most certainly was and that I had a good job, he said; "After you are married, I will put you in business with a friend of mine." I thanked him and didn't ask any questions. From that moment my future had been decided. I was happy. I had had so much uncertainty in my life, I was grateful to Don Manuel for ending that for me. But he would never have agreed to me bringing Carmen to Australia, so far away from her home.'

'Oh Papá, Mamá had some good times here too. Now, tell me about the ladies.'

'Oh that. I tell you another time. Do you want a biscuit?' Coco is looking up at me, dribbling, waiting for another biscuit.

'No. I already said I don't want one, I want to know what you were going to tell me.'

'I don't want you to think I don't miss your Mamá.'

'I would never think that, Papá.'

I miss her more than my daughters can ever imagine. My heart has lost a piece that will always be missing. Carmen was my wife, my best friend. I don't talk about this with my daughters. I don't want to make them sad.

Now I feel worried about saying this to Lola. I get up and walk to the sink and wash two cups for our coffee. I know I must tell her. I go back to the table and sit across from Lola, I take her hand in mine.

'Lola, you know the ad that Betty put in the paper? I don't want you to worry, I don't want to get married again.'

Lola frowns. I cannot understand how this girl can frown so much. I look at her dark eyes, almost black. She has the eyes of the *Charruas*, in the shape of an almond. We think it is from my side of the family, but we will never know. When the Spanish came to our country the *Charruas* were slaughtered. Wiped out and cattle and sheep were put on their land. They say my great grandmother married an Indian.

'I know Papá.'

I pull my hand away and get up to pour the coffee. I pour it very slowly, giving my daughter her favourite cup, then I go to the buffet and pick up the sugar bowl. It is a ceramic bowl my eldest daughter Malena made in art class in high school. It is not very good, but we keep it because she made it.

Lola is very quiet. I look at her as she sips her coffee.

'Lolita, your sister is trying to help in the way she knows.'

It was our fault Betty was like this. Perhaps we gave her too much freedom. Lola is angry that her sister denied her culture. I am not. You can't move to a different country and expect that your children will not adopt the culture. This is what happens in life when you migrate.

'Why does she always do things without talking to us first?' She picks up the elastic band from the table and stretches it with both her hands until it is about to break.

'Do you want to know something?' I take a sip from my short black coffee.

'What?' The elastic band remains stretched, between her hands.

'Four ladies rang me. Two on the first day the ad was in the paper.'

'Four? What did they say?'

'One Argentinean lady rang me. She sounds very nice. She likes dancing. You know she said she is sixty-four and she goes dancing every Saturday. We talked a little, about politics, our children. She has three children and five grandchildren.'

I take another sip of coffee. Delicious.

'Are you going to meet her?'

'No, she will kill me, all that dancing.'

Lola laughs. 'Ok anyone else?'

'Aah, now you are curious. You know it is funny, they are all sixty-four. Maybe I say I'm seventy, not seventy-two.'

'And what do they sound like?'

'One was too old fashioned and religious.'

'How do you know she is old fashioned?'

'She said she is a very good woman, who goes to church every Sunday. She likes knitting and cooking.'

'So why is that old fashioned?'

'A bit boring, don't you think? What would we talk about? Knitting, God?'

'What did you say to her?'

'I say I am sorry, but I am an atheist, and my daughter is a lesbian.'

'You what? What did she say to that?'

'She hung up the telephone'.

I had not heard Lola laugh so much in a long time. It was good to see her smile.

'That is very cheeky of you Papá.'

Carmen hated the church, the lies, the hypocrisy. She refused to let the girls enter a church. Once Malena had cried because she wanted to go to a church in the country town close to where Carmen was born. But Carmen stood there, holding her hand, and told her, 'Look at that building, it is huge and inside it has gold and outside people sleep on the street and are hungry.'

Lola was twenty years old the first time she entered a church. The daughter of our good friends, Alfredo, and Rosa, was getting married. Carmen refused to go. She couldn't understand why this girl was getting married in a church. Her parents were atheists, political people. Betty argued that it was a celebration of love, and it didn't matter where it took place. Each person had the right to celebrate wherever they wanted. Lola talked about liberation theology and how not all churches and clergy were right wing. Look at the churches in El Salvador, they were for the people. Oscar Romero died fighting for the poor. Carmen stood her ground. She was a stubborn woman. Her beliefs guided her life. We watched the girls drive away and Carmen and I stayed home.

'What about the other two ladies?' She puts her coffee cup down.

'One is called Manuela, and she has two cats, Felix, and Freddy. You know I don't like cats and what will Coco think?'

'Papá, you're not going to take the cats and Coco when you go out.'

'Yes, but if I visit her and Coco can't come?'

Coco always likes to go with me, he gets lonely if I leave him. He is my faithful companion; I can't abandon him.

'Anyway, you know I don't like cats. And the names, so silly, Freddy and Felix, like little cute twins.'

'And the other woman?'

'You want another coffee?' I get up to make another coffee.

'No, I just want you tell me who the other woman is?'

'She is Italian. She lived in Argentina for many years. She was a teacher. Now she is old and looks after her grandchildren. Five grandchildren'.

'Are you going to meet her?'

'No. Too many grandchildren. What will Alex and Daniel think?'

'Papá, you have seven grandchildren. What does that matter? You are just going out with her, we're not all going.'

'Yes, but think of Christmas, how will I buy so many presents? Any way not an Italian for me. I don't like pasta too much. She sounded like a nice lady. Very educated.'

'So, we have to wait and see who will ring you next.' Lola smiles.

'Now you are curious.'

'If you're happy about it, then I'm happy for you. I know it doesn't mean you loved Mamá less. It might be good for you to have someone to go out with. Haven't I always said, go to a group, meet people?'

'Yes, but this isn't going to play bingo with some old people.'

'I know, but it will get you out. I'm happy for you Papá. I mean it. I still think Betty did the wrong thing not asking you first though. Does Malena know yet?'

'No, I will tell her when she rings.'

She will probably find it hard. She was very close to Carmen.

'Enough of me. How is Leo and the boys?' Lola has got up and is stretching. She bends down and her clasped hands are behind her, high up in the air. How can she do that? She lowers her arms and unclasps her hands.

'Good. Leo is going to Canberra next month on a tour with the band.'

'Canberra that is very nice. Are you going too?'

We took the girls to Canberra one year. Malena was studying about the Australian government at school, and she would come home and explain to Carmen and me how the Parliament worked. It was complicated with the lower and upper houses. We could not understand why Australia had the Queen in their politics. To not be a republic was shameful, how this country was proud, was incomprehensible. One Saturday it was very cold, and we were sitting at home drinking *mate* and talking about what Malena wanted to do when she finished school. Carmen was making *pollo con arroz* and as she was stirring the pot, she looked at us and suggested we go to Canberra. Thirty minutes later we were in the car. When we arrived in Canberra, we found out that the Parliament was not open to the public on Saturday. Malena suggested we go to the Art Gallery instead.

'No, I don't want to leave the boys. I think they need me. Alex has broken up with his girlfriend.'

'I can stay with them; you go to Canberra with Leo. Remember when we went to Canberra, and we went to the art gallery? We saw that painting called Blue Poles, that looked like someone had splattered paint everywhere. Malena said it was art and we didn't understand it. Betty said she could paint that, and Malena was upset that we couldn't appreciate art.'

'How could I forget; we spent the night in the car, freezing. You said we couldn't afford a hotel and it was too late to drive home.'

This makes me laugh. It was an adventure, more than I ever had in my childhood. During the night we stopped in the parking lot of a shopping centre. As soon as the shops opened, we were there drinking coffee and eating bad croissants. Lola frowns.

'Lola it was funny, remember how we told jokes until we fell asleep?'

'We were embarrassed Papá, and I was scared too.'

'But we made it a good memory. You can't take everything so serious, that is what makes you stressed. Life is long and many difficulties will happen. It's not good to be upset about every small thing. Go to Canberra, enjoy yourself.'

'I don't want to go to Canberra with Leo, I'm going to stay with the boys. I don't think you and Mamá understood how hard it was for us.'

'Because you cry all the time Lola, you don't understand how lucky you are. We took you on a holiday and you complained. You went on a camp for school, and you cried and wanted to come home. You have food and clothes; you have education and a family. You live in a country where you are safe. Think of all the good things in your life, *mija*.'

She gets up, the elastic band in her hand now broken, stretched to destruction by despair and despondency.

'I better get going. I'm meeting Kerry. Do you want to come for dinner tomorrow?'

'No, I'm going to Betty's for Grandparents Day at the school *mija*.'

'What! You didn't tell me that. You're driving up there tomorrow?'

I thought I told her last week when Betty rang me. Maybe I forgot.

'You don't need to worry Lola. I will leave very early. I take my food and I stop at the rest areas with Coco. He keeps me company and Gardel of course. I have all my tango CDs ready in the car.'

'Ring me when you get there and stop every two hours.'

I get up from the chair. Coco pricks his ears as soon as he hears the chair scrape on the floor. He stretches, gets up and gives himself a little shake.

We walk through the lounge room and to the front door, Coco behind me.

I give Lola a big hug. I wish my love was enough. She manages to smile slightly.

I walk her to the car, and she opens the door and gets in her old Toyota. I helped her find that one, it's been a good reliable car.

'Keep me up to date with the lady callers too.' She shouts out as she waves goodbye.

'I will. Bye Lolita.'

I wave as she drives off down the road. I feel relieved that she is not so angry about the ad. I don't want to add to her worries.

Carmen was the love of my life. Nobody can replace her, Lola knows this. Nearly forty years until that cancer took her away. She didn't smoke, she didn't drink, didn't even like to play cards. But she loved to dance. Oh, how we danced. Every Saturday before the girls were born, we would go to 'La Sala', one of the biggest dance halls in the city. The bands played everything, rumba, salsa, cumbia, a bit of tango. Carmen would be smiling, her long black hair tied up into a bun. Afterwards we would go for pizza. When we got home, we were exhausted and happy.

She was a good woman. Australia killed her. Ate away at her, month by month, year by year. It was my decision to come here. She hadn't wanted to. But I knew it wouldn't be safe to stay. Her brother was missing, our friend Elena was in jail.

Lola was nine. She complained she had been robbed of her culture. But she was alive; and she didn't see the violence, the blood that I saw on my brother-in-law's wall.

I wanted to protect them. I wanted to go as far away as possible from the horror I saw. Australia was an unknown, it was far, it would be safe.

Three days after we arrived, I went to work. I went to a factory and said, 'me job'. Only two words and I was on the assembly line, pouring hot plastic into moulds.

Greeks, Turks, Latinos, Macedonians, we all work together. Here we are all the same, 'wogs', here to work.

BETTY

Lavender Oil
Ingredients:
- Dried lavender
- Carrier oil of your choice (I use olive oil and almond oil)

As I open the shed door the smell of lavender jumps out. The drying plants hang like purple fairy lights.

Last night Papá rang to tell me he will leave early and should be here around six in the evening. The kids, especially Sunshine, are excited. She told her teacher her Grandad speaks Spanish. She is so proud about this.

We talked about the ad too. He is chuffed that women are ringing him. I'm so relieved. It could have backfired on me. When I spoke to him, he sounded excited. He was like a child telling a story, amazed that it was real, that it was happening to him. He told me about the Cuban woman. She was a widow. He said they had been talking about their grandchildren. The sports the kids played; how terrible it was that they didn't speak Spanish. How beautiful Australia was, how clean the parks, not like in Latin America.

He told the Cuban woman about his tomato plants. She seemed to know about the various types of tomatoes. This pleased him greatly.

I pull the dry lavender bunches down and place them on the bench. I cut the flowers gently. The smell is heavenly. A floral, woody smell that makes me feel like I'm floating.

The Cuban woman told him she owned a restaurant in Paddington she had opened with her husband and now her son had taken it over. They talked about food, what they loved to eat and how hard you had to work in Australia to start all over again.

They were arranging where to meet. She suggested her restaurant. He didn't drive to the city. There was nowhere to park. He didn't catch public transport either. It confused him.

I line up the glass jars and start filling them with the purple flowers, each one about three quarters full.

The Cuban said the public transport in her country was a disaster since the dictatorship. She wished it would end, so people could live decently again. What did she mean the dictatorship? There were no dictatorships in Latin America now. What is she talking about?

Cuba of course.

What! Fidel has given the people of Cuba everything. Free education, free health care, decent housing.

She called him a communist. And he called her a Yankee arse-licking *gusana*. He was still fuming when he told me the story.

I told him that it shouldn't matter what the politics of their countries were. They were both migrants living in Australia. They probably had more in common because of that.

Papá said I'm naïve. 'You think like an *Australiana*. Politics is not voting on election day; it is in your blood. You're either on the left or on the right. With the people or with the bosses.'

I take a bottle of almond oil and one of olive oil. I mix them together, the sweetness of the almond with the richness of the heavy olive makes it perfect for skin care.

My parents, well, now just my father, have a black and white view of the world. I don't like it. Everything is right or wrong, good, or bad. Religion is bad, making money is bad, unions are good, public schools are good, private schools are bad. My parents complained when I decided to send my children to a Steiner school.

It's a private school; it goes against everything we fought for. Education should be free for every child; you shouldn't be supporting private schools; my father had yelled down the phone.

It's an education system I believe in. The public school system is harsh; children are made to grow up too quickly. They're institutionalised. They lose their creativity and uniqueness. Steiner schools nurture the child; they let them learn at their own pace. They don't push them or rush them.

I like it that my children are not rushed like my sisters and I were. Rushed to bed because our parents had to get up early for work. Then rushed to school, rushed to read because our parents couldn't read English, and someone had to translate for them. Poor Malena, being the eldest, was pushed to grow up too soon. My parents needed her to interpret their new country. Malena went with Mum to the doctor. She had to explain what a pap smear was. She went to the bank with Mum and Papá to take out a mortgage. At sixteen she had to translate interest rates, variable and fixed interest rate loans, and how much they could borrow.

When I had my children, I decided I wanted to have time for them, and enjoy their childhood. I stayed home. I didn't want to be a part-time mother.

When the kids were little, we baked carrot and zucchini cakes and made playdough. We went for walks in the bush. We painted together and danced. They didn't grow up with technology. We've never even had a television.

When Skye was old enough to go to school, Chris and I decided that a Steiner school was the best choice. It was an education system with similar values to ours. The school was set in bush land and the classrooms were made from stone and timber. They had huge windows that looked out onto the bush. The teachers were kind and never shouted at the children.

In kindergarten they baked bread and learnt French knitting. They played music and sang. Skye settled in well and was happy. When it was Leif's turn to start, I worried as he was a very energetic boy. The teacher took the class on bushwalks and gave them lots of opportunities to move around. Leif loved school and adored the teacher. Then it was Sunshine's turn to start. She was a very bright girl who had taught herself to read. She became the teacher's helper and was allowed to go to Leif's class for some of the time to do the work they were doing.

I pour the thick oil mixture into each jar. The flowers are submerged in the oil yet floating. Slowly I screw the lids on the jars. I pick up each jar, turn it upside down and give it a vigorous shake.

Tomorrow is Grandparents Day. Papá agreed to come up. I didn't think he would agree with such short notice, but he did. I'll roast some vegetables for dinner as I know he will like that, though he'll probably complain about roasted tofu.

I take each jar and carry them over to the shelf, outside, near the shed, where it is sunny, and the oil can be infused beautifully.

Papá can teach the kids some words in Spanish and the kids and teachers will appreciate meeting someone from a different background. There are barely any migrants or refugees in Mullumbimby. The closest thing we have to multiculturalism is the German backpackers. Initially I liked that. I felt I was in a different country, the cultural melting pot I came from became the past.

I had drifted away from my family throughout my adolescence. It was difficult navigating two cultures; I couldn't slip in and out as easily as my sisters could. I resented it. When I had an opportunity to leave one behind, I took it and moved in with my boyfriend. I felt like a snake shedding skin, ripping the layers. I couldn't get rid of them quick enough. I didn't want the culture that had been plastered on me to leave any marks as I tore it off.

My new life had no boundaries or limits, and I threw myself into it. My boyfriend was loving. His parents were English, and he too was wriggling his way out of a difficult adolescence, young and unsure of his identity.

We fucked and smoked.

After lectures we would have a beer and smoke joint after joint. Most days friends would come over. We listened to Bob Dylan, Joni Mitchell, Van Morrison while we drank cheap wine out of a cask and smoked. Our conversations were often philosophical and full of yearnings or despair. Probably wanky, but at the time it seemed deep and important. Necessary too as I needed to understand the world in my own words, think of it with my own thoughts, as I disassembled the imported worldview of my upbringing.

Some weekends we'd drop acid and take a train out of the city to the Blue Mountains. During these times everything felt so alive, the trees looked like they were reaching out to touch our faces through the train windows. Holding hands was mystical and pure and our skin felt velvety.

I cried and laughed. I felt real for the first time in my life.

Some weekends it was speed and parties. Long, long nights of dancing, smoking and conversations.

During this time, I rarely saw my parents. Lola sometimes came out with us and told me what was happening at home. But I didn't want to know, I didn't care, it was a lifetime away.

Malena was judgmental. I didn't see her during those years. She had finished university and was working in a law firm in the city. She had met some Italian bloke and was thinking of marriage.

I didn't want to get married. Marriage was too serious.

The laughter and chatter of the kids coming home from school takes me away from my thoughts. I close the shed door and go out to greet them.

'Hey guys.'

They park their pushbikes outside the house, leaning them against the verandah. Sunshine runs towards me and jumps into my embrace.

'I told Melissa that my grandpa is coming to school tomorrow and she said he can teach us some Spanish. He can teach your class too Leif.'

'Yeah maybe. I'm hungry. Mum, what's there to eat?' His tall slender body, caught between a boy and an adolescent, constantly needs feeding.

'Make some avocado and bean paste toasties. I haven't had time to make anything, I've been in the shed most of the day making oils.'

'I'll do it.' Skye volunteers. She likes mothering the younger two. Always has.

When I go inside the house, the three of them are sitting around the old oak table, chatting, and eating. I pick up a basket from a corner of the kitchen.

'I'm going to pick some vegies for dinner.'

Sunshine jumps of her chair. 'I'll come with you Mumma.'

We go out into the garden and wander through the vegie patch. We pick purple beans from the vines, some silver beet and a small blue pumpkin. Sunshine seems to be eating more beans than she is putting in the basket.

'I'm going to swing,' she says and skips off then climbs onto the old tyre swing Chris has put up in the sycamore tree facing the vegie garden. The tree was there when we bought the land and when Chris saw it, he immediately thought of the swing. He put it up when we lived in the caravan while we built the house.

I take my basket of vegies and go inside to cook. Skye is doing homework at the kitchen table and Leif is sitting on the sofa playing guitar. Soon Chris will be home.

'Leif, can you go and get some wood and start the fire?' He looks up at me, still strumming the guitar.

'In a minute.'

Five minutes later he puts the guitar down and goes out the back to get wood. The kitchen is warm as the vegies cook in the oven. I take out some sourdough that Wendy, my neighbour, gave me in exchange for limes. I cut thick slices and brush each one with an olive oil and garlic infusion I made. Skye dips a piece of bread in the oil and pops it in her mouth.

'Yum. Mum can I go to Willow's place on the weekend? She's having an early Winter solstice party.'

'That's very early, we've only just begun Autumn.'

'It's her birthday and she really wants a Winter solstice theme. We're going to dress as witches and sleep out by the fire.'

'Interesting. I guess you can go.' Willow and Skye have known each other all their lives. I met Willow's mother, Kara, at a nursing mothers' group when the girls were babies and we've remained good friends.

'I can hear your dad coming.'

Chris walks in and hands me an enormous bouquet of rosemary as he bends down to kiss me.

'For your next oil batch. We have so much growing at the moment.'

I take the bouquet up to my nose and inhale the piney, woody aroma.

'I'll throw some in with the vegies in the oven. Go take a shower, my Dad will be here soon.'

'This was in the letter box.' He hands me a post card of the Eiffel Tower. I turn it over. It's from Malena.

'Hi Betty, Chris, Leif, Skye and Sunshine,

Greetings from Paris. The kids and I tagged along to GC's work trip. It's been so long since we left Rome. Paris is a beautiful city. I hope you get to visit it one day. The kids have not stopped eating crepes since we arrived. You buy them on the streets, full of hazelnut, just like Nutella. Hope you are all well. Lots of love Malena.'

I put the card down, on the kitchen bench, Eiffel Tower side facing down.

They probably flew there too. No regard for increasing emissions.

As I'm cutting up some of the rosemary, I hear a loud horn and a dog barking. Papá and Coco have arrived. The kids run outside.

He walks through the door. Between the kids, the dog and all the bags he is carrying, I can barely see him. I take the bags and give him a kiss. Coco runs off with the kids, as they throw a ball for him.

'How was the drive?'

'*Bien mija*, no problems, traffic was good. I'll ring Lola to let her know I'm here, so she won't worry, you know what she's like.'

While I set the table, I can hear him talking to Lola in Spanish, I catch something about coffee in the *termo* and at the park.

When we sit down to eat, I see how tired he looks. He looks older than when I last saw him, maybe even a bit smaller, like he has shrunk. His shoulders slightly hunched. When he smiles the creases around his mouth deepen. His light brown eyes, however, still hold a mischievousness as well as the secrets of his youth.

'How is the nursery business, Chris?'

'It's going really well, Juan, we have a couple of big contracts, so we may need to expand. What about your garden?'

'I have some wonderful tomato plants, I brought you some to try. They're very sweet and juicy.'

'I look forward to it. I have some heirloom seeds you can take with you too.'

'What is this heirloom?'

Chris smiles. 'They are seeds, which have been grown in one area for a long time, and the same seeds, so you could say they are purer. These ones I have are from a farmer up the road, his family has grown these tomatoes for generations.'

Chris is very patient with Papá. He is warm and kind to him.

I look at these men in my life. They come from such different places, one from privilege, one from poverty. They have been brought together by me. Two worlds, which otherwise would have never crossed.

After dinner Chris and I clean up and Papá sits with the children and Coco in the family room. When Chris and I go to join them, Papá is asleep, on the old blue sofa. Coco lays sleeping at his feet, Skye is reading a book next to him. Sunshine is drawing quietly at the coffee table and Leif is softly strumming the guitar.

The next morning, we get up early as usual. I'm surprised to see Papá up and with his head stuck in a cupboard.

'Betty, I can't find the *café*. All morning I look for it. I woke up very early, a rooster woke me up with the *kikiriki*.'

This makes me laugh. 'You know in English it's cockle doodle doo?'

He pokes his head out of the cupboard and looks at me seriously. 'A rooster is a rooster, they speak rooster, it's *kikiriki*.'

We both laugh at the ridiculousness of it. He's right whatever country they are in, roosters make the same sound. We just describe it differently, must be something to do with the sounds of each language. I wonder how Chinese or Japanese people describe a rooster's crowing.

'We don't drink coffee any more Papá. I don't have any.'

'No coffee? Why? What is wrong with coffee, you don't have high blood pressure?'

'No, I don't. It's not good for you, makes you edgy, irritable.'

'You think I'm irritable?'

'No, I didn't say that. I'm talking in general. Have a cup of tea.'

'Tea, only the English and the sick drink tea.'

'I like tea and I'm not sick or English,' says Skye as she enters the kitchen.

'Of course not, *amor*. What do you have for breakfast?'

'Porridge. Do you want some Grandpa?'

'Okay. I will have some porridge with my granddaughter then I will find my *termo* to see if there is any coffee left from yesterday.'

We drive the ten minutes to the Steiner school, passing by old Joe's dairy farm first. His family has been here for generations. Then comes a stretch of open fields, the solid rain this summer has turned them into an emerald green. Before we turn off for the school we go past a few houses. One of them is where Lily, Sunshine's little friend lives with her two mothers and brother. I turn right onto the dirt road, towards the school. Papá makes a comment about a dirt road to get to a private school. I pretend not to hear it.

I park the car and the kids jump out. I wait for Papá as he pushes his old legs out the door. Skye sees Willow and they run towards each other and walk to the high school buildings.

We go to the hall for the introduction. The chairs are in two circles, one inner and one outer and the school coordinator, sits at the front of the circle, the stage behind her. The school does not have a Principal, Cathy is called a Coordinator. She stands up to speak.

'I would like to begin by acknowledging the traditional custodians of the land on which we gather today, the Bundjalung people. We honour First Nations people's culture and connection to the land, sea, and community. I pay my respects to Elders past, present and emerging and any Aboriginal people here today.

'Welcome, parents, grandparents, and children. Grandparents, you are so important in the lives of the children. You hold the stories of our families.'

Cathy smiles. Her voice is calming. She is a great leader, strong and gentle at the same time. She guides with love and warmth.

'Children ask your grandparents about these stories. Ask them what life was like for them as a child, what games they played, what school was like.'

I think of Papá and his childhood. He played football with the neighbourhood kids; the ball was made of layers of newspaper tied together.

His only toy was a block of wood. He said it was a great toy because it could be whatever he wanted, a truck, a horse, a person. Every day he could have a new toy and go wherever his imagination took him.

Cathy talked about celebrating the richness and diversity in the room and sharing our stories.

I watched Papá as Cathy spoke. He sat with his hands in his lap looking up at her. For Papá teachers were practically gods. Neither he or Mum had been to high school, but they had wanted my sisters and I to go to university. It didn't matter that they didn't know what you did at university, what mattered was that we became *un profesional* as Papá put it. *Un professional* could earn money and have a good life. *Un professional* didn't have to get their hands dirty with grease, stand in an assembly line or clean other people's mess.

Malena was the first to go to university. Papá drove her there on her first day. He woke up whistling. Emotions erupted, joy, pride peppered with longing and nostalgia. Malena was a smart young woman and was granted her first choice of arts/law.

A lawyer my parents understood, but why did she have to do painting as well? She had never been good at drawing.

Lola followed in Malena's footsteps and went to Sydney University. She did a combined degree too, science/arts. By now our parents understood that arts meant humanities and you could do political science, which they were pleased about. My mother told all her friends she had two daughters at Sydney University. Neither she nor Papá could contain themselves, the pride they felt was overwhelming. It was too big for just the two of them.

I was the least academic in the family. I did nursing. My parents said I should have studied harder and got into medicine.

A morning tea has been organised for the grandparents. The children have baked scones in the school's earthen oven, which was built by some of the parents a few years ago. We go outside for the morning tea and sit on picnic blankets under the shade of cypress pines.

Papá is very impressed with the oven.

'This make the best pizza,' he tells one of the teachers, who smiles politely in agreement.

Pots of chai tea are brought out with the trays of scones. As one of the children pours Papá a cup of tea, he asks what it is.

'Chai tea, it's made with spices, it's very nice,' the child explains.

Papá looks unsure as he brings the cup to his lips.

'It smells like cat wee,' he says too loudly.

'Don't drink it then.'

He is so closed off to anything new, it irritates me.

'These scones are delicious,' he says. Jam dribbles on his chin as he eats the scones with gusto.

He congratulates the children on their cooking, saying how wonderful it is that they are taught to cook.

'Betty why are some of the children not wearing shoes?'

'They probably don't want to wear them.'

He looks puzzled. 'They are allowed at school with no shoes? That is very strange. When I was a boy my brother and I had much shame about our old, broken shoes and we still wear them to school.'

Leif's class recites a poem and sings two songs with Leif playing the guitar. In the middle of one of the songs, Papá whispers in my ear, 'I need to go to the toilet.'

I point to the toilet and explain it is a compost toilet and doesn't flush. 'That's what the sawdust in the bucket is for.'

When he returns, he asks me, 'Why does a private school not have money for a proper toilet?'

'I'll explain later.' Was I always going to need to explain everything about my life to him? Even a fucking toilet. It's exhausting.

Following the concert, the grandparents are invited by their grandchildren to visit their classes. Sunshine is the first to run up to Papá and take his hand.

'Come to my class first Grandpa.'

The classroom is spacious, with high ceilings and large windows looking out onto the vegetable garden. On one wall is a mural the children painted with a local Aboriginal artist. Sunshine proudly explained to Papá and I that the artist was an Arakwal man from the Bundjalung Nation. She said he taught them to say *jinggiwahla*, which means hello. 'Say it Grandpa, *jinggiwahla*.'

Papá repeats the words. 'I like it. Better than English. See how you open your mouth to say the word, not like in English, where people speak with their mouth half closed.'

Sunshine smiles at him, takes his hand and leads him over to another wall, decorated with the children's art. She shows him her artwork. She has drawn a tree, with a long trunk, detailing knots on the bark. The roots can be seen under the ground and the branches are dotted with leaves in brown, yellow and red.

'For this picture we sat outside and looked at the tree and drew it. Melissa said mine was very good.'

'*Mi amor*, how did you see the roots of the tree? The other children didn't see them, look at their drawings.'

'Grandpa, I imagined it. You can't see the roots under the ground, but they are there, I didn't want to miss it in my picture. Otherwise, it would not be the whole tree. How can a tree exist without roots?'

'You are right, Sunny, there is so much we cannot see when we look at life.'

'Come and meet my teacher.'

She introduces him to her teacher, Melissa, who asks him where he was from and how long he had been in Australia and why had he come.

Papá is used to these three questions. He is asked them almost every time he speaks to someone for the first time. He answers obediently, the answers sounding rehearsed, from how often he repeats them. Why he had come to Australia is always a tricky one for him. He told me he didn't want to say for a better life because that wasn't always the case. A safer life yes, but if you gave this answer you always got a smug nod; developing countries are so backwards, they are always at war about something. Mostly he lies and says to be with family here.

Melissa calls the class to attention and tells them she would like to introduce Sunshine's grandfather, who is from South America, where the toucan is from, and that he speaks Spanish. Papá immediately turns to me and softly says, 'There is no toucan in Uruguay, do I look like *un pajaro*? Do these *gringos* ever learn?'

She asks Papá to say hello to the children in Spanish and introduce himself.

'*Hola niños*. My name is Juan.'

The children are asked to say *hola* Juan. Melissa asks if he could say how are you? If he is asking the children he would use the plural, *como estan*.

However, the children would need to reply using the singular, *come estas*, but he is an older person, so they need to use the formal command, *como esta*. This I know. Spanish is fucking confusing, and Lola expects me to teach it to my children.

'I say to you *como estan*, because there is many of you, but you say to me *como esta* because there is only one of me, okay. If you are good, you say *bien*.' He simplified it. Smart.

'*Como estan niños*? Now you say *bien*.'

A chorus of *bien*, fills the room.

'You ask me now.'

Sunshine jumped up, with '*Como esta?*'

Melissa asks the class to repeat after Sunshine. Following the chorus of *como esta*, Papá, replied '*muy bien gracias*'.

On Melissa's lead, everyone claps, and Papá bows. I can feel his pride.

One of the grandmothers comes up to him and tells him she has been to South America, that she loved the beautiful people and the culture.

'Did you visit the slums too and do you think they are beautiful?' he replies. The woman's mouth falls open and her eyes are wide. She stares at him, not knowing how to reply.

I quickly whisk him to Leif's class before he goes off on one of his political rants.

Leif's class has a deck overlooking the valley. We stand and look out to the horizon. Papá finds it hard to talk to Leif. When they are together, they often stand in silence. The silence now is broken by Papá commenting on the amazing view. Leif wants to connect with him, I can see it, but neither of them seems to know how to reach the other.

Leif takes him to see his class's vegetable garden. I watch them as I talk to Ruby's mother. Ruby is in Leif's class. They only moved to Mullum this year.

I can see Papá examining every vegetable; the Lebanese cucumbers, the purple eggplants hanging like baubles, the Queensland blue pumpkin, and the tomatoes.

'Your father is very charismatic,' Ruby's mother tells me.

I've never heard that description of him before.

'Very good garden,' I can hear Papá say. Leif smiles at him and nods.

That evening Papá says it is good that the children do cooking and gardening at school. This is quickly followed by, 'Do they have time for reading and writing?'

'Papá, of course they do. But they also do other things. Practical things that connect them with their world.'

I cook a cauliflower soup and a lentil dhal. Papá eats quietly. Speaking English all day tires him.

We go to bed early, and I can hear him farting until his digestion gives way to sleep and snoring.

I'm happy that my children see their grandfather but I'm always happy for him to go home.

I don't hug Papá, the way Lola does. I kiss him on the cheek to greet him when he arrives and then kiss him on the cheek goodbye when he leaves. There is nothing in between. Sometimes I want to hug him, but I can't.

I'm afraid that this will happen with my children. I'm always kissing them, hugging them, almost as if I can't get enough of them.

Leif is beginning to feel awkward. He stays still, surrendering to the hug, his arms hanging by his side.

Chris and I are always hugging, caressing each other. Leif protests when we hug and begs us not to do it in front of his friends.

I find this difficult to understand, living in a place where so many of the adults show few inhibitions. We go skinny dipping in the river with friends in summer. Leif feels uncomfortable now that he's older and he wears his swimmers. He tells us we are disgusting hippies.

I know that modesty arrives with pre-pubescence. But I hate it. I tell Leif everyone's body is beautiful and there is nothing to be ashamed of. He says he isn't, but it doesn't feel right to be nude in front of everyone. He hates that his father sometimes walks around the house naked. It embarrasses him.

Ten minutes after Papá leaves, the phone rings. It's Lola.

'Has he left yet?'

'Yes, about ten minutes ago. Lola you're as bad as he is.'

'I'm worried. He's old; it's a long way to drive. Did you remind him to stop every two hours?'

'Lola he's not a child. You are not responsible for his safety.'

'You can be such pain, Betty. I bet you didn't even pack any food for him. You know he won't buy food. '

'Why won't he buy food? He's got money.'

'He says what you get on the road is rubbish and he hates sitting by himself to eat in a coffee shop.'

'Lola, your mothering doesn't help. He'll only get more dependent on you. You know that. Why do you do it?'

'I'm worried about him. If he doesn't eat, he'll be tired and if he's tired, he could have an accident. He would have been better off with your horse food. How was he anyway?'

'Exhausting as usual. He barely talks to the children or Chris.'

'Well, he would if you taught them Spanish.'

'Lola, we live in Australia, where English is the official language if you have not noticed.'

'You just don't get it do you Betty?'

Both Lola and Papá are hard work. When I was younger, I would put up a fight, but not anymore. It's arduous. But maybe a new female challenge will help Papá to chill out slightly.

JUAN

Quien tuviera dieciocho años
To be eighteen years old
Y anduviese en las reunions
And go to parties
Conquistando corazones
Conquering hearts
Con su porte juvenil
With that youthful demeanour
    '*Quien tuviera dieciocho años*', Guillermo Desiderio Barbieri
    y Carlos Gardel

As I look up at the night above, I see Venus but not the array of stars I see at Betty's night sky. The sky there is like a painting so bright and clear.

Last night I came back from Betty's house. It was a long drive, but I am happy to sleep on my bed. Betty has one of the beds they call tofun, or futon, whatever it is, it is very hard and uncomfortable. I don't tell Betty this. I enjoy seeing my grandchildren. I wish they understood Spanish. Sometimes it is hard for me to find the words in English. My memory is like a long dark tunnel, and I walk further and further down the tunnel hoping I will find what I am looking for. When I'm in there I find pictures and words that I don't want to remember among the mess of jumbled English words.

Tonight, I go to Lola's place to eat. It is easier for me to relax at Lola's, there's familiarity. I lock the door and Coco looks up at me. I know he wants to come.

Yesterday when we came back, he ran to the backyard and dug up Carmen's rosebush. That was very bad. I have to punish him. He will stay home alone tonight.

I start the car and the voices of Los Olimareños greets me. One of my favourite songs, *Cielo del 1969*. I remember that year . Malena had started school. She was so proud in her white tunic with the big blue bow.

The night is cool. Lucky, I have my coat.

I park the car on Newington Road. It is a busy street. Cars and buses drive past fast and noisy. I walk from the car to Lola's. The footpath is old and cracked. I find myself in the cracks of the footpaths of Montevideo. Carmen is with me, her arm linked with mine. She is laughing.

I knock loudly at Lola's front door. When I'm about to knock again a bus goes past. I try again. Still no answer. On this busy street, they can't hear the door. I have my own key, but I don't want to use it when Lola is home. That can be rude. I am not a rude man.

I hear music coming from the side window. Alex's room. The boy is always in his room. I tell Lola, it's not good, a boy his age in his room by himself too much time. The boys, they don't listen to Lola.

I try again, hitting hard with my fist. The paint is peeling off the door and a bit comes off as my knuckles knock on the door.

Lola comes to the door. 'Hola Papá. Why did you knock so loud?'

'I have been standing here for ten minutes. You are all going to go deaf with that music. Lola, ask him to turn it down.'

'I do but he won't do it.'

'Then make him do it. You're too soft on those boys. Tell their father to act his age and be the man of the house.'

I walk inside and Lola closes the door. At least the traffic noise is gone.

'Please, Papá, don't start. Where's Coco?'

'I didn't bring him. He was bad today.'

'What did he do?'

'He dug up the rosebush I put in for your Mamá.'

After Carmen died, I went with my daughters to a nursery, a big one, past Liverpool, to choose a plant for their mother. We bought a rosebush, with white roses. We came home and planted it together. I look after the roses very well. I prune them, fertilise them and every year I can pick roses to put in a vase next to Carmen's photo.

'I say to Coco, today you stay home, no visiting Lola and the boys. When I closed the door to go, I could hear him inside crying. I must be firm.'

'Good for you. A dog needs to know who the boss is.'

'So do children Lola, so do children.'

My daughters bring up their children in a modern way. They give them too much choice, always asking what they want to eat, what clothes they want to buy and wear. The children think they are the boss. Alex needs to respect Lola. Malena and Betty have strong husbands, their children know the father is in charge.

We walk through the hallway, past Alex's room. The music is very loud, and it makes my ears hurt. I thump loudly on his door. 'Alex, *mijo*, turn that music down.' After a about a minute, he finally turns it down and comes to the door.

'*Hola* Abuelo,' he says as he kisses me on the cheek. His head is hidden inside a black hoodie.

'Here take this to the kitchen.' I give him the shopping bag with the wine, the meat, and the tomatoes. I pull the hood down on his jumper so that his head is exposed.

'Why are you hiding in there *mijo*?'

He looks at me, takes the bag, pulls his hood back up and walks to the kitchen. He puts the bag on the table, then he goes back to his room. Lola looks at me and shakes her head.

The table is covered with dirty coffee cups, a notebook, a tin of Milo, and one of the boys' jumpers.

'Dinner's nearly ready, he'll come out to eat,' she tells me as she picks up the coffee cups and unpacks the bag I brought onto to the table.

'The tomatoes are from the garden and look I buy these *chorizos* really cheap from the Chinese butcher.' I pick up the chorizos and show her.

'They're not Australian ones. They're tasty ones. The butcher said, "You like South American sausages? I have very cheap for you." So I bought some. I cooked them for dinner last night. They are very good.'

I got some crusty bread rolls from the Coles bakery, then I cut the roll in half and put it in the pan to absorb all the tasty *grasa*. I put the chorizo in the bread, added some chimichurri and I had a *chori pan* better than the ones sold on the streets of Montevideo. Coco enjoyed it too.

'Wow they smell so strong, I can almost taste the garlic from here.'

Lola looks at the bag of chorizos, her wide nose flared, like a horse.

'Put them in the bottom of the fridge Papá. I'll make the salad and we're done. I'll keep the chorizos for tomorrow. I've already cooked *albondigas con arroz*.'

'Keep them for the weekend and I make a barbeque for you. Invite Kerry and her family.'

'We'll see.'

'Why not? Kerry likes my barbeques.'

'Do I have to decide now?'

'Lola, you are too stressed. You need to relax. I'll come and cook the *asado* and you don't have to cook.'

'Okay, Papá.'

I open the wine and pour her a glass as she stirs the pot on the stove, 'A cabernet sauvignon. Smell.' I hold the glass up to her nose. 'Good, ha?'

'*Si* Papá.'

We hear the front door open.

'Good, everyone's here. Let's eat. Dinner's ready.' Lola shouts out as Leo and Daniel walk into the kitchen.

'*Hola* Abuelo.' Daniel gives me a hug. 'I'm starving.'

'Juan,' says Leo as he shakes my hand. He walks over to Lola and kisses her.

At the table I sit next to Alex. I always sit next to Alex at dinner at Lola's house. Alex is my favourite grandchild. I don't tell the other grandchildren. That would not be kind. Alex was my first grandchild and I was there when he was born. Leo was away on a tour with his band. He was coming back for the birth in two weeks. Lola rang us at one in the morning. She sounded anxious. She told Carmen she felt like the baby was exploding inside her and she had wet herself. Carmen and I came over straight away, and I drove Lola to the hospital. I know Lola was very scared. It was her first baby and Leo was not there.

Carmen held her hand while Lola pushed. I stayed outside. I walked up and down the corridors. I didn't want to go inside. Women's business. We were there for twelve hours. I went and bought food and coffee for Carmen. The next afternoon the baby was born. Poor Lola was exhausted. Carmen too, looked like she ran a marathon with her.

Alex was a beautiful baby. A boy. That made me very happy. He was very long and had lots of black hair. When I held him, I cried. I never held a baby boy before.

I ask Lola what she will call him.

'Alex.'

'Alejandro, you mean?'

'No, just Alex.'

I find this very strange, like half a name. But Lola and Leo like it.

'How is school Alex?' The boy needs to talk, he is there eating not saying anything.

'Okay.' He does not look up; he continues looking at his food.

'You know you are very lucky; I had no more school after I was thirteen.'

'I know Abuelo, you already told us.'

'What about you, Daniel?'

'I'm in a band for school, you'll have to come and see us.'

'I will love to go. These meatballs are very good.' I look over at Lola, she is eating quietly. She looks tired.

Leo tops up my wine glass. He looks over at Daniel.

'You didn't tell me that Danny. When did that happen?'

Leo lives in another world. He is a father, but Lola has all the responsibility.

'Last week.'

'And are you playing bass?'

'No Dad. I'm the pianist.' He looks up from his plate and his mouth is red from the sauce on the *albondigas*. I give him a serviette. Daniel has been playing bass since he was seven years old. He has a gift, like his father. They hear a tune, and they can play it.

'Very funny. Well, what's the band called?'

'It's the school band. We do all the official gigs.'

'That's great Danny. I want to come and hear you play.' Leo takes a piece of the crusty bread and mops the sauce on his plate.

'What about you Alex? Is there anything I don't know about?' he asks, mopping up the sauce.

'No, Leo. No secrets from you.' Alex doesn't look up from his food.

'Alex, stop calling him Leo,' Lola tells him.

'That's his name.'

'I don't mind Lola. Don't worry about it. How is Alison going? I haven't seen her lately.'

Why doesn't he agree with Lola? The mother and father must be a team, otherwise the children will divide and conquer, like the Spanish did to the Indians in South America.

'We've split up.' Alex does not look up from his food.

'You didn't tell us that,' Leo said.

'What's there to tell? We're having a break. I told Mum.'

Lola stops eating and looks up at Alex. 'You didn't tell me if it was her decision or yours?'

Why does Lola ask this. They already split up.

'Does it matter?' Alex puts his fork down and gets up.

'Of course it does, did you want to split up?' Lola continues with the questions.

Alex has been going out with Alison since he was fourteen. They are always together. Probably a good thing to have a break. I think Lola is upset because she likes Alison. She is like a daughter to her. Lola buys her clothes; they talk and watch movies. She sits on the sideline with Lola when Alex plays football, cheering for him.

'Yes, Mum, I did, okay. I need a bit of space. Anyway, I gotta go get ready. I'm meeting Johno.'

'Where are you going?'

'There's a party at Aiden's.'

'Will his parents be there?'

'I guess so.'

Alex walks away to his room. Lola asks him too many questions. She is like a military interrogator. This makes Alex angry.

'What's for dessert, Mum?' Daniel asks.

'Crème caramel, I made it especially for you.'

'Dessert, you don't need it. Look at that little belly you're getting.' Leo leans over and taps, Daniel's stomach.

'Dad, you're being mean.'

'The girls won't look at you if you get fat.' Leo tells him.

Daniel is getting a little *gordito*. He will grow out of it as he gets older.

'I don't care. I don't like any of them.'

'Do you want dessert, Papá?'

Lola is standing, holding a flan.

'Of course I do.'

'Did you make a real crème caramel or out of a packet?'

'Papá, of course I made a real one. You know I don't cook out of packets.'

'You made the tin one that your Tia Gladys make?'

'If you mean, did I use condensed milk? Yes, I did. Do you still want some?' Now Lola sounds angry like Alex.

'I will try it. You know, Lola, your mamá she make it without a tin. She do it very quickly.'

'I know, but I'm not Mamá.' She gets up, pushes her chair and moans to herself.

Lola is always on the defence. I'm not trying to kick a goal, I only want to help her. She takes everything too seriously. Everything is not a problem.

Alex comes back. He has wet hair, blue jeans, and a black jumper. He looks older than fifteen years. He is a good-looking boy. Tall, dark hair and eyes. In the last few months, he looks more serious. Maybe this is good. A man must have a bit of mystery about him.

'Do you want a lift?' Leo asks him.

'No.'

'I take you, Alex.' I get up as quickly as I can in this old body.

'No, Abuelo, I'll walk.'

'No, no, I take you.' I don't want the boy walking around at night by himself.

'Do you want to have a coffee before you go, Papá?' Lola asks as she stands and walks towards the kitchen.

'No, I'm okay.'

'Are you coming back?'

'No, no. I have to go home. Coco is inside, he will need to go the toilet. Thank you for dinner. You know the crème caramel was very nice.'

'*Gracias* Papá.'

I get up to leave and kiss Lola and Daniel goodbye. Leo shakes my hand. Alex and I go to the car. He walks in front of me, his shoulders hunched.

He opens the car door and sits in the passenger seat. His long legs stretched in front. He puts the seat back, so he is almost lying down.

'What music you like, Alex?'

'Just the radio is fine, Abuelo'

'So where is this party?'

'Not far, just keep driving, I'll tell you when to turn.'

'You're too young for a serious relationship with a girl, now you can have some fun. This is good you are not with Alison.'

'Maybe.'

We listen to the music for the rest of the way. I tap along to the beat on the steering wheel. Alex taps with his foot.

'How you get home?'

'Don't worry, I'll ring Dad.'

'Alex, don't take drugs. Little bit of beer, wine, ok, not drugs, you go crazy. Remember what happened to Mauricio?'

Mauricio is the son of Cristina and Mario. Good friends. We came to Australia together. Same plane. They, like Carmen and I, were leaving our country, unable to understand the monster it had become. They were both in the Communist Party and feared for their lives. Mauricio was their only child. He was Malena's age. We all met on that plane, none of us knowing what would become of our lives. All we knew was that we had to leave, and Australia was a safe country. We could never have imagined the wounds of migration.

Our bond that started on the plane grew once we landed in Australia and we became family. Mauricio was like a son to me. I taught him how to change a tyre, how to check the oil on a car. When he was about fifteen, he started smoking marijuana. The boy we knew left and was replaced by a shadow that grew until darkness ate him. One day he went crazy. He got a knife and he wanted to kill his father. Cristina, his mother is a psychologist, and she couldn't help him. They put him on the pills to get better and he got very fat and stupid. The drugs kill his brain. I don't want that to happen to my grandson.

'Yeah, I know. Thanks, Abuelo. *Adios.*' He kisses me on the cheek and gets out the car. 'Abuelo, don't drive too fast.' He winks at me.

'Don't worry, Alex, you enjoy yourself.'

Alex smiles. Good. I haven't seen that Alex smile for many weeks.

He will be alright. Maybe he can come and stay with me next weekend. Alex sometimes mows the grass for me. I give him some money and tell him not to tell Lola. Lola will not like it. But the boy needs some money.

He is good company for me. We drink short black espressos and eat the Tim Tams. I practice my English with him, and he corrects me when I pronounce words wrong.

We watch old cowboy movies. Sometimes I fall asleep on the sofa watching the movie and Alex covers me with a blanket. I know he likes to come to my house. Lola is a good mother, but she wants to know everything. She doesn't understand men are not like women, we don't need to say everything we do and how we feel.

Alex is a good boy. He is very good with his hands. He fixed my old television and helped me to fix the washing machine. We do things together.

Lola just wants to talk to him all the time. She is very bad at doing things with her hands, so she is not interested in what Alex likes to do. She can't even hammer a nail. I try to teach her, but she shows no interest. She tells me if she needs to hammer something, she asks Leo to do it. But Leo never fix anything for her. Too busy with his guitar.

It is important to be able to do things with your hands. I go to work when I was thirteen. I work in a mechanic's shop, cleaning the tools, putting them away, sweeping. My first pay I give to my mother. She was very happy. My father was drinking more than working. She gave me ten pesos and told me to buy myself a treat. I go to the *almacen* on the corner and buy myself a litre of milk. I sit on the kerb and drink the cold fresh liquid, every mouthful bliss.

At home I fix everything for Carmen. Betty's husband, too, is very practical. That hippie can build, he has a fantastic garden and fixes everything. He even built their house. They made each brick, from mud. I don't understand why they can't buy the bricks, but Chris say the mud is better for insulation. Some of their friends help them too. I went with Lola and Leo. While we made the bricks, Leo played the guitar for us.

Malena's husband is not practical, no, he likes to talk. The Italian loves to talk and he likes to cook pasta *putanesca*. Carmen liked him. A good left-wing lawyer did lots of work for the unions. He makes good money and he makes Malena very happy. He doesn't need to fix anything; he pays the tradesman to do it.

When I get home, I feel tired. Coco jumps at me, almost knocks me over. I bend down to pat him, and he licks my face. He is very happy I am home.

'I know, I know, you need to walk. Let me drink some water first and then I take you.'

Coco understands. We both go to the kitchen, and he sits down to wait until I am ready to go. It is late but I will take him for a short walk. We always go to the same park. It is not a very clean park, but it is big. There is a very big tree in the middle of the park. Betty told me it is called Moreton Bay fig. A magnificent tree, commanding and strong. There are smaller trees in the park too. I pick up Coco's leash and he jumps excitedly.

As I'm about to close the door the phone rings. I don't want to go back in but what if it is the children in an emergency.

'*Hola.*'

'Malena, *mija, como estas?*'

'*Si*, very good.'

'Did you see the Eiffel Tower?'

'I wish I could have taken your Mamá to Paris.'

Do I tell her about the ad?

'When?'

'That is good *mija*. Finally, those *Italianos* recognise your degree.'

Coco is pulling the leash I am holding. He pulls so hard I have to hold onto the table to stop me from falling.

'*Mija*, I have to go. Coco is desperate for his walk.'

It's better I don't tell her about the ad yet. Nothing has happened so there is nothing to tell.

'*Si*, I love you too. *Abrazos* for my grandchildren. *Adios*.'

Coco practically pulls me along all the way to the park. I find a stick for him to fetch then we sit down on the usual park bench. Today I feel very tired, and it is dark. The lights in the park are not very bright and there are not enough of them.

I notice that Coco has gone, and he is taking too long. He likes to go and explore and leave his mark. But he doesn't go too far. I get worried so I get up take a few steps and, in the distance, I can see a small white dog yapping at Coco's feet. The light at the park is not good, nor is my eyesight. A woman is calling the dog, but the dog is not obeying.

I walk towards Coco and as I get closer the yapping dog comes up to me and growls. I try to kick it away and as I lift my leg I slip and fall onto my backside.

The woman calling the dog comes running. 'Here, let me help you. Are you okay?'

She tries to hold my arm to help me up, but I pull it away.

'Are you hurt?'

'No. I am okay, but it is your fault. You cannot control your dog.' Coco sits next to me. He knows I hurt myself. He licks my face.

'I beg your pardon. It was your dog that came up to mine.'

'To play. My dog he likes to play. If your dog is not friendly you need to keep him on the leash.'

I look at this crazy woman. She looks like she is about seventy. Her hair looks very bad. Too many colours. Like one of Sunshine's paintings. Her skin is like one of those *Australianas*, who has been too much in the sun. Even in the bad light I can see this.

'You are very rude,' the woman tells me.

'I'm not rude. You are a stupid woman that cannot control her *little* dog.'

'I've a mind to push you right back so that not only is your old arse on the ground but your whole bloody body.'

I don't know why but I start to laugh. She looks so ridiculous. The idea of her pushing me makes me laugh instead of being angry. This small woman trying to push me! It was strange to be laughing but I could not stop.

She laughs too.

'Why are you laughing at me?' I ask the woman.

'Why are you laughing at me?' she asks me.

'Because you look ridiculous.'

'Well, you look more ridiculous, laughing there on the ground. Let me help you up.' She puts out her hand for me to hold.

'I can get up by myself.' I stop laughing.

'You're a proud and stubborn old thing aren't ya?'

I realise it is hard to get up. I turn my body slowly until I am on four legs like Coco. The small dog starts to bark at me again.

'Quiet, Churchill,' the woman tells the dog.

After much panting and twisting, I manage to get up. The dog is still yapping so I yell at it. 'Shut up, Churchill.' The dog looks up at me and it stops yapping.

'Churchill. What a stupid name for a dog. Why do you call him that?'

'What's your dog called?'

'Coco.'

'That's not much better. Like Coco Channel. Churchill is a good strong name.'

'Yes, but he isn't a strong dog.'

'How do you know?'

'Just look at him,' I tell her. 'Come on, Coco, we have to go.'

'Are you alright to walk?'

'Why? You want to carry me?'

The woman laughs. She has a very gregarious laugh. 'I'm Frances.' She puts out her hand for me to shake it. I don't want to touch her hand, but I don't want to be rude, so I shake her hand. Her skin feels *aspera*, harsh.

'I'm Juan.'

'One', she says very slowly. 'Like the number?'

'No, of course not. My name is not one or two or five or any number. My name is Juan.'

'Well then, One, do you live around here? I'm sure I've seen you before.'

'Yes, I live five minutes from here.' As I go to walk away, I feel the pain in my knee from the fall.

'Where are you from?'

'I just told you; I live five minutes from here.'

'No. I meant what country do you come from?'

'I come from Uruguay. You probably don't know where that is?'

'I do. That's in South America. You know why I know? Because I like watching the soccer and Uruguay did well in the last World Cup. That beautiful boy. What is his name? It's For, For Forlan, that's it.'

'Yes, he is very good. You like football?'

'Yes, I love it. I used to be more of a league fan but I'm really liking the soccer. Forlan, so good and so cute.'

We are now standing underneath the light, and I can see the wrinkles on her neck.

'You say that to your husband?'

'He's gone, long time now.'

'He left you?'

'Yeah, he left me, he died on me. In the middle of dinner. Went to pick up a potato with his fork and bang. Heart attack. Five years ago.'

'Sorry.'

I put my hand on my back, it is hurting from the fall too.

'Yeah, me too. But life goes on. Can't sit and cry for the rest of me years.'

'My wife died too.'

'What she die from?' She has picked up the silly dog and is now holding it like a baby.

'Cancer.'

'Oh, the poor love.'

'I have to go.' I look at Frances looking at me. Her face is thin, marked with the lines of a long life, like the many rivers of Uruguay.

'Maybe I see you around 'ere soon, One.'

'Maybe.'

I am smiling to myself as I walk away. What a *loca* woman.

LOLA

18 March 2012

I don't need a job for stimulation. I read. I love reading anything, novels, biographies, magazines, cookbooks, newspapers, even the junk mail in the letter box. I do crosswords, anagrams, I keep a journal. Originally it was a dream journal. Part of a Jungian therapy program. Now it's a journal about my waking hours. A mundane sort of journal. It's a relief, not to strive anymore. I stopped trying to be clever and no one really noticed, except Papá of course.

I like my job at the supermarket. It's real. People need to buy food and I scan it for them and take their money.

Kerry is always asking me; how can you keep working there? It must be boring.

It's not boring. It's not challenging, but this doesn't bother me. There are no big expectations, you don't need to achieve anything, and you can daydream while you work. You've got a science degree, for God's sake, Kerry says.

'A waste, all that studying for nothing.' Papá's words. Not that he really understands what my degree is about. He knows I studied a lot and I'm supposed to work in a 'luborratorri'.

I like the safe working-class world of the supermarket. But if I'm honest it's not the life I imagined for myself. I wanted a big life, with travel and adventures. Mental illness stopped that. It created fear where there should have been excitement.

I rest my head back against my favourite cushion, the purple one with the mandala. It's 11am and I'm still in bed. Leo brought me a coffee earlier. I know I should get up. A slight fluttering just below my sternum is holding me back.

I put the pen down and look at the wall in front of me and notice the paint is peeling in the corner and, just above it, is what looks like mould. Shit.

The phone rings.

'Do you want silver beet? I'm at the fruit shop and it's very cheap. Ninety-nine cents for a bunch.'

'No Papá, I don't need any silver beet.'

'Why not? You can make *pascualina*, or *canelones*.'

Papá exhausts me. He's like a shadow. Always there. He stands next to me while I cook asking me questions about what I'm making or telling me about what he has read in the paper and how I really ought to read the article.

When I go shopping with him, he tells me what I should buy and complains about the price of things.

Kerry says its old age, fear of letting go of life, of those you love. The old need to cling on like a leech, sucking the blood from the young to keep them alive.

What does she know? Her mother lives two hundred kilometres away and she only sees her at Christmas.

Leo says Papá is lonely and I need to be patient, then he goes back to strumming his guitar.

'What about capsicum, they are cheap too. I'm at the Chinese shop, you know the cheap one.'

I know the shop he is talking about. It's owned by a Vietnamese family. He calls every Asian person Chinese, no matter how many times I tell him that is racist.

'No, I don't need any vegetables. I brought some home yesterday from work.'

He hangs up. I turn on the small television in my room. The midday movie will be on soon.

Men are bloody hard work. I grew up in a house dominated by women. Now I'm in a house full of males. They all leave the toilet seat up. They watch soccer and basketball. They leave cups lying around and socks that smell. They burp and they fart. They eat quickly and a lot. They grab me, they hug me, they shout at me.

I wash their clothes, change their sheets, and cook their meals.

60

I had wanted daughters. When I was pregnant with Alex, I was expecting Leyla. I had imagined a motherhood of chatting and watching silly romance movies together, of shopping for clothes and drinking coffee in cafés and talking some more. A house full of dolls and bags, and silly shoes.

Instead, the house was full of cars and light sabres, swords, soldiers and Lego Bionicles. Ugly monsters and soccer balls.

When Alex arrived, Leo was ecstatic. He said the next one will be Leyla.

Four years later Daniel was born. I became depressed and entwined in debilitating anxiety. The thought that I would drop Daniel when he was in my arms would not leave my head. When I went to pick him up, the thought surfaced. It became stuck like a piece of old chewing gum under a school desk. I picked him up quickly and put him in the pram. The thought twisted itself and told me I would upturn the pram and Daniel would fall out. I wanted to scream and leave my head. I went to therapy, where the counsellor told me feeling cheated of mothering daughters had manifested into a fear of hurting Daniel.

Leyla became entangled in the storm of my unconscious. I hated Leo. After all wasn't it the man's sperm that determined the sex? Papá said I was irrational. Leo said I was ungrateful. Malena told me to give it time, that this would pass. Betty suggested homeopathic drops and Mum, who now was always tired, held Daniel, as she sat on the old blue couch. Between them, Leo and my parents cradled Daniel, giving him the closeness a baby needs.

Three months later I still panicked when I had to pick up Daniel. My doctor sent me to an anxiety disorders clinic, as the counsellor with her theories on the manifestation of repressed emotions wasn't helping. At the clinic I had to hold a baby doll and pretend it was Daniel, while I learned to calm my breathing down. After a few weeks I had to bring Daniel with me. Papá or Leo would drive me. They would wait outside while I went in with Daniel. The psychologist would ask me to pick him up. Slowly I would bend down and take him out of the baby carrier. I was terrified. We did this every week and he watched me while I sat holding Daniel. My heart rate was so fast I thought I would have a heart attack. The psychologist was kind but firm. He said this was exposure therapy. The goal was to let the thoughts be there but not respond to them and they would start to quieten. When you're in the midst of it, you can't imagine that storm of thoughts will leave. I had to practice at home too, first for two minutes, then five, then ten, then twenty. Leo would time me, while Alex watched cartoons on television.

Eventually the terror started to shift, and I would hold Daniel close to me for hours. I bought a pouch so that I could carry him everywhere with me. I didn't want to put him down. I adored my sons, but I still felt envious of mothers with daughters. Like Kerry, whose Ella was born three months after Daniel. I couldn't see them. The first time I saw Ella she was nine months. Betty had a daughter. Kerry had a daughter. I felt cheated.

After a year and three types of anti-depressants, the anger finally lifted. I cried for the next three months and wrapped myself in guilt for having emotionally abandoned Daniel for much of his first year of life. Alex was about to start school and I had not even noticed.

Gradually I made myself comfortable in the male world I'd been assigned. I tried to kick a soccer ball, even when I thought football was the dumbest game ever invented. I read books about pirates and watched *Star Wars*. I read books about raising boys and cooked bread in the shape of dinosaurs with them.

Sometimes the anxiety came back, and I stayed in bed for days. When it passed and I was able to join the world again, I spent days cleaning up the messes the boys had created.

Leo escaped into his music. Music is his life. We are a mere distraction from it. When he needs a break from playing or writing songs, he spends time with us. Often, he's on tour with the band: Carlos, Rafa, Tim and Lisa.

The band has been together for over a decade. It's like a marriage. The ups, the downs, the arguments. When I first met Leo, I went on tour with them. At first it had been fun and then it became tiresome, the same faces every day, arguing, Rafa's disgusting jokes. Lisa's ego, needing the boys to pep it up continuously.

When I first met Lisa, I envied her. She was beautiful and she could sing. She and Leo had lived together for two years, six months of it in Paris. I hated her for that. I hated her for having had Leo before me. It didn't matter that Leo adored me, or that Lisa and Tim had been together for more years than anyone could remember and had two kids.

It was irrational. I ripped up any evidence I found of Lisa and Leo's history. The two of them on stage, singing to each other, the two of them holding hands in Paris. Lisa in a red bikini. I felt sure that Tim would approve, even if Tim didn't seem to be bothered by their past. He loved them both, he even asked Leo to be his son's godfather. It was incestuous, it bore holes in my gut, but Tim just smiled, hugged Leo and wrote songs with him.

I met Leo at a barbeque at the Latin American Cultural Centre. He was eating a *chori-pan*, made from the sausages full of spice and fat that we ate every weekend at our backyard barbeques. He was sitting by himself, feeding bits of sausage to the dog by his side.

He had thick black hair just above his shoulders. He caught my gaze and smiled. I looked away and went to sit with my parents. They were at a table with some of their friends. Some were the same friends they had flown to Australia with. On the plane they had bonded on their flight into uncertainties and unknowns, and their friendship had remained.

'Go and get something to eat Lolita,' Mamá said. 'There's chicken.'

'I know Mamá, I'm not hungry.'

Then I heard a guitar weaving its way through the chatter and laughter of my parents and their friends. I looked up to see the man who had been eating the *chori-pan* and feeding it to the dog was up on the stage tuning his guitar. His bandmates were also getting ready, checking microphones. A woman and three other men.

I wondered if the woman was his girlfriend.

They were introduced as Los Salseros and began with a popular salsa from Colombia.

People got up to dance.

'Come on Lola, let's dance.'

It was Diego. One of the kids I had grown up with. Our parents were friends.

Diego and I had grown up dancing together. At first with the South American Spanish Saturday School's folk group. Then as teenagers at the Uruguayan club. We could dance anything, the tango, rumba, cha cha. And boy could we salsa.

I looked up and saw the guy on the guitar looking at me. I quickly looked away as Diego took my hand to spin me around. When the music stopped, we clapped. Diego kissed me on the cheek gently as he always did after we danced.

I looked up to see if the guitar guy was looking. He was. He got off the stage and walked straight towards me.

'*Hola*, I'm Leo,' he said as he leaned in and kissed me on the cheek.

'*Hola*, I'm Lola.'

'Lola and Leo, I like it.'

I laughed nervously. 'I liked the music.'

'You're a good dancer.'

'I like dancing.'

'Was that your boyfriend?'

I laughed. 'Diego, no. I've known him since I was ten years old.'

He parked his gaze on my eyes. I tried to work out the colour of his. They were light brown, maybe even green.

'Would you like a drink?'

'Ok, just a Fanta.'

'Where are you sitting?'

'Over there.' I pointed to the table.

'Are they your parents?'

'Yes.'

That was over twenty years ago.

The phone rings. This time it's work asking me to come in to cover a shift. It gets me out of bed and out of my head. I get ready quickly, grabbing a piece of toast to eat in the car.

When I get there, Sue, who's been working there for over ten years, tells me there's been a change of plans and we are wanted in the office.

'The new manager is here and he wants to talk to all the permanent staff,' she tells me.

We quickly make our way to the office. All the staff are there and the new manager is talking. I try to sneak in quietly.

'And who have we here?' he asks smiling. 'Lola, I'm Lola.'

'Nice to meet you Lola.'

He walks over to me and shakes my hand. 'I'm Nick.' He thanks Sue for going to get me. He doesn't look much older than Alex.

'Sit down please. Now as I was saying I like to think of my staff as one wonderful team made up of diverse parts, all working together to make the team function effectively. I want to get to know you, find out how you like to work. If you have any ideas for improving how we work, I want you to tell me.'

He sounds like he has just come out of business school. Who is this young bloke trying to fool? It's a suburban supermarket for God's sake.

He asks everyone to say how long they have worked here and what they like best about their work.

Daniela, an older Italian woman, who works in the deli, and whom I really like says, 'It is good; I like to make the customers happy.'

Craig, who has worked here for more years than anyone remembers replies, 'Keeps me busy, out of trouble.'

Sarah, a new young woman, looks over at Nick. 'I love working the check outs.'

Sam, with Down syndrome, on the special employment program, says he likes all the friendly people he works with.

When it comes to my turn, I can't think of anything. So, I say, 'It's real, there are no pretensions, people have to eat, and we sell food.'

When the meeting is finished, Nick asks me if I can stay back for a minute, he wants to talk to me.

'Lola, I found your reply very honest. I appreciate honesty in my staff.'

I look at his blue eyes, his dark hair. He is attractive, and very young. 'I like honesty too, I don't like pretensions, they bother me. I like people to be who they are.'

'And who are you, Lola?' His eyes fix on mine, and they don't look away. I feel a shudder. 'What do you mean?'

'I mean, none of us are really who we present to the world are we? There's always more, you know, the iceberg theory that you only see the bit on top.'

'Maybe.' He is making me feel uneasy.

'What made you decide to work here?'

'It's a job, I needed a job, and this was a good one.' I take a breath. 'Are you having this little talk with everyone, or are you just picking on me?'

'Sorry, Lola, I didn't mean to pick on you, I was just intrigued by your answer. I like to know my staff that's all.'

'I better go; I've got shelves that need packing.'

'Yes, sorry to keep you.'

He brushes against me as he walks to the door. I feel something, almost sexual. The feel of his skin on mine stirs something.

Fuck, fuck, fuck. I can never let myself feel like that again. I cannot allow myself to come undone again. I've got my father. He depends on me. The boys need me. It scares me to even think I might feel like that once more.

LOLA

10 April 2012

Life is what you make it. Bullshit. I hate all that new age, blame the victim stuff, with its dumb slogans. 'Stay positive better days are coming.' How do you know that? Or 'don't be pushed around by the fears in your mind but let the dreams in your heart lead the way.' Easy to say if you don't have an anxiety disorder, or you are not worried about paying your rent, or having enough money to buy your son's school uniform.

I put the pen down and go and have a quick shower. As I turn on the hot water tap, my eyes settle on the mould growing in between the tiles. The bathroom fan has been broken for weeks. When I step out of the shower I open the window, then walk to the bedroom.

My old jeans are on the chair by the bed and I pull them on. The green T-shirt I wore yesterday is there too. I pick it up and smell it before putting it on. I'm just going to Papá's and back.

The house is eerily quiet. Leo and the boys left early. Leo suggested taking them out to breakfast before school. He leaves for Canberra tomorrow.

Outside, the air feels heavy as if it's about to rain. The car is parked up the road and I look up at the clouds as I walk to it. Once in the car I take a deep breath. My eyes follow the windscreen wipers moving from side to side, clearing the grime from the windscreen.

I look at my father holding the apple in his hand. A bite has been taken out of it. He turns it like he is examining a precious piece of gold. He shakes his head; in the same way he does when he's watching the news.

'Papá, what are you doing with that apple?'

'It is no good, not fresh.'

He places the apple in a plastic bag.

'I'm taking it back to the Arab that sold it to me.'

He shakes his head again.

'Well, are you taking the whole bag or just that one apple?'

'I buy only two apples.'

'What do you mean you only bought two apples?'

'I feel like eating an apple. You know apple is a very good fruit. It has lots of chemicals to fight the cancer.'

'Antioxidants, they're called.' Since Mamá's cancer, Papá has become obsessed with 'fighting the cancer.'

'Yes, that one. I read it in the newspaper. I not have apples so I go to the shop and buy two apples. But this apple is brown inside. The Greeks always had good fruit. The Chinese too have fresh fruit. The Arabs, they just want to sell you anything.'

I admire my father's resolve but scorn his racism, although like today his determination isn't always fixed on something worth pursuing.

'Let's go. Are you coming or staying?' He was adamant.

Do I really want to go with my father to return one apple? I know that once he has something in his head there is no point trying to persuade him otherwise.

'As long as we don't take too long, I need to leave soon. I'm working this afternoon.'

I wait while he takes Coco out into the backyard. The dog looks up at him in disbelief that he isn't coming with us. I watch him lock the front door. I fall into step beside him as we walk along the cracked footpath. He is slow. I sometimes forget he is old. He seems to have become bow legged in his old age. Maybe he was always that way; I just didn't notice it before. It's only since Mamá died that I've spent so much time with him.

The fruit shop is a short stroll. The place has really changed from when I was a kid. The Greeks have left, and new waves of migrants and refugees have taken their place. The milk bar where we used to go and buy chocolate milkshakes, from Con and his wife, Demetra, is no longer there. On our way home after school, when we had some money, my friend Debbie and I would pop in and order our milkshakes. If Christos was working after school, we sat in one of the booths with the red enamelled tables. Debbie liked him. Chris, as everyone called him, was in the year above us at school. He was part of the popular group, but unlike most of the others, he was never mean to anyone. We thought he was so cool, smoking cigarettes outside the school gate.

The fruit shop is spilling out onto the sidewalk. Boxes of eggplants and spinach greet us. As we reach the counter, I see fresh dates and pastries.

A young woman in a hijab is feeding a baby behind the counter of the shop. She calls out to the man packing shelves in what I assume is Arabic. He comes over to us.

He is young. I expected him to be older.

Papá takes out the apple.

'This apple is bad. Inside brown, look.'

He holds the apple up, too close to the man's face. The young man steps back.

'You want to change it?' the man asks. I smile to myself as I think of changing apples like you change tyres.

'No, maybe all apples you have are bad. I want my money back.'

The man turns to the woman and talks to her in Arabic. She puts the child down, in the pram, next to her and opens the till and gives my father fifty cents.

'I pay fifty-five cents,' he protests. 'One dollar and ten cents for two apples.'

Heat creeps up my face until I'm burning with embarrassment.

'Papá, *dejalo*. Leave it,' I tell him.

He does not move, nor look at me. The Arabic man speaks to the woman again.

She opens the till and gives him five cents. He places the bitten apple on the counter and walks out victorious.

I look at the woman and mouth, 'Sorry.'

'No problem,' the man replies.

I suddenly feel sad. It is only the little injustices that my father can fight. A lifetime of oppression is too big for all of us. I think of the little battles that are played out on suburban streets, with religions and politics colliding and how they can grow into big battles as young people fight for the passions of families' homelands and the right to exist in a world where no space has been made for them.

'I need to go Papá, I'm working this evening. What time is Betty coming?'

'I don't know, tonight some time.'

Coco is looking up at us and I bend down to pat him.

That night I scan and pack an older Vietnamese man's shopping, he reminds me of my father. When I ask him how he is and if he would like the laundry detergent in a separate bag, he nods and smiles. Everyone seems to be doing their shopping and I'm tired after standing on my feet for eight hours. The Vietnamese man is my last customer. I look at Sue at the register next to me. She too looks tired as she packs up her register. She's older than me, a good-natured thin woman, who life has treated unfairly.

By the end of the night, the staff have left, except Shauna, the assistant manager, and I, and Nick of course. In the office, Shauna is finishing up, counting cash. I help her, then we bag the money, and she puts it in the safe. Once we finish Nick thanks us for staying back. He is always very polite with the staff.

Shauna is headed toward the breakroom to get her bag. 'Coming, Lola?'

'You go. I need to go to the bathroom.'

'Okay, see you tomorrow.' I like Shauna, she is one of those no bullshit working class Australian women.

That's what I found so difficult at university; the amount of bullshit middle class people put out. They could never say anything like it was. How they dressed things up too, so many words to say something relatively simple.

I feel a little uncomfortable being left alone with Nick after our talk the other day, but I'm busting for a pee. When I get back Nick is waiting for me to lock up.

'Lola, I need to make some changes with the staff in the next couple of weeks and I'd like to run something by you. I was thinking, do you want to go and grab something to eat and maybe I could pick your brain a bit?'

'Sorry my brain ain't for picking tonight. I'm exhausted.' I look down and pretend to fix the zip on my handbag. I feel a rush of heat on my face. I'm turning red, and I can't stop it. Think of icebergs, I tell myself, and cold ice, maybe imagery will trick my brain to cool my face.

'What about just a short chat then? I promise not to talk about work for too long.' He looks at me, half smiling. Is he flirting with me?

What the hell would we talk about then? 'I gotta get home.'

'Oh, come on, just a coffee.' I look at his boyish face and the way his brown hair falls over his forehead. Fuck he looks good.

'Why? Don't you have someone to get home to?' Maybe the question was out of place. Too late.

'No, do you?'

'Yes, I do. My husband and children.'

'Can I drive you home then? I notice you catch the bus sometimes.'

'You are perceptive, aren't you.' I say, leaning back against the wall. 'But why do you think I'm the person you need to talk to?'

'You're smart, you know the staff and they like you.'

'Yeah, yeah,' I say with a snort of derision. 'Flattery won't work'.

'By the way, I meant to ask you, are you Spanish?'

'Depends how far back you go I guess.'

One side of Nick's mouth quirks up in a smile.

'Tell me over coffee, my shout.'

'One coffee only.' I can feel myself blushing, come on, icebergs. I smile slightly, unable to hold it back.

I don't know why I agree to go with him. He intrigues me somehow. He excites me too. He is so fucking attractive. Leo will be packing for Canberra. Danny will be watching television. Alex is spending the night with Papá, his Abuelo.

'Great, let's go. What sort of café do you like? I know. Something really arty, bohemian?'

'Are you stereotyping me?' I say as I follow him to the door. I observe him lock up and set the alarm. My eyes are on his slender neck.

'No, not at all.' He says it like he genuinely means it.

'Take me somewhere you like to go.' I'm curious to see what he chooses. My stomach is tingling with butterflies. This is ridiculous.

I'm surprised by his car. I expected something fast and modern. I open the passenger door of his Camry sedan. As he turns the engine on, he looks at me and smiles, a warm but cheeky sort of smile. Drake is singing. I've heard this music coming out of Alex's room. He taps along on the steering wheel. We are flirting and I like it.

We drive to Leichhardt and stop outside Tony's. An Italian café I know well. 'Why this place Nick?'

'Do you know it?'

'I do,' I say, opening the car door. 'Tell me what you like about it?'

'I like good coffee and I know I can get that here.'

71

'Good, me too.'

Tony's is an institution. The owner, Anthony Moretti, opened the café when going to cafés was the pastime of postwar immigrants and Australians looked on suspiciously. Older Italian men would come and drink coffee, play chess and talk football. On the weekends they would bring their wives and children to eat cannoli and gelato. The walls are plastered with football posters of every Italian team there ever was. Leo loves this café. He introduced me to it. Tony often calls out to him, '*Ciao* Leo, how's the music?'

'*Molto bene*,' Leo answers.

We find a table in a corner, near the window. I feel guilty and hope no one I know is here. I sit with my back to the other tables and look out the window. A young waiter, I recognise, takes our order. Nick orders a macchiato. I expected him to be a latte man. I order my usual piccolo.

'Did you grow up drinking coffee?' I ask him.

Macchiatos are for serious coffee drinkers. I think you can tell something about a person by the type of coffee they drink. Cappuccino drinkers are ordinary, mainstream, not questioning the order of things. Flat whiters are not totally mainstream, but not alternative either. They like to have a foot in both and often go where the wind blows, unlike the decisive, self-assured short black drinkers. Us piccolo drinkers aspire to be like a short black drinker, but it's too bitter. We need the sweetness of the milk, a little bit of whiteness to fit in, to be liked and accepted. We crave approval.

'No way. My parents were tea drinkers, we didn't even have coffee in the house. The first time I drank coffee was when I went to uni.' His gaze is on my eyes as he speaks.

'Where did you grow up?' I'm curious about him too.

'Waverton. What about you?'

'Fairfield, in Southwest Sydney.'

'Yeah, I know where that is.'

'You ever been there?'

'Umm, actually I haven't.' He looks down at the table and taps his fingers.

'Thought so.'

'What do you mean thought so?' I want to explain that when I see him, I see privilege, entitlement. A life not knowing what it's like to be on the outskirts of society. A life not having to explain everything, what you eat, or your name and where you were born, why you are here. Explaining to your parents how to access services. Where you never get a break. It is fucking draining.

'Well, you've probably never had a reason to go to Fairfield. People go to Fairfield because they live there or their relatives live there, or they need to buy something you can't find anywhere else.'

'Maybe you could take me someday,' he smiles as he says it, brushing his hair away from his face.

'So how far back does the Spanish in you go?'

How many generations does it take before people stop asking about your background. With the English, after the first generation was born in Australia, I'm sure this question was no longer asked.

'I was born in Uruguay.'

'In South America? Isn't that the country where the Australians went, the idealists, who went to set up a commune or something like that?'

'No, you mean Paraguay. They wanted a Utopian community.'

'Well, I was close.'

'Actually, you were about one thousand kilometres out.'

We are sitting opposite each other. The table is small, our knees are almost touching under the table. I move my legs to the side and cross them. I feel the high of flirting and the guilt of enjoying it.

'You like making me feel stupid. Why?' He looks offended and looks away.

The young waiter brings our coffees. I watch as he puts sugar in his coffee. On one of his fingers, I notice a small tattoo. I can't quite make out what it is.

I don't mean to make him feel stupid but his white middle classness annoys me.

'Sorry, it's not personal. Anyway, where are your parents from?'

'They're good English stock, very boring. My Dad was born in Brookvale and Mum's from Adelaide. Dad was a bank manager and Mum stayed home. We had roasts on Sunday, you know the usual. Tell me about your family, they gotta be different.'

'Actually, we had barbeques on Sunday too. We eat, we shop, we work, we shit, so not really that different.'

He laughs. His laugh is loud and open, unlike Leo's chuckle. This is his world, he owns it.

He leans back in his chair, holding the small coffee cup, studying me. 'Lola, are you going to tell me why you work in the supermarket? Did you finish school? Your parents didn't want you to study?'

'Nick, my parents were not some peasants stuck in the patriarchy. Of course, I finished school.'

'So, what happened?'

'Nothing happened.'

'You got married young?'

'No, but I am married. I have two sons. What about you, do you have a girlfriend?'

'Sort of. What's your husband's name?'

Why did he want to know that? 'Leo.'

'Leo, is he from Uruguay too?'

'He is.'

'Are there a lot of people from Uruguay in Australia?'

He is firing questions at me, eager to know, thirsty for my world. 'Nick, there are thousands of Uruguayans in Australia. Like other South Americans, most of them came in the 1970s and 80s, escaping military dictatorships. I was a child, my parents wanted to protect us.'

He taps his long fingers on the table between us 'Have you been back?' I look at the tattooed finger.

'A couple of times. A long time ago, before I had children.'

'Did you like it?'

I shrug and take a sip of my coffee. 'It was strange. Like a mix of loss and yearning. I imagine it must be like what adopted children feel when they meet their biological parents for the first time. You're home but you don't belong, who you would have been has died, who you are is a foreigner.'

'Whoa, that's heavy.'

I look at his hand resting on the table. It is very close to mine, almost touching. I can feel the electricity run through my body. Suddenly I want to cry.

He puts his hand on mine. 'Lola, I'm sorry, I didn't mean to upset you.'

'No, no it's not you.' While I like the feel of his hand on mine, I pull my hand away and wipe my eyes with the back of my hand. 'Tell me about you. Do you like being a manager?'

'It's all right. Maybe I'm naïve, but I really want to manage in a way so that people feel involved.'

'You're serious, aren't you?'

'Of course, I am. I thought I could make a difference, but maybe you're right. I'm just the young manager with the bright new ideas, which no one gives a shit about.'

I was coming undone. For so long I have been going, responding, doing. Now this young guy, who I don't even know, is going to make me fall apart. What the fuck was happening to me?

'Nick, I don't know what you want to change but remember you can't ask staff to do more than what is required of them. They just want to come in do the job and go home. That's what they're paid for.'

'What work did your parents do?'

He is devouring me with questions, and I'm letting him. I don't know how to stop it. 'My mum worked in a factory. My dad was an electrician.'

'What about your husband what does he do?'

'What does it matter?'

'Just curious.'

'He plays music. Come to think of it, I have to go; he's going on tour tomorrow. Early.'

'What instrument does he play?'

He is a monster; he doesn't know when to stop. 'Guitar.'

'Do you play too?'

'Nick, I really have to go.' I stand up.

'Of course, sorry. Let me get the bill and I'll drive you home.' I let him pay.

In the car the same music is playing. It's soothing. Maybe because of the familiarity from it spilling out of Alex's room.

He puts his hand on my leg as he drives. I awkwardly place my hand on top of his. His skin is soft. I keep my hand still, afraid to move it. It feels good. I want to cry forever.

I give him directions to my house. The front light is on. He stops the car and turns the engine off.

'I really enjoyed spending time with you Lola. I hope we can do this again.'

'Maybe,' I mumble. I get out of the car, close the door, and run inside, my heart is beating so fast and loud I can hear it.

BETTY

Rose Essential Oil
Ingredients:
- Pressed rose petals
- Jojoba and almond oil

Rose essential oil has anti-depressive properties. It's the sweet and spicy aroma. As the nose takes it in through to the olfactory nerve at the front of the brain, information is sent to the amygdala and hippocampus, where the emotions live. Rose has a beautiful calming effect. I'll take some oil for Florencia.

I walk over to my work shed. The cupboard where the oils are kept is made of camphor laurel timber. Chris made it for me. The second shelf has the rose oils. I take out a small bottle and walk back to the house. I'm nearly packed.

I'm going to Sydney. A funeral. Tia Gladys died last week, quickly and unexpectedly. She woke up feeling nauseous and dizzy. She called my cousin Florencia who picked her up from her house and took her to hospital. An hour later she was dead. Flo said it was quick and painless. Poor Tia Gladys. She was Mum's only relative in Australia. A big woman with a strong hearty laugh. The type of laugh that enfolds you and yields you to a warm familiar place.

I loved Tia Gladys, and I also liked her. Her house was a respite from the slogans brandied around mine. I never felt guilty at my aunt's house for not believing in all the things my parents did, nor for not finishing my dinner when there are children in South America that don't have enough to eat. At Tia's house I could just hang out and be a normal kid. In the school holidays I would go and stay. She used to give Flo and I money to go up to the shop and buy hot chips. When we got back, she took half the chips, added beaten eggs to them and turned them into a *tortilla*. The rest of the chips Flo and I ate while we watched the midday movie.

One year I went camping with Tia Gladys, Flo and Tio Ricardo. We camped by a river somewhere down the coast. There were no other campers and I remember the vastness and feeling like we were the only people on earth. I'm sure it wasn't even legal to camp there.

Tio Ric taught me to fish that weekend. My line was caught and Tio Ric came to help me. He slipped on a rock and fell in the water. Tia was the first one to laugh, and then Flo and I started and couldn't stop. I can still hear Tia's laugh. Tio Ric often took us out on camping trips. He liked the outdoors. He said it was important for our health to disconnect from our busy lives and connect with nature. Sometimes Lola came too. In the evenings we sat around the fire, drinking *mate* and listening to stories about Tio and Tia's childhood, and how they met. In Uruguay, Tio had been an engineer, here he worked for an imports business. Tio had grown up in a middle-class household, his mother was a teacher and his father an accountant. He learnt English and played water sports as a teenager. His privilege had allowed him a bigger view of the world than my parents. Life hadn't forced him into black and white. He could see the grey and he could choose. He chose to be on the side of the people as Papá would say. The choice had cost him his job.

There was a lightness at Tia Gladys' that I never felt at home. In my house nostalgia pierced the air, breathing was heavy. Malena's moods were suffocating. Mum's silences felt like screams in my head. When I was with Tia and her family that weight was gone.

I'm sure that Tia too suffered the losses she and Mum had lived through, but Tia didn't seem to carry them the way Mamá did.

Tia Gladys was Mum's older sister. She was the last surviving sibling of the four. Tio Mario disappeared during the dictatorship. His body was never found. Mum refused to believe he was murdered. She had always hoped that he had escaped and one day he would turn up.

My parents returned to visit Uruguay when the dictatorship ended. I think they had to see it for themselves, they couldn't believe it was over. They joined thousands of others outside Montevideo's parliament house as the new democratic government was sworn in. It was a bittersweet victory; families had been destroyed; relatives were missing, families were spread across the globe, no longer even sharing a common language. Cousins didn't know each other. Some families had stayed in the same neighbourhood but had been broken by differing ideologies, never to speak again.

When my parents came back, Papá said he never wanted to return. Mum said that while she was in Uruguay, Australia had been erased from her memory. The only thing she had to remind her that she had been in Australia was the English *thank yous* and *sorrys* that escaped her in shops and buses.

Mum's youngest brother Ramoncito was killed when he was thirteen. He was playing with a group of friends out in the street. They were throwing rocks, a popular game for teenagers who had nothing, and he was hit by a rock on the head. The police wanted to take the boy that threw the rock, but Mum said her mother wouldn't let them. Her mother told them it was an accident and destroying another life would not bring her son back.

Now Gladys, the last chapter of their story, and we are left with the remnants. Yet their story is imprinted in us, we carry it somehow, whether we want to or not.

The funeral is tomorrow. I will go with Papá and Lola. I am driving down today on my own. It takes me about ten hours, and I can be in my own headspace as I cross from the kids' chatter to Lola's doubts and insecurities and Papá's questions. I'll stay with Papá. It will give Lola a break.

I wake up early. It's one of those clear days, where you can see into the distance. The sky is a sharp blue, like a tranquil, smooth lake, not a cloud in sight. I can see Mt Chincogan. I want to leave before the kids get up, otherwise they'll want me to take them to school and I won't get out of here until mid-morning. I make myself a green tea and sit out on the verandah. I adore living here. It's the place where I feel most myself, where I feel whole. Here everything makes sense. It's like all the pieces of world fit together and there's a purpose. Maybe even in a spiritual sense. I was denied that growing up. Mum had such distrust and despised the Catholic church that she banned us from experiencing any scripture or spiritualism. I understand her dislike and anger at what Catholicism did in South America, how it was used to repress and control, but spirituality is bigger than one religion. It can help people to find peace and connection. Mum couldn't see this; she couldn't see beyond the pain and damage.

I eat some chia pudding that I made last night, with creamy oat milk and fresh blueberries picked from the bushes we planted three years ago. The kids will love that for breakfast.

When I finish getting ready, I go into the bathroom, to say goodbye to Chris, I can hear him in the shower.

'I'm off Chris.'

'This early, the kids won't see you before you go Betts.'

'That's the idea, otherwise I'll never get out of here before midday.'

He sticks his head out of the shower, and I kiss his wet lips.

'Drive safely. Remember to take your dad those seedlings I left out for you, the Kumato tomatoes?'

'Yep, in the car. I'll ring you when I get there. Love you.'

'Love you too Betts, take care.'

I sneak out quietly, so the kids won't hear me.

The east coast of New South Wales has to be one of the most beautiful places in the world. I'm so tempted to take the coastal route, but I know I have to do it all in one drive. I can't really afford to say in a motel overnight, nor do I have the time.

Listening to Norah Jones, I set off and don't stop until Bulahdelah. It's a little town, not too far off the highway, where I can get a smoothie and keep driving. I've got my almonds to munch on the way.

Last stop is just before Sydney for petrol, and luckily there is an Oliver's among the crap fast foods, where I can get a yogurt.

I get to Papá's at about 8.30pm. He is waiting for me with a small feast. He has bought the flat Afghani bread from the Afghan bakery. You need to eat it warm otherwise it becomes hard and chewy, he tells me. He has made guacamole, and he has bought hummus, baba ganoush, tabouli and Lebanese oregano pizzas. He has cut up tomatoes, from his garden, in quarters and drizzled them with olive oil. There is a bottle of Argentinean red, a Trapiche. He pours me a glass and I look over at Coco stretching into a downward dog.

When I sit down to eat, he tells me proudly, 'no meat.'

'Thanks Papá, this looks delicious.' Coco comes over and places his head on my lap. I stroke his head softly.

The tomatoes are sweet and juicy. The oregano pizzas are a treat. I have never had them before.

'Where did you get these pizzas from? They are amazing.'

'From the Lebanese shop. You like them? They are called manoosh.' He exaggerates the *oo* sound.

'The man who makes them his name is Ahmed. He is very nice. He came here because of the war in Lebanon. He tells me his whole village is gone. He was a student. He went to Beirut, to university. When he came back his village was blown up. His mother, father, sister all dead. *Una tragedia.* He makes very good coffee too. While I wait for the pizza, he always makes me a coffee. And the pizza is very cheap. Two dollars for one pizza.'

'I really like them. Maybe I could make them. We can't get this type of food where I live.'

'That's because where you live there are no migrants, too many *Australianos*. Why you not bring the children?'

'I didn't want them to go to the funeral and anyway this gives me some time with you.'

'I like to see the children.'

'They sent you some drawings.' I walk over to my bag and take out the drawings that Skye and Sunshine sent. I give them to Papá. He looks at them and smiles. Sunshine has drawn a picture of him in his garden, among the tomato plants. Coco is by his side, with a toy in his mouth.

'My ears are not so big. Coco looks very good. Sunshine's drawing is better than Skye's.'

Why did he have to say that? Skye has drawn a lovely landscape with sunflowers.

'I'm going to bed. The drive and the food and wine has made me very tired.'

Papá gets up and kisses me on the head. 'Goodnight *mija*.'

JUAN

Yo no quiero que nadie a mí me diga
I don't want anyone to tell me
que de tu dulce vida
vos ya me has arrancado.
that you have now torn me
from your sweet life.
      '*Soledad*', Alfredo Le Pera y Carlos Gardel

Last night I spoke to a woman from the ad. She rang me. I was preparing all the food for when Betty is here and the phone rings. When I answer I hear a woman's voice, with an accent, ask, 'Is that Juan?' I say yes and she tells me her name is Agnes and she is answering my ad, she says this in Spanish. I am a bit shocked, and I don't know what to say. So I say, '*Muy bien, muy bien.*'

She is very well spoken; it is not the accent or language of the *barrios* I come from. At first it is awkward, and the conversation is like a choppy sea, words tossed around within waves of thoughts and silences. After a while there is calm as we find familiar spaces in the music and movies of our youth and all that was destroyed by the military governments forced on our *pueblos*.

We arrange to meet, in a few days, after Gladys' funeral.

'Coco let's go for a walk.' I pick up his leash and he jumps excitedly. I like to walk before it gets hot and Coco can do his business in the park and not the backyard, on my tomato plants. Besides he needs a good walk before we go to the funeral and leave him here alone.

As I walk out, I look over at Betty. She has rolled out her yoga mat in the backyard under the lemon tree. From the kitchen window I can see her long arms reaching out into the sky and then she bends down. It reminds me of the Muslim man I worked with at the factory. He had a little mat and at morning tea and during lunch breaks he would find a quiet corner to pray to Allah. Some of the men laughed at him. I admired his dedication.

I shout out to Betty that I'm going, and she gives me a wave. She is not moody like her sisters. She is balanced, strong and confident. I have never heard her shout at her children like Lola does to poor Alex and Daniel. Lola shouts and they ignore her. Betty asks her children calmly to do something and they do it.

At the park there are some women, pushing prams with babies. I cannot understand how they can be so covered in this weather and in this country. The men walk in front, speaking loudly in Arabic. South American men have a reputation for machismo, but we don't cover our women like that. Carmen and I were *compañeros*, I didn't tell her what she had to wear or do.

'One, one...'

I hear someone calling an Australianised version of my name. I have heard my name pronounced like this many times. I cannot understand why the *Australianos* cannot say Juan. They can say ham, hello, and everything else with the Spanish J sound, but they cannot say Juan. At the factory they called me John. At first when the boss says John, I don't answer. After some weeks I get used to being John. When your name is changed it is very difficult, like you lose part of your identity. I was split into two. John went to work, and Juan did everything else.

Luckily the girls have names that are easy to say in English. Betty is also an English name. I chose the name, from Betty in *The Flintstones*. That program made me laugh and I liked Betty, Pedro's wife. Carmen chose Lola and Malena. Lola for a Spanish friend she was very close too. Her parents had come to Uruguay after the civil war was lost and then had left like us because of the dictatorship. Carmen and Lola worked together at the textile factory and Lola taught Carmen to make paella. Malena's name is from a tango we both love.

I turn around and see that little dog from the other day and behind him is that crazy woman. She is waving.

As she comes closer, I can hear she is nearly out of breath and her stupid little dog off the leash again. The dog goes up to Coco and Coco chases him playfully, both with the tails wagging. What was her name?

'How are you One?'

'My name is not one, it is Juan.'

'Hooarn,' she says it slowly and exaggeratedly as she catches her breath.

'I was good, enjoying the park, until you and your dog arrived.'

'Well Churchill and Coco seem happy to see each other.' She sounds short of breath, almost panting. I don't want this woman to fall over and die here.

'Are you okay?'

'It's my asthma, I need to find my puffer.'

'Sit down, woman, before you fall down.' I take her arm and walk her over to the nearest bench. She puts her hand in her bag and searches for her puffer.

'I can't find it. I think I may have left it at home.'

'Empty your bag.' Women can never find anything because they carry so many things in those bags. Many times, Carmen had to empty her bag to find her keys.

She empties her bag onto the bench.

'It's here,' she says as she picks up a small green plastic tube, shakes it and sprays it in her mouth.

I feel calmer as she breathes easier. Her face has softened but she looks tired. I notice that her skin is an olive colour, like mine. I still cannot remember her name. Her little dog is sitting at her feet, looking up at her.

'Thank you, Juan.'

'Does this happen to you often?'

'No, I think it was from walking fast to catch up to you. Let me buy you a cuppa as a thank you.'

'You almost died because of me, and you want to thank me?'

She laughs, that loud hearty laugh.

I'm worried about leaving her alone so soon after her asthma attack, so I agree to the coffee. I have some time before we have to be at the funeral.

She suggests we go the Lebanese café across the road. I know this one because I have been there with Lola and the coffee is very good.

We cross the road and find a pole to tie the dogs to. I look at Coco. He puts on the face, with the droopy eyes that tells me; I am sad that you are leaving me. I pat him on the head. Churchill sits quietly looking up at the woman.

'You know I didn't name him Churchill? My husband did. He admired Churchill, said he was a strong leader. Funny thing is most Australians hated him.'

I nod. I don't know what Churchill did. I know he was an English man.

'I wanted to name him Benji.'

I don't know who Benji is either. I know that if Carmen and I had owned a dog, I would have let Carmen choose the name.

We sit down at the small wooden table closest to the door, so that we can see the dogs.

The moustached waiter takes our order. I order a short black and she orders a cappuccino. Most of the people in the café are men. I like the simple tables and the plain décor. There are a few framed photos on the wall of Beirut. It must have been a beautiful city before the war. It sits by the sea, like Montevideo.

'Are you feeling better?' I ask her.

'Yes, much better, now that I can breathe properly.'

Our coffee arrives and the familiar smell relaxes me. I look at this woman in front of me, as she picks up her cup and takes a sip of the coffee. The chocolate sticks to the top of her lip.

'You have a moustache, like the waiter, but a chocolate one.'

She laughs as she wipes the chocolate off her face. She laughs so loudly I think she might have an asthma attack again.

'What is so funny?' Her laughter is warm and comforting and I smile.

'You. You are funny, Bud.'

No one has ever called me Bud before, but I like it.

'Do you have family close by Juan?'

'Yes, I have my daughter Lola and my grandsons. What about you?'

'I'm on my own. I still miss Malcolm, that was my husband. You never quite get over losing someone. You move on but there's a part of you that goes with them.'

She looks down at her shoes, her hands clasped on her lap. I know exactly what she means.

She picks up her cup and takes a sip. 'I have my brother; he lives in Queensland. I see him a couple of times a year. He and his wife come and stay with me.'

'Is that where you are from, Queensland?'

'No, we grew up in Dubbo and I came to Sydney after I got married. Malcolm had work here. What about you, when did you come to Australia?'

'Long time ago, in 1976.'

She smiles at me. I see the creases around her eyes.

'That must have been hard for you, new country, new language.'

Her question makes me think of our first months in Australia. It was hard, but I was used to hard. I had grown up in poverty, with an alcoholic father. Lining my shoes with newspaper in winter to keep the cold slipping in through the holes in the soles. But Australia was a different kind of humiliation. Treated like an imbecile because I couldn't speak English. My children speaking to doctors, to salespeople, for us. There I was the father, but here I was like the child.

'A little,' I say.

When we finish our coffees, she gets up and goes to the counter to pay. I get up as fast as my old knees let me and stand next to her. As she takes out her purse to pay, I give the man a twenty dollar note.

'You didn't have to do that; I was going to shout you.'

Does she want to shout at me because I paid? We walk out, past a dying plant near the doorway. When the dogs see us approaching, they start yelping and jumping. She gathers Churchill in her arms, like a small child. I smile at her, and Coco starts pulling the lead. He is ready to go. We walk across the road to the park, so the dogs can have a run before we go home.

'This was nice, Juan, let's do it again soon.'

I look at her, in her blue tracksuit pants and flowery blouse. I like her honesty; how she is direct and unpretentious.

'Yes, I would like that.' Her name evades me still.

Almost as if she can read my mind, she says, 'In case you forgot, my name is Frances.'

BETTY

Lemon Balm Soap
Ingredients:
- Lemon balm
- Olive oil
- Coconut oil
- Water
- Sodium hydroxide
- Grapeseed oil
- Shea butter
- Lemon essential oil
- Turmeric powder (for colour)

The day of Tia Gladys' funeral is one of those perfect Sydney Autumn days. Sunlight is streaming through the kitchen window. It reminds me of a poem we learnt at school, which for some peculiar reason I still remember. 'Australian Spring', about jolly Spring, letting loose her tide of bees. At the time I found the image frightening as I thought of hundreds of bees on a mission to get to the flowers, no regard for anyone in their way.

I drink a glass of water and take in the smell of coffee that's lived in the kitchen for as long as I remember. Papá comes in and kisses me on the head. He walks over to the stove, turns the percolator off and pours himself a cup of the thick black liquid. He offers me a cup and I remind him that I don't drink coffee. I watch him as he smothers his toast with sweet thick quince paste. He noisily slurps his coffee.

'I bought you some lemon balm soap, Papá. It's great for dishwashing.'
He looks up from his coffee. 'Okay.'
He gets up slowly. Age is invading all parts of his body, an unwanted visitor.
'I'm taking Coco for a walk before we go, do you want to come Betty?'
'No, I'm going to do some yoga.'

Papá struggles to put the collar on an excited Coco.

I pick up my yoga mat and go out to the backyard. I need some sun salutes before I can face the day ahead. I find a bit of grass and roll out the mat and stand in *tadasana*, mountain pose. Inhaling I lift my arms up into *urdhva hastasana*, exhale into *uttanasana*. Then into plank and exhale into *chaturanga*, followed by downward dog. Inhaling I jump back to the front of the mat, exhale sweeping arms out to the side and back to standing with hands in prayer pose. After twenty rounds of sun salutes, I can feel the blood circulating to every part of my body. Feeling energised I cross my legs, hold my hands in prayer and give thanks for all that I have in my life. *Namaste*. As I roll up the mat, I look over at the tomato plants. They look healthy and heavy with fruit. Nature is good to us.

Back inside I eat the muesli with the soy milk Papá has bought for me.

I listen to the radio as I do the dishes. Papá's old cassette player with its radio must be over twenty years old. The sound is a bit grainy but comforting.

The phone rings. It's Lola.

'I can't drive. I've tried but I just can't.'

'What do you mean you can't drive Lola?'

'It's the thoughts; they're back. I get in the car and when I go to start the engine I keep thinking I'm going to run someone over. Or maybe I have run someone over.'

'For Christ's sake Lola if you had run someone over you certainly would remember. They're just thoughts Lola; don't let them have so much power over you. Just get in the car and let the thoughts come and go as you take deep breaths.'

'If it was that fucking easy, I wouldn't have a problem. I can't stop, I'm shaking.'

'Where's Leo?'

'In Canberra, remember, he's touring in fucking Canberra.'

'Lola, just take the train.'

'I can't I'm too scared to go outside.'

'Rescue remedy Lola, have you got any?'

'I don't need those stupid drops, I need drugs, I need Valium or Xanax and I don't have any. I can't go Betty, what do I do?'

I had forgotten that when Lola has one of her episodes, she becomes totally disabled and dependent, like a small child. The first time it happened was some years after she and Leo were married. It was Leo who rang me, he didn't know what to do. He told me she woke up in the middle of the night, screaming and she didn't know where she was. I was already living in Mullumbimby; I couldn't just drive down. He didn't want to ring Malena or my parents. I told him to take her to a hospital.

He said you could almost feel the fear in her eyes.

I look at the clock in living room. It's the clock we girls bought our parents on their twentieth wedding anniversary.

'Betty are you there?'

I can hear the panic in Lola's voice.

'Yes, I'm thinking what to do. We have just over an hour. I'll pick you up. You just get ready. And Lola don't drink any coffee, it will make you feel worse.'

I hang up and race to get changed into the only dress I have that can be worn to a funeral. It is dark blue, about knee length with three-quarter sleeves.

I decide to grab some clothes for Papá. He can get changed at Lola's. I go to his wardrobe and pull out the first shirt I see. It's light blue with short sleeves. There are pants hanging in the wardrobe too, next to Mum's dresses. I can't believe he still hasn't thrown them out. It must be reassuring to have something physical, something she wore. He has her favourite blanket on the sofa to put over his lap when he watches television. The red and blue one she knitted. She used to cover herself with it when she was barely strong enough to get out of bed and sit on the couch. He refers to her mug as Mamá's mug whenever he offers me a drink in it. He often uses the pronoun 'we' to talk about the present. In his mind she is always there.

I drive to Fairfield Park. We used to come here to hang out and share cigarettes after school. He has to be here. Oh shit, we are going to have to leave Coco in the car at the funeral. Hopefully we can leave him at Lola's. As I'm getting out the car, I see him talking to a woman. She is holding a little white dog in her arms.

As I approach, I can hear her voice. It sounds throaty, like a smoker's voice. They don't hear me, and I am almost touching Papá before he turns around.

'Betty, I thought you said you didn't want to come.'

'Lola rang we need to pick her up.'

'Is she alright?'

'Sort of, but we'll have to go now otherwise we'll be late.'

The woman is looking at me.

'This must be your daughter; Betty, is that right?'

'Yes,' Papá replies.

'Your father has been telling me all about you.' The woman smiles at me. I'm confused. 'Is that so?'

'Yes, and I'm sorry to hear about your aunt.'

'Betty, this is Frances.'

She extends her hand out and I take it. Her skin feels leathery and hard.

'Your father and I first met in this park a few weeks ago.'

She must have read my bewilderment. My father doesn't talk to strangers, especially Australian women in the park.

'Yes, we did, our dogs have become friends.' Papá smiles as he says this looking down at Coco.

'And we have too,' Frances adds, winking at Papá.

Now I'm confused. Who is this woman, standing in the park, dressed in blue track suit pants and a blouse with bright yellow flowers, holding a fluffball in her arms and winking at my father?

'Papá we better go.'

'Yes of course. See you Frances.'

'Bye Juan. Take care love.'

Love? She probably calls everyone that.

'Thank you, Frances.' It almost sounds tender.

As we are driving to Lola's, I ask him about Frances. He tells me how they met.

His voice is animated as he recounts the story. He tells me how he couldn't stop laughing at the ridiculousness of the situation. I smile as I imagine Papá on all fours, laughing, trying to get up.

When we get to Lola's, we find her curled up on the sofa with a cup of tea. Coco goes up to her and licks her. She pats his head.

'*Lolita, mija, que paso?*' Papá asks as he puts his arms around her. She is crying.

'It started with thinking about the funeral and then I couldn't stop thinking about Mamá's funeral and then I kept thinking of dying and that I would run someone over if I got in the car and now I can't stop.' She speaks fast and is almost breathless. The sobs seem to be coming from somewhere that I'm thankful I've never been.

'Lola you are a good driver, you do not do that.'

'I know Papá, but even though I know it's not rational it still makes me upset and it's the fact that I can't stop thinking about it that's distressing.'

Lola is a rational person, she's a scientist. She knows these thoughts are totally insane but she still gets anxious about them, and it makes her worse. They go around in her head; it becomes a merry-go-round she can't get off.

This is a bad combination. Lola's anger and frustration at losing control, Papá's lack of insight, a funeral we need to be at in thirty minutes and Lola's fear of killing someone.

The funeral is not a good place for Lola in her current head space, but neither is leaving her here alone. 'Let's go, you need to get out of here Lola. Have you eaten anything?'

'I can't my stomach is cramped.'

I need to get food into her, or she will most likely faint. I mash a banana and practically spoon-feed it to her.

Somehow, we manage to get in the car and drive to the service on time. We enter just as the doors to the chapel are about to close.

A photo of a young smiling Tia Gladys greets us as we sit down. Lola sits between Papá and me. Her back is hunched, she is a scared child. Papá takes her hand.

The service is run by Maria. I remember Maria from visiting Tia Gladys as a child. She is a very strong woman with dark brown eyes, almost black, and long grey hair tied in a loose bun. She wears bright red lipstick and silver bracelets. Mum used to say she was a gypsy. She didn't trust her.

Tia Gladys had met her at the chocolate factory where they both worked just after they arrived in Australia.

Papá leans over to us and whispers, 'Why did Flo ask this crazy gypsy to do the service?'

'Because she was Tia's friend,' I whisper back.

Maria is a clairvoyant. You give her something you are wearing, like a ring or necklace; she holds it in her hand, closes her eyes and speaks to you in a Spanish unlike the one my parents spoke at home.

When I was about fifteen, she told me I would have three children and live in a very green place with lots of trees. When I did have three children, I wondered whether it was because Maria had told me it was my future.

She told Tia Gladys about Tio Ric's car accident. He didn't believe her. Tia Gladys told him Maria said the accident would happen in May so he shouldn't drive for the whole month of May of that year. He did drive and he did have an accident. It was a small one. Someone drove into the back of him and he got whiplash and had to take two weeks off work.

Tia Gladys believed everything Maria told her. She said Maria even foresaw Lola's breakdown. Mum said it was ridiculous. I think Mum was secretly envious of Maria for being closer to her sister than she was.

Maria spoke of Tia Gladys' generosity and love of life. A woman, whose house was always open and where many lost souls found refuge. It was true; there were always visitors at Tia's. She always had the *mate* going and many conversations took place with rounds of *mate* and toast with *dulce de membrillo* or *torta fritas*.

At the end of the service Maria led us through a meditation where each person was asked to focus on the love that Tia Gladys brought to their lives. We took that love with us as we said goodbye.

The meditation moved me greatly. I felt energy blocks shifting and when we finished, I felt much lighter and almost joyous. It felt like Tia Gladys was there to soothe and heal all those there.

Lola was crying softly into a tissue and Papá was fidgeting. I could tell he was uncomfortable and eager to go.

Maria invited everyone to a nearby community hall where there would be refreshments and the Latin American women's choir that Tia Gladys belonged to would sing.

Papá and Lola did not want to go. Lola's anxiety and Papá's intolerance of anything spiritual had made the decision for them. I wanted to go. We had to be there for Flo.

LOLA

13 April 2012

I haven't been to work for three days.

I put the pen down. Work. I can't face Nick. Somehow, he managed to reach a part of me I thought was buried. The anxiety episodes are draining. The funeral is a blur. The worst thing about it is it feels like a weakness, I can't control my own thoughts.

I can hear Alex in the lounge room.

I walk into the lounge room and see him sitting playing video games.

'What are you doing here, why aren't you at school?'

His eyes don't leave the screen in front of him.

'Alex. Alex. Hello, Alex, I'm here.'

He doesn't look away from the screen. 'Hi Mum.'

'Alex, why are you home so early?'

He gets up turns the television off and walks away. He doesn't look at me. I hear his bedroom door close loudly.

Leo is in the back room listening to music.

I put the kettle on and go to see my husband.

'Alex is home, and he won't say why he is back from school so early.'

'Maybe he had a free period?'

'Or maybe there's something wrong.'

'Leave him alone Lola, he probably needed some space. Don't smother him, just mother him.'

Leo takes me in a big bear hug. I wriggle free.

Leo needs to be there for Alex. He used to be and then Alex stopped talking to him – and to me too. Not that long ago they were talking about football, who were the best players on the Uruguayan and Australian teams, the best coaches, the difference between South American football and English football. The living room seemed like a boy's club. I felt excluded. Even Papá joined in.

Now they barely exchange words. Alex comes home and goes to his room. He only comes out to eat. Sometimes he watches a bit of television or plays on the Playstation. He then goes back to his room and closes the door. When I knock to ask him something, he tells me to go away. I don't know what to say to him. Everything seems trivial. Leo should try and reach him, but he doesn't seem to know how.

I'm always saying, 'Talk to him Leo.' When a boy becomes a teenager, he begins to move away from his mother, and he needs his father.

I know that Leo tries sometimes, but Alex pulls away.

Leo tells me Alex is like me. We're both hard work. I know that sometimes I put walls up. I've had to become like this in our relationship to survive. When I first met Leo, I was totally open, I gave him all of myself. He didn't. It took him longer to trust me. In the early days, I would spend nights waiting for him. He would tell me he was coming over after a gig and then didn't turn up or he would come really late, too late to go anywhere. He later told me he was testing me, to see if I really loved him and would stick around. I was madly in love, and I forgot myself when I cried over him. My sisters told me it was unhealthy, and the relationship wasn't right for me. I didn't listen and I persisted. Leo always put his needs first, whereas I squashed mine to be with him. Until that day when it all poured out in an ugly mess, and I was left trying to put all the broken bits back together.

That day I had felt an overpowering anxiety. It happened after speaking to a counsellor about a weird sensation of too much saliva and the need to keep spitting it out. She asked me what it felt like and the word sperm came out of my mouth without thinking. I went back to work but couldn't focus. I was at Sydney University, working on a research project. By the afternoon I couldn't even read. I would read the same page over and over again, without understanding any of it. When I got home, I burst into tears. Leo asked me what was wrong, and I couldn't answer and just cried. He sang all my favourite songs as he played his guitar, while I lay on the old blue couch in our living room.

I tried to sleep. After tossing and turning for what seemed hours, I fell asleep. Then it happened. One minute I was lying in bed and the next a terrifying dream woke me. I kicked and screamed as the rage of my entire life surfaced. This was madness. I couldn't focus, I couldn't think, I heard voices, I couldn't stop the images that were flooding my mind. There it was, scattered in front of me, the pain, the hurt, the anger, the loss. I needed to mop it up, to bundle it up and put it away, the precious and the wounded. Leo could not understand what had happened to me and I couldn't explain it.

I had to leave him, but I loved him. Part of me wanted to run and part of me wanted him to hold me and tell me everything would be okay. I was too scared to be alone, too vulnerable in the state I was, so I stayed. He began to let most of his walls down, as I began to build mine up. To survive in the relationship, I had to start protecting myself, so that I would never come undone like that again.

Now Alex is going through something and neither of us are able to reach him. Leo doesn't understand how hard adolescence is in this culture. He grew up in a different place at a different time. Montevideo just before the dictatorship. The student movement was growing. There was a lot happening; demonstrations, sit ins at the high school. There was barely anytime to study. It was a time of hope, change was imminent. There was a purpose; you were part of something big. The social goals of Leo's youth kept him focused. You knew who you were and where you belonged.

Alex and his friends don't have that. Now Alex is struggling. This culture is harsh. Often there are no real connections.

Leo struggles with fatherhood. His own father stopped being part of his life when he was seventeen. He hasn't spoken to his father since the day they argued, and Leo moved out. His father didn't want him to be involved in student politics. He told him he was wasting his life. Leo very rarely talks about his father. His mother tried to reach him. For years she sent Leo letters. He still has them all. He has never replied. After Alex was born, he sent his mother a photo of the three of us. By then we had a new address and he sent it without a return address. I'm sure she would have written back.

I think if we go to Uruguay together as a family it might help all of us. I want to show the kids where we come from. I want Leo to see his parents. I think it would help heal some of the wounds we all carry.

When I suggest it to Leo he says, what for? To show them what? A country so poor and damaged that half of its population left.

He tells me I romanticise it. I still have the picture of a childhood playing on the street and sitting with neighbours at night drinking *mate* and telling stories. Leo tells me I should be grateful that my parents shielded me from the horror that overcame our country and that I have no idea of the pain I was saved from.

It's true. When I think of Uruguay, I feel love and security I don't feel the pain that Papá or Leo feel.

Maybe we can all go back when we take Mamá's ashes. Papá keeps her ashes on his bedside table. We decided that when Papá was ready, he would go to Uruguay with Betty, Malena and I and take Mamá's ashes back to the town where she was born. We are going to scatter the ashes on the land where the house of her birth used to stand.

JUAN

Mírame! Nunca te olvidaré
Look at me! I'll never forget you!
Con tu partida voló mi ventura
With your departure, my happiness flew away
Donde hubo dicha quedó amargura
Where there was joy, bitterness remained
    '*Quiéreme*', Carlos Gardel y Alfredo Le Pera

I decide to ring Lola. I know it is early. I need to talk to her. This is very unlike me, pacing up and down the house, Coco following me. I know Lola will answer the phone. It seems to ring for a long time. Finally, she answers.

'Lolita, I am going to meet one,' I blurt. I know I am talking very fast. My head has been so busy with thoughts, like a train speeding out of control.

'What?' She sounds very sleepy.

'Lola I'm meeting one.'

'*Que* Papá? What? Meet who?'

'The lady Lola. A lady.'

'What are you talking about Papá?'

'A lady from the ad, I'm going to have *café* with one. In a coffee shop.'

Lola seems to have forgotten. She takes a few weeks to recover when she gets sick, and the pills give her the brain of a ninety-year-old. Slowing my words, I start again.

'Lola, remember, the ad I told you that Betty did.'

'Of course, sorry. I'm half asleep. Tell me, when are you going and who is she?'

'Today. That is why I not sleep all night. I think all night, do I go? Lola what should I do?'

This is very strange me asking my daughter what to do, asking Lola who can never decide anything. Usually, I'm very good at making decisions.

Once I decide, that is it, I don't think about it anymore. I like to move forward. Not Lola, she tortures herself, thinking and thinking whether it was the right decision, thoughts are like gymnasts in her brain, jumping, somersaulting, rolling everywhere, springing, and spinning.

'Go. Go of course.' This time she sounds very certain.

'You are sure?'

'Of course, I'm sure. Who is she? Tell me, tell me.' Lola no longer sounds sleepy.

'Her name is Agnes. I know the name is horrible, but she sounds very nice. I talk to her on the phone, and we laugh. She comes from Argentina. We like the same music, same movies.'

'Sounds good, Papá. When are you meeting her?'

'At 11.00am.'

'What are you wearing?'

'My pyjamas. Why?'

'Not now, when you go to meet her.' She laughs loudly.

'I don't know. What do you think I put on?' Before Lola asked me, I did not think about what I would wear. Now I have a new problem.

'Do you want me to come over and help you get ready?'

If she is offering to come, she must be very sure she wants me to go, and it will make her feel better.

'Where is Betty?'

'She went to meet Flo.'

I am relieved Betty is not here. I don't want her bossing me with what to do, making me take those rescuing drops she has for nervous people. Telling me this is about new beginnings.

'You are okay to come Lola, what about the boys?'

'Daniel's going to soccer with Leo and Alex. Alex will probably stay home.'

'Is he alright? He not taking drugs?' When children don't go out with the family and are always in their bedroom, maybe they are taking drugs.

'No, Papá. He's not taking drugs.'

'Good. You remember what happened to Mauricio.'

'Papá, I'll have some breakfast, and I'll drive over,' Lola tells me.

'Okay. *Gracias*, Lola, you are a good daughter I'm very lucky.'

While I wait for Lola, I sweep the kitchen floor and wipe the dust from the cupboards.

I feel silly, an old man, so nervous. Am I doing the right thing, Carmen? I will always love you. I was with you until your last breath. You died in my arms. It was a cold Winter afternoon and she had been sleeping most of the last few days. Betty and Lola were in the kitchen making *pasta frola*, the way Carmen had taught them. Malena was in the bedroom with Carmen, reading and holding Carmen's hand. Chris was here too. He was playing with Daniel and Leif in the backyard. Malena suddenly shouted out to us to come quickly. Carmen was making strange noises, like a gurgling creek. Betty told us, she was leaving, the gurgling was the fluids building up. The girls sat on the bed, and I held Carmen in my arms. She opened her eyes and looked up at me. I could see tears. I kissed her softly on her mouth and she was gone. Her face softened as both life and pain left her body.

The phone rings as I'm about to put the coffee on. It will be Lola, she can't come.

'Malena, yes *mija*.'

'It was alright. That crazy gypsy, Gladys' friend, did the service.'

'Lola? She is okay now. You know she gets better after a few weeks when this happens. She's coming over soon.'

I cannot tell her where I am going.

'I have to go *mija*, I can hear Lola. That is good you are going back to work. *Besos*.'

I look out the window and see Lola getting out of her car.

'Lola, why did you take so long? I thought you had an accident.'

'I didn't take that long. I had to eat something before I came.'

'Why, you think I won't give you food?'

'No, I just need to eat when I get up. Anyway, why have you got a dusting rag in your hand and a coffee jar?'

'I'm taking away the dust. It is very dusty.' I often keep the widows closed because it is always getting very dusty.

'Why are you doing it now?'

'Because it is dirty now.'

'Papá, do it later. Let's sit down. I need a coffee.'

'You just said you already eat.'

'Yes, I said I ate, but I didn't have coffee.'

'I make one for you.'

101

When I go to the kitchen, I forget what I am doing. I pick something up then put it down again. I go to the fridge and open the door and look. I close it and I forget to get the milk out.

Lola gets up, goes to the fridge, gets the milk out and gives it to me.

I take the bottle of milk from her, and I drop it. '*Mierda.*'

'I'll clean it, Papá, don't worry. Sit down, try and relax.' She pats my hand. 'Your hand is sweaty. Do you want to go and have a shower?'

'Now you tell me I am dirty.'

'No, I think you are nervous, and a shower will relax you. While you do that, I will find something for you to wear.'

'Ok, I have a shower.'

I feel like a little boy sent to have his bath.

When I come out of the shower, I go to the bedroom and Lola is there, holding one of her mother's dresses and smelling it.

'Lola, what are you doing?'

'I was looking for a shirt for you to wear and saw these. I didn't know you kept them.'

'This one was her favourite.'

'I can see her wearing it,' says Lola. 'We were in the Chilean cake shop buying empanadas. Mamá was talking to the shop attendant; she was a fat woman with big hips and one of those dark broad faces of the southern Andes. They were talking about John Howard and the Tampa. Mamá said, this was a country without a soul. The shop assistant had agreed and said Howard was like Pinochet without the army.'

'I can't throw them out, Lola. They were her favourites. When I see her dresses hanging in the wardrobe, for a few minutes I can forget that she has gone.'

'What about this shirt?' She is holding a light blue shirt.

'Yes, I like it.' It is the one Carmen bought for me at David Jones. Very expensive.

'I'll wait in the kitchen while you get dressed.'

As I button up the shirt, I imagine Carmen standing in front of me. She is smiling, her hands on her hips. Her hair is no longer black, it is grey and falls onto her shoulders.

When I go to the kitchen. Lola is sitting at the table crying, and the kettle is whistling. I go and turn it off.

'If you don't want me to, I won't do this.' I don't want to make Lola cry.

'No, no, I think it's the right thing. The dresses made me think of Mamá and how much I miss her.'

'I know *mija*.' I put my arm around her small frame.

'I'll make us a cup of tea. I don't think we need coffee now. Do you have tea in this house?' She says this, sniffling as she gets up.

'Lola, I don't drink tea, why would I have tea?'

'Maybe Betty brought some.'

I look in the cupboard and see some peppermint tea bags. I give them to Lola. They are the ones Betty brought when she was here last year.

'They are a month out of date. Should we use them?'

'Lola, they are herbs, how can herbs go bad? You know what your Mamá said, the use-by-date is for the first world so people will throw out more and buy more.'

'Papá, you look fantastic, ten years younger for sure. Sorry I had not even noticed. Is that aftershave I can smell?'

'Of course, it is aftershave, what do you think I wear? Your mother's perfumes?'

'That colour looks very good on you.'

'This was your Mamá's favourite shirt for me.'

'I didn't know when I picked it. Let's have the tea. It will help us feel calmer.'

'Ok, but don't tell your sister I drink this tea.'

The tea is bad, but I drink it quietly. I don't want to further upset Lola.

'I better go there could be too much traffic. I don't want to be late.'

'I'll drive you, Papá.'

Lola stops outside El Rincon, a popular Latin American café in Horsley Park. It's owned by a Salvadorian couple. Miguel was a teacher in El Salvador and Elena was a lawyer. Good people. Both had been jailed and had been lucky to escape. They opened El Rincon about five years ago. It is a small café, with very good food.

Lola and Leo love coming here when they visit me. Leo even played guitar one night. It was to raise money to send to orphans in El Salvador. During the war many children lost their parents. In El Salvador, like in other parts of Latin America, people had to take up arms to fight the fascist governments. Many lives were lost, families were destroyed and the *hijos de puta* stayed in power. They got to stay in our countries, and we had to leave.

'Papá, I won't come in. You can read the paper while you wait for her. What time will I pick you up?'

'One hour.'

'Ok. But what if you're still here talking to her? I know, I can walk past and look in the window. You better go and sit next to the window. Go in and sit down and let me see if I can see you from outside.'

'What if I want to go and she is still talking?' I'm worried I won't like her.

'Wave and I will come in.'

'If I want you to come in, to rescue me, if she is boring, I can wave to you and say, look, *mi hija* is here. You come in and say we must go; lucky you find me, your son is sick.'

'Isn't that a bit melodramatic?'

'Ok, you say your car is broken down and I have to drive you home.'

'I can't lie. See this is why I tell you it's good to have a mobile phone. You can just excuse yourself, get up and ring me.'

'Lolita, if I wave, you come in.'

'Ok, see you later. Good Luck!'

I kiss Lola and get out of the car. As I walk into the café, I see Miguel wiping down a table.

'*Hola* Juan,' Miguel, calls out to me. '*Como esta?*'

'*Bien, amigo.*'

I go to the table, next to the window, order a short black from Miguel and pick up the Spanish Herald. I see Lola waving from the car. I wave back and she knows she can leave.

I'm up to the sports pages, about to read about the football game between Uruguay and Peru, when a thin elderly woman with glasses comes up to me.

'Juan?'

'*Si.*'

I get up to shake her hand and pull out a chair for her.

'I'm Agnes.'

'Agnes, sit down, *How are you?* What would you like to drink? Would you like to eat something?' I realise my words are crashing into each other.

I'm talking in Spanish and too fast.

'I'll have a *café con leche* and a *media luna*.'

The *cono sur's* croissant, the *media luna*. She is definitely Argentinian. I hope she is not arrogant like so many from Buenos Aires.

'Miguel, *un café con leche y media luna for la señora*.'

'*Si, si*.'

The Salvadorian smiles at me, as if to say I know what you are up to old man.

'Have you been waiting long Juan?'

'No.'

I didn't think she would be so skinny. She sits with her shoulders back, her posture is excellent. She looks like a *burgesa*. I don't think she ever worked in a factory like my Carmen.

'So, Juan, tell me, how long you have been in Australia?'

I feel like the teacher is asking me a question at school. 'Thirty-six years next month. Soon I will be more in Australia than in Uruguay. That is sad, to think more life here than in my country.'

'Australia is our country now. I have been here twenty-eight years. I have come to accept this as my home.'

'Do you ever feel like you want to go back?'

Carmen had wanted to return to Uruguay. She wanted us to retire to the town where she had spent her childhood.

'*Claro*, I like to go back. But I am happy to live here. I have my son and my daughter and my grandchildren. I can't leave them.'

'I know what you mean.'

For Carmen the pull of her roots had been stronger than the pull of her children. Not for me, I wanted to be close to my daughters. Now I only have Lola nearby.

'How old are your grandchildren, Juan?'

'Malena's children are ten and fourteen. They live in Italy. My daughter Malena married an Italian and he wanted to go back. He couldn't adapt to the life here. Then I have my daughter, Lola, she has Alex. He is fifteen and Daniel is eleven. My daughter Betty has three children. Her youngest is seven.'

'Have you been to visit the ones in Italy? I would love to go to Italy.'

'No. I will go one day.'

'I like this café.' Agnes said, looking around. 'The croissants are the best in Sydney. Nearly as good as the ones in Buenos Aires.'

'You know they don't make them here. They buy them from the Argentinean bakery. From Jose, you know him?'

'Yes, I do. Our children went to Spanish school together.'

'When did they go? My daughters went to Spanish school too.' I look at her drinking her coffee. Her thin lips barely touch the cup.

'Maybe 1978 or 1979, I can't really remember. It was so long ago.'

'What did your children study?'

'My son, Ricardo, is an engineer. My daughter Silvia is a music teacher.'

'My son-in-law plays music. Not a good job for a man. He never has enough money.'

'Silvia teaches in a high school, so she is very lucky.' Of course, her daughter would be doing well.

'My daughters all went to university. Sydney University. Except for Betty, she is the youngest. She went to a different university. She likes to be different to her sisters.'

'What did they study?'

'Malena is a lawyer and Betty is a nurse. But she doesn't work. She stays home to look after the children. Lola studied science.' I don't want to tell her Lola now works in a supermarket.

We talk like we are playing tennis. Throwing the questions from one side of the table to the other. After about an hour, two coffees and three croissants, I look out the window and see Lola. I wave hard with both hands so she can see I want her to come.

'Oh, there is my daughter. I will ask her to come in.' As I get up Lola is entering the café. 'Hola, Lola. What a surprise, what are you doing here?'

Lola looks at me. She looks at Agnes, then back to me. 'I ... I'm shopping.'

'Agnes, this is my middle daughter, Lola. This is my friend Agnes, Lola.' The women give each other a kiss on the cheek.

Then Agnes asks her. 'Would you like to join us?'

I worry that Lola say the wrong thing so I answer for her. 'No, no Lola is very busy. I can drive you home Lola. She crashed her car last week, so she must catch the train.'

Lola stares at me. I know she is not happy. 'Agnes it was lovely to talk with you.'

'Yes, maybe we can meet again.' Agnes stands up and goes to take out her purse.

'No, please, I invite you.' I cannot let a lady pay.

I go to pay Miguel and leave Lola and Agnes talking. Then quickly walk to the door to open it for the women. Agnes walks out first. Lola follows.

'Adios, Agnes.' I shake her hand.

'*Chau* Juan.'

We watch Agnes walk away from us.

'Let's go. Where did you park?'

'I don't have a car. I crashed it apparently.'

Suddenly we both start laughing.

'I hope you're not too far. I don't want to walk too much. My knees are hurting. It's the cold.'

'No, the car is close,' Lola says as we weave between people on the street. 'Well, tell me, how was she?'

'Don't you think she is too skinny? Even her lips are thin?'

'There's nothing wrong with being thin.'

'Yes, but that is too thin. She has no hips. She looks like a schoolteacher.'

'What did you talk about? Was she nice?'

'She is very educated, very polite. I am a simple man, Lola.'

I think of Frances and how she laughed as she drank her coffee. So comfortable in her own skin.

'That is nothing to be ashamed of. You are a good man, Papá. Anyway, how do you know? Did she say she was a teacher?'

'No. But she sounds like one. Anyway, I don't like how she eats. Your Mamá, she ate with gusto, she savoured the food, enjoyed it. This woman she holds her food like she has to eat it, not like she loves it. You know what I am saying?'

'Yes, I still don't know anyone that can leave a chicken leg as bare as Mamá could.'

Lola does not understand what it is like to go hungry and how that feeling can stay in your body.

Once in the car, Lola puts on music. It is Mercedes Sosa singing, *Gracias a La Vida*, and we both sing quietly to *La Negra*, the Argentinian icon, as we drive back home. I think of Frances, drinking her cappuccino.

BETTY

Cinnamon Oil
Ingredients:
- Olive or almond oil
- Cinnamon sticks

Cinnamon oil for comfort and peace. I take the small bottle, along with the rose oil and put them in my bag to take for Florencia.

Flo and I are meeting in a café near her house. Flo lives in Glebe, in the inner city. Glebe Point Road is full of cafés, bookshops, restaurants. It's across the road from Sydney University. As I walk past Badde Manors, I remember meeting Lola here years ago when she was at uni. We would catch up for a coffee, in between her lectures. In those days, Lola and I told each other everything. I can still see her laughing at my dumb stories. Like the time my friend Steph and I talked our way into some rich private party at a club pretending to be writers for the social pages of a new magazine and we drank ourselves silly and flirted with way too many guys. Steph made a fool of herself on the dance floor when she slipped, fell and ripped her skirt. She was left standing there with half a skirt on and her g-string showing. When I told Lola these stories, at first she would smile, the corners of her mouth turning up, then she would bend over howling. When she laughed, she was free. I loved seeing Lola like this. She was happy, her whole body would relax. I miss the old Lola.

Glebe has morphed into a sophisticated adult, no more old grungy cafés where you can sit and read for ages over one coffee, or the old fish and chip shop with the plastic table and chairs outside. Trendy restaurants have moved in. There seem to be quite a few vegetarian places, as people move away from the meat-based diet most of us were brought up on, which I'm pleased to see. The rhythm here is very different to Mullum. Faster, younger. It's in the way people move, the clothes they wear, their hair. In Mullum, if you walk barefoot without brushing your hair, people don't think you have a mental illness or you're homeless. It's organic, beautiful, comforting. The comfort you get when you drink a cup of tea, wrapped in a blanket, looking out into the bush.

The mix of people has changed here too. More Asian students. It makes sense Australia is in Asia, regardless of how it clings to its Britishness. I think of Papá, complaining how Fairfield and Cabramatta are full of *chinos* and *arabes* now. He says it like he has a right to because he was here first. The arrogance of ignorance. Mum used to say that Australia had an Aboriginal soul and even though everyone else came and trampled over their land, that soul was strong. No matter how much land was ripped out by mines, destroyed by farming, and claimed by invaders, Aboriginal people would always own that land because no one else could understand it or connect to the land in the way Aboriginal people could. I don't know how she came to believe this. She could barely read English. Maybe she believed that was the case for Indigenous people in South America, so it must be the same here. I might not connect to land like Aboriginal people, but I do have a connection with the land. I can feel it when I walk on it with my bare feet, when I touch the soil to plant, even when I look out at the gum trees in their expansiveness. Mum said we could never belong here, it is not our land. I don't agree. I feel I do belong. The sense of belonging and grounding came when I moved to Mullumbimby. I didn't have it before. Mum was stuck in longing and that stopped her from accepting where she was. Nostalgia clouded her life.

Flo suggested we meet at Poets and Poppies, near Gleebooks. I can see it now. As I walk in, I'm greeted by a young woman with green hair and a boyish face with a smile that radiates innocence. I tell her I'm meeting someone, but I can't see them. She tells me there is a garden, out the back. The café is one of those inner-city terraces, narrow and long. In the garden, sitting at a small metal table with two vintage wooden chairs is Flo, looking out into the distance. I call out to her.

'Betty,' she gets up and greets me with a big hug.

'How are you doing Flori?'

'I'm okay. She looks down and when she looks up at me, I can see the tears rolling down her cheeks. 'It's really hard, Betty. This morning, I was thinking about something, and I went to ring Mum, then it hit me, she's gone forever.'

'Give it time. It's so raw still.'

'Thanks for coming to the hall after the funeral, I know Tio Juan and Lola didn't want to come. It was important for me you were there. You're like a sister to me.'

'Of course, I was going to be there. Las Palomas choir sang such a lovely tribute.'

'God, Mum had been part of that choir for so many years. She loved singing with all her Latin-American friends. Many of them were like aunties to me.'

I think of the choir singing and Papá rolling his eyes as he whispers in my ear, they sound like howling cats. He could be so fucking inappropriate. Then he complained about the empanadas, they were cold and must have been made by the stingy Chilean in Merrylands because they didn't have enough filling. They should have bought them from Jose, at the Argentinian bakery.

'It was a beautiful service. Maria was sensitive and spoke so lovingly about Tia. I could almost feel her. She was loved by so many people.'

We order our chai teas from the waitress with the boyish face. I feel closer to Flo at times than to my own sisters. Flo is more accepting and kinder. Maybe it was because Tia Gladys was like that too.

The waitress brings our teas. Flo puts a teaspoon of honey in her tea and stirs it. She looks exhausted. Grief does that. It rips everything out of a person. I saw it when I worked in palliative care. Families at the bedside of their loved one, as life slowly leaves their bodies. The pain of watching someone die, day by day, gradually ripping away at the energy and soul of the family, waiting for death to come and take them. Exhausted and devastated. I remember an Italian woman, who had been at her mother's bedside for three weeks. One day, she shouted, "I wish she would just die,' as she stood in the hallway just outside her mother's room. People looked at her. They understood. She expressed what many of them were feeling. It's the watching and waiting that eats at people. At least Flo didn't go through this as Tia Gladys died suddenly.

I wanted to tell Flo about Papá and the woman at the park. It had made me uncomfortable.

'You need to be gentle with yourself Flo. Are you taking some time off work?'

'Only a week to pack up Mum's house. I want to go back to work, it will distract me'.

'I'm here for a few more days, I'll come and help you.'

She reaches over and takes my hand. 'Thank you, I would really like that.'

Packing a life away, that's not something anyone should have to do on their own. Tia Gladys had lived in her house at Merrylands for as long as I can remember. Now all she had ever touched, held, sat on, eaten from in that house had to go until the house was once again empty like when they first moved in, before their story settled there.

'On the day of the funeral I went to the park, near Papá's house, to pick him up and he was with a woman. An Australian woman. They spoke like friends, it was weird.'

'Tio Juan, friends with an Australian woman? No, he probably just met her there and was being friendly.'

'No. She called him love and she knew who I was.' I can still picture the woman in her tracksuit pants holding the little white dog. The incident unsettled me. It usually takes something pretty big to shake me. I'm surprised how affected I was by the sight of my father with this woman. I won't tell Lola until I know more. In her current state she doesn't need this too.

I get up to pay while Flo goes to the bathroom.

The waitress with the green hair takes my card.

'We are having a poetry slam here next Wednesday night if you want to come. It should be really good, there's some awesome poets. Take a flyer.'

The last time I went to a poetry slam was at uni when my friend Steve performed. His poetry was about being gay, coming out and life during the AIDS epidemic that had fallen at our doorstep. Steve was studying nursing with me. We hit it off straight away, we had the same sense of humour, both escaping oppressive family backgrounds. He and I nursed AIDS patients together at St Vincent's Hospital in Darlinghurst. Some of the boys had no visitors as families rejected them at a time when they needed them most. I remember holding the hand of Mark, a country boy from Coonabarabran, as he died. He called for his mum as he took his last breath. Steve died ten years later. He was thirty-four. The funeral was in the Hills in Western Sydney where he was from. His parents held a religious service which Steve would have hated. He was buried next to his grandfather's grave. No one spoke of why he died.

I take Flo's arm and we walk down Glebe Point Road.

'I talked to Teresa Maldonado at the funeral. She was happy to see Papá. They had not seen each other since Mum's funeral. She said Papá was looking good, there was a glow about him, and she invited all of us to a paella at her house on Saturday. You never know what could happen.'

'I can't believe you're trying to hook Tio Juan up. He and Tia Carmen were soulmates, he's never going to be with another woman. I was surprised to see Teresa, she usually avoids going anywhere where there's a lot of community.'

Teresa and her husband Franco had been friends of our parents, from the Latin American Cultural Centre, the little piece of Latin America created by those who had fled dictatorships in Uruguay, Chile, Argentina, and other countries. They gathered there on weekends to listen to the local musicians singing the songs of Victor Jara, Mercedes Sosa, and Daniel Viglietti, about struggles in their homelands. Unlike Malena and Lola, I didn't want to go. It wasn't my world. I didn't want to hear the music or see the films showing the atrocities happening on the other side of the world. When Mum and Papá were at the Centre, they were confident, Mamá spoke passionately about what was happening in Uruguay. She was no longer the mother who relied on her daughters to understand the world, nor another factory worker.

Papá joined the *asadores* outside, as they slowly roasted the strips of beef over the fire, brushing it with the rich chimichurri marinade. I remember Terresa's husband, Franco, because he wasn't like the other men. He would talk to the kids and listen to what they had to say. He was the Spanish teacher at the Centre and he spoke English very well. He was always the one to interpret for the people on the stage so that the Australians who came to hear the music could understand the stories behind the songs.

'Poor Teresa has never gotten over the humiliation. You know she came to visit us often after Franco left. She and Mum drank *mate* late into the night as they talked. Mum was always good at comforting people.'

'Tia Gladys was the best. She made me feel safe and loved.'

Some years later, after I had moved away to Mullumbimby, Mum told me Franco had met a Spanish man and left to live with him in Madrid. The community was shocked, and Teresa humiliated. Mum said it had taken Teresa years before she was able to face the community, and she never returned to the Latin-American Cultural Centre.

'Flo, Papá was excited about the ad, so you never know. I like Teresa.'

He seemed open to meeting someone and that gave me hope. I knew he was still grieving like a splinter had become stuck, and not removing it made him exist in pain. A new adventure might just start to dislodge that splinter, so that memories could replace grief.

'Flo, do you remember the *asados* we had at our house?'

I loved it when everyone came together at our house. During the day, the women settled in the kitchen and made salads and desserts as they drank sweet *mate*. The gourd was passed from one woman to the other. One woman was the official pourer, refilling the gourd with hot water and sugar as she passed it to each woman. They talked, joked, and listened to music. Mum was happy on those weekends.

Outside, the men cooked the *asado* on the barbeque someone had welded at work. It would take hours. Not like the *gringo* barbeques, Papá would say. These *gringos*, throw the meat and turn it over and it is all over in five minutes. Cooking *asado* was a ritual, and it was the men who did it as they drank their bitter *mate* and talked football and politics.

We kids, played outside, speaking in English, except for the ones that had just arrived and were still struggling to get their tongues into the unfamiliar positions that English required.

In the evening the women made *torta fritas*, big round fried pastries. We would eat them before they had time to cool down. The men played cards and drank whisky in the next room.

The adults forgot about Australia until the next day when they all went to work.

'Of course, I remember. Tia Carmen always had fruit salad for dessert, with heaps of strawberries. Mum took that awful *torta de jamon y queso*, with the puff pastry because she couldn't be bothered to make the pastry. Tia Carmen would put it in the fridge and every time she said to Mum, '*Harina, agua y sal* Gladys. *Basico.*'

We laugh.

'I know Mum complained about Tia Gladys' cooking. She said it was laziness combined with Australian packets.'

'Mum was a crap cook'.

As Flo says this, we look at each other and laugh again. I love this woman.

LOLA

16 April 2012

I can't stop thinking about what happened. His hand on my thigh, my hand on his. His skin soft. There was a gentleness about it, a comfort, yet an excitement at the same time. It destroyed me. It's now been a week since the funeral and I'm in clean-up mode, grasping at fragments of myself, following the cyclone that hit my mind. This time it hit hard, tearing at places long buried. I hadn't even seen it coming. No warning. After nearly two years of being quite well.

I put the pen back in the draw in my bedside table. I can't put the journal back in the drawer. Leo might see it. Instead, I open my sock drawer in the tall boy and put it under the piles of socks. It feels like I have committed a sin.

Nick was the trigger. I wanted to squash it, but then the funeral, Alex so distant, Leo going away, it was all too much to deal with and it hit me like a torrent. It overpowered me. Anxiety does this, it's a beast, a bully and it takes over.

The mess in the bedroom mirrors my mental mess. Clothes and blankets are strewn over the floor. I pick up the cups lying all over the room and walk to the kitchen. I wash them as I look out the window, facing the neighbour's wall. The droopy geranium on the windowsill is a piece of nature among the concrete and brick walls. I water it slowly, observing the water as it enters the soil and is absorbed, so that like myself, it can ease back to life.

Dishes spill out from the sink to the bench, to the kitchen table. I begin collecting and washing them, cleaning, and tidying my mind as I clean up the house.

The past week has been a blur of sleep, terrifying thoughts, and chamomile tea. No work. I don't even know what Alex and Daniel have been up to. But my thoughts are beginning to return to ordinary existence. The obsessive thoughts are petering off. I knew they would. Soon they will be like small drips interrupting my stream of the mundane.

The tablets helped. And Leo is back. His presence is reassuring and complicated. I'm so fucking confused. Do I genuinely love him, or do I need him because I'm too scared to be alone?

I take a few deep breaths. Music is coming from Alex's room. It must be Saturday.

Leo comes up behind me and puts his arms around me. I turn around and snuggle into the familiar spot just below his shoulder. I belong here. Or do I? Nothing else can exist, not even time. I am that young woman, surrendering. I feel his first kiss, with yearning. The moistness of his lips, his tongue confident as it meets mine, interrupted by the image of Nick's hand on my thigh.

'Mum, can you drive me to Caleb's?' Daniel is standing beside us.

Leo kisses me gently on the head, as he releases his embrace.

'Oh, gross guys.'

Leo walks over to where Daniel is standing and takes him in a bear hug. Danny struggles to free himself.

What the fuck was I thinking? Nick. What was I looking for? Everything is perfect as it is.

'What about football Danny?'

'We've got a bye.'

'Let's drive him and then we can go and have breakfast, Leo. I'll see if Alex wants to come.'

'How has the invisible man been?'

'Leo!' How can he even joke about it? Alex is drifting away from us, and he can't take it seriously.

I knock on Alex's door.

'Want to come out for breakfast *mijo*?'

'No, go away Mum.'

'Come on Alex, we haven't been out together for ages.'

'Well, you've been in bed all week.'

'Alex, I was sick, come on, it will be fun. You can have pancakes or bacon and eggs.'

'No.' His voice is firm.

'Please Alex, darling, do it for me. Can I come in?'

'Go away Mum.'

'What are you going to do if you don't come with us?' I know I should stop but I need him to be okay.

'Go with Leo. Now that you've managed to come out of your room.'

'Why don't you come out of yours too?'

'Mum, leave me alone. I don't want to go out with you and Leo.'

'Have you seen Alison?'

'NO! Fuck off and leave me alone.' His voice is loud and definite.

'Alex, please, respect! See you later. We won't be long.'

I don't know if this phase will pass or if it is the beginning of something worse. How can I help him if he won't talk to me? This is more than a broken heart.

Leo is singing as we drive off. Daniel joins in singing about the streets of Montevideo. Leo is tapping along on the steering wheel to the beat and Daniel improvises on the back of my seat. I look at them and smile, wishing it was always this simple.

We drop Daniel off and drive to Tony's. Leo insisted we come to Tony's. He says it's the best coffee. He's right. I can't tell him why I don't want to come here. And I can't lie. I have never been a liar.

When I was seventeen, Betty and I went to a party instead of the movie we told our parents we were going to see. When we got back, and they asked about the movie. I ran to my room and left Betty there telling them how good the movie was. I knew my face would give it away.

Leo looks relaxed. He always does after a tour. I don't know if it is getting away from me and Alex or just being out playing music, smoking pot, and joking around with Rafa.

I steer us to a table on the opposite side of the café to where Nick and I sat. 'So how was it?' I ask after we sit down.

Being a Saturday, the café is busy, and the smell of coffee and bacon penetrate the air, a strange fusion of two foods.

'Great, lots of fun. You know what Rafa is like. He never stops.' Leo answers as he taps his long thin fingers on the table. Leo is always tapping a tune.

'I bet there was weed too.'

'Not much. Lisa's pregnant. Not drinking, or smoking.' He looks over to see if the waiter is coming.

'What, another child? I suppose Tim's Mum will look after that one too.'

'She's a good mother, Lola.'

He is always defending her. I can't understand it.

'You wished you'd had kids with her, don't you?' I blurt it out, without thinking.

'Lola, please. It's a nice morning, we're together. I'm back home. Let's enjoy it. How is your father going? Anymore dates?'

'One Argentinian. Oh yeah and today, Betty organised a dinner at Teresa's house. Remember her? We haven't seen her for years. Bumped into her at Tia Gladys' funeral. We're all invited. She's cooking a paella. I told Betty we'd all meet at Papá's.'

'Why can't the old man go alone? He needs Mummy again. A *viejo* like him, still horny and needs Mummy.'

'It's not like that. And he's not horny, he's looking for a companion, someone to go out with and talk to.' Leo could be so crass.

'They're just going to hold hands? Open your eyes Lola, the *viejo* is horny. And good for him. He needs to be choosy, doesn't want some dried-up old woman, with a walking stick. A nice wet fanny, that's what he needs. Someone who'll give him a good fuck.'

'You're disgusting.'

'I'm realistic. I still want to fuck when we're old.'

Sometimes I think I hate Leo.

A young waiter comes and takes our order. I've decided on a croissant with my coffee and Leo orders a cheese and ham toastie.

'How's the happy hippie doing?'

'Haven't really had a chance to talk to her, I've been so out of it this week. Anyway, I'm worried about Alex. What if he's depressed? We need to be doing something now, before it gets worse.'

Images of Alex slitting his wrists had invaded my mind in the last few weeks. They scared me. Sometimes I think irrational thoughts can skip into reality. It is a frightening space. If I waver for even a second, I can get stuck, unable to see reason.

'He has friends, Lola. He goes to school; he goes out to parties. It's just us he rejects. That's normal. He still loves you. You need to let him become a man.'

Is it really that simple? Why couldn't I just let it be? No. I had to claw and scratch and rip it apart. Find pain, when maybe there was no need to.

I couldn't let go of Alex. I still needed him. I needed him to walk, to exist near me. When your children are born, you don't realise that one day you will release them. You will have to let them go to live their lives, to be out there feeling everything on their own. And the worst part of it is you can't fix things when they don't turn out like they want them too. You can't run to their boss and tell them to stop bullying your son and give him the promotion he deserves. I won't be able to ask his colleagues at work to be kind to him, nor his wife not to leave him, or be unfaithful. I can't stop what will happen or the pain he might feel. I hate knowing that I can't do anything. I give birth to this being and then I have to let go. It's almost a punishment. You are granted so much power and control and then it is taken away and you're left with nothing.

I could feel my face tightening. My forehead frowning.

'All you need to do is be there. You don't need to do anything else. When he needs us, we will be there. More than my father ever did. Just let him grow up. Lay off him. When he's in his room he's most likely wanking.'

'Why does the focus have to be so, down there for you?'

'Why is yours so up here?' He says it, tapping his head with his index finger.

Our coffees arrive and the smell greets me like an old friend. I watch as Leo stirs sugar into his short black.

'Leo, what would you think if I left my job?'

I take a sip of the warm, comforting liquid.

'Lola, if you want to leave your job, leave. I can't understand why you want to work there. I want you to be you, Lola. Do whatever it is that makes you happy.'

'What about money? Your income is so unpredictable, we won't be able to budget.'

'Money comes and goes. So, we'll live on rice and potatoes, like in South America. Millions of people in the world live on bread and beans or rice.'

'Yeah, try telling the kids that. And that millions of people don't have new shoes and football t-shirts and cars to drive them everywhere.'

'They'll cope. What do you want to do Lola?'

Leo doesn't think about the future. To him you live day by day with what you have. I look at him as he drinks his coffee. How does he never seem perturbed?

'I don't know.' It was true, I didn't know. The supermarket job gave me routine, and I needed that. But I didn't need the feelings that I had when I saw Nick.

I don't truly know myself; who I really am? So much of my life has been surviving and coping, there hasn't been room for much else. And whenever I do see a space, I fill it. Really full, stuffing and stuffing so there's no room for any kind of contemplation. When you're empty anything can happen, it's a dangerous state to be in.

That's what happened with Nick. A little gap, exposed, naked.

'Maybe I could become a botanist. I like plants. I already have a science degree so I would get some credits.'

'Back to study. Think about it. The stress of the essays, deadlines. If that's what you want, I'll support you, but please think carefully. You tried the masters and remember what happened.'

Of course, I remember. It wasn't the study, it was the students. Those arrogant snobs. The red-haired one, who drove a BMW. He knew I was nervous. I had said yes to tutoring because I needed the money. The scholarship was not enough.

'This will be different. I won't have anything else, and the boys are older. Alex was just a toddler then.'

Leo stayed home with Alex when I was at university. He was so good with him. He sang to him, took him to the playground, they danced to the Wiggles, played with toy cars on their hands and knees pushing the little cars along. Leo had drawn a service station, a supermarket, and a garage for each car, with chalk, on the carpet.

I was angry when I saw it. The mess on the carpet. The two of them just looked at me while I had a minor tantrum. Alex got up and walked away. Leo followed him. I just sat there, on the service station and started to cry.

On Saturday, the day of the paella at Teresa's house, Alex refuses to go. He says he is going to a friend's house. I offer to drive him, but he wants to walk. Is it true he is going out? Or is he going to stay home and play video games?

We stop at the bottle shop and buy wine to take. One red and one white. Leo is driving and I look out the window at the rows of houses, wondering what family dynamics are going on in the different houses. Is anyone really happy?

Daniel is telling Leo about a movie he saw.

We stop outside Papá's house. At the door we are greeted by Betty and Coco.

'Hi guys. Daniel, you're looking handsome. You've scrubbed up pretty well too Leo. Did you see Papá? He just went out to get some milk. I told him we didn't need it, but you know what he's like. He insisted on driving to the shop. He said he doesn't want to buy it from the Arab down the road, something about bad apples.'

Betty was talking fast. Three days with Papá and even she, the calm hippie, was hyper.

'Let me get these shoes out the way. He keeps putting these shoes here. I tell him they're in the middle of the way. Put them near the door but he keeps on leaving them there. He has to have everything the way he wants it, even if it's inconvenient. He can't see it.'

'It is his house, Betty.' She visits him once or twice a year and wants to tell him how to live his life.

'That's not the point. He has this wacky order. He puts things where they don't really go and doesn't want to change them. Oh yeah, and did you know that he still has Mum's clothes in the wardrobe?'

'I know. He's sentimental.'

How can she be spiritual and pragmatic? A spiritual pragmatist. Is there such a thing? Don't spirituality and pragmatism oppose each other?

She is dressed in a long stretch-knit purple skirt. The type that clings to you but looks messy. A matching scarf is wrapped around her head and her long black hair flows out from under it. From her ears hang a pair of silver earrings with lapis lazuli stones. The ones Flo brought back from Chile for her. I remember the night she got them. Betty, Malena, and I went to Tia Gladys' house to see Flo. She had just come back from South America. It was the first time she went back since she left at six years old. Flo was radiant. She spoke to us in really fast Spanish, strewn with new words and phrases that we had never heard. The only Spanish we were used to was the fifteen-year-old Spanish that our parents and their friends spoke. Imported and planted without much growth.

She brought new music and stories. A new generation. The adolescence and youth we would have lived burst out of her suitcase. I welcomed it, taking what was rightfully mine. Malena savoured it, not wanting it to escape again. Betty played and joked with it, like a new friend.

We went home drunk on Latinness. Adorned with silver and amethyst, singing the words of a new generation.

'I'm back.' Papá walks in holding a big bouquet of flowers. Coco runs up to him.

'Lola, *mija*, how are you feeling?'

'*Bien* Papá.'

'Leo how was your tour?'

He spoke with an unfamiliar confidence. He even seemed to stand taller, with his shoulders back.

'Great Juan, really good.'

He kissed Daniel and rubbed the top of his head.

'I have something for you.'

'What Abuelo?'

'Close your eyes.'

He put the flowers down and went out of the room. Was he taking Teresa flowers? He really is taking the ad seriously.

'Put the café on Leo,' he shouted.

He sounded happy, jubilant almost.

'Why the tie?' I whispered to Betty.

She shrugged.

'Horny,' Leo said, pointing to the flowers.

He came out holding a poster. He put it in Daniel's hand.

'Open your eyes.'

'Wow, Abuelo, where did you get it?'

'I have my ways.'

It was a signed poster of Luis Suarez, a star of Uruguayan football.

'Where's Alex? I have something for him too.'

'At a friend's.' I'm beginning to resign myself to Alex no longer going anywhere with us.

'Good. It will be boring for him at Teresa's.'

'Are we ready then?' Betty asked.

'The coffee, Betty.'

'Again. Papá, you've already had two coffees today.' Was she really counting how many coffees he drank?

124

'Leo and Lola want one.'

'I'm okay Juan. I like the tie.' Leo commented.

I couldn't remember the last time I had seen him wearing a tie.

'Why so formal Papá?'

'What you mean, formal?'

'The tie.'

Betty glares at me.

'You like it, Lola? It's Italian. Malena sent it to me. For Christmas, a few years ago. Now you are all here. I will tell you. I cannot go to Teresa's house. I have an appointment I must go to. Tell Teresa I am sorry. You all have a good time, enjoy the paella.'

He picks up the flowers and quickly walks out, leaving four flabbergasted faces.

JUAN

A veces cuando pienso que vivo solitario
Sometimes when I think I'm living alone
Me parece un calvario la vida sin tu amor
Without your love, life is tormented
Y en medio de esta pena que aviva mis deseos
And in the midst of this pain that fuels my desires
Me parece que veo tu rostro encantador
I think I see your charming face
   'Ansias de amor', Guillermo Desiderio Barbieri y Carlos Gardel

I see her. She is sitting on the bench we like to sit on after we've walked the dogs, the one under the Moreton Bay fig tree. But no Churchill today.

As I get closer, I can see she is wearing a dress. I have never seen her wearing a dress. Usually, when we walk, she has the tracksuit pants. The dress has flowers. Big red ones. Too big, I think.

She smiles when she sees me. I wave at her with my left hand. In my right hand I am carrying the flowers. The flowers are tiger lilies. That is what the woman in the shop told me. I think this is a stupid name. Tigers and flowers do not belong together. When I went to buy the flowers, I saw many beautiful ones. Roses, violets, carnations. Roses are too forward. They are the flowers of young love. Carmen's favourite flowers were carnations. I did not want to buy Carmen's favourite flowers for Frances. That would be wrong. So, I look at the tiger ones. Nice, big open flowers. Not scared to be in the world. Maybe that is why they have been called tiger; the animal is strong, a powerful predator, parading its dominance and beauty. The conqueror. The tiger lilies may conquer hearts.

I think Carmen was like the tiger lily before we came to Australia. She was fearless and strong in the world. Here she became the carnation, closing in and squeezing her life as small as possible.

127

Frances is walking towards me. She has a big smile. Her hair does not look like the rainbow today. It is all brown.

'*Señorita.*' I say to her, as I give her the bouquet of the tiger lilies.

'Oh, Bub, they're beautiful.'

She looks like she is going to cry. Now I worry that she is allergic to flowers. 'Thank you.'

She kisses me on the cheek.

'I feel so silly,' she says wiping her eyes.

I take out my handkerchief from the pocket of my shirt and give it to her. This seems to make the crying worse.

'Frances, what is wrong?'

She starts to laugh. Not her usual big laugh, but giggles like a child.

'You are such a gentleman. I have never been given flowers before or a man's handkerchief, either, for that matter.'

'No!' I cannot believe her husband never give her flowers, but I don't want to tell her that. She takes my arm. It was her idea we go out for dinner. For many weeks we have been meeting every day at the park, walking our dogs. Sometimes we go to the pub for a lemonade. I enjoy her company. At first, I was uncertain, but the more we talk, the more I like Frances. She is wise and strong, like the big tree we sit under in the park, with deep roots, standing strong, grounded. She is very kind too, always helping a neighbour or a friend. Frances doesn't judge other people, like my daughters do. When I am with her, I feel lighter, happier.

'Let's go, Juan, you old romantic bastard, making me cry.'

I pull my arm away.

'What you mean bastard. You are upset?'

'No of course not Juan. Bastard can be like mate or friend. You know in an affectionate funny way.'

'So, you use it for an insult and for a friend?'

'Yeah, that's right.'

'You are sure? You do not lie to me; you are not upset? I find this very strange that you can say this insult to a friend, and it is not an insult.'

'Of course not. I am happy. Now let's go and get some dinner.'

She takes my arm again. We walk to the RSL Club. It is not far.

When we get there, I stop outside. I have not been inside an RSL club, never in my life.

'Come on then, what are you waiting for?'

'Frances, you never have flowers before, I never go to the RSL before.' Carmen and I always pass by this club, so close to our house and we never went inside.

Now she does the big laugh.

'Well, it's the beginning of new things for both of us.'

We go inside and we sign our names. This I know, because all the clubs have it, even the Uruguayan one. The carpet is a reddish brown. It looks old. To go to the restaurant, we take the escalator to the first floor.

It is very bright and noisy. There are huge television screens, and the rugby is on.

We find a nice table next to the window and Frances puts the flowers on the table. 'Frances, why is it called RSL?'

'It stands for Returned Services League. They were formed after the war, for returned soldiers to have a place to get together. Now they make money from the pokies and bars.'

I cannot believe what Frances tells me. I am in a club for the military! What do I do? Do I say something, or do I stay quiet, we eat, and I never come back.

'But now it's not just for the soldiers? Anyone can come?' I worry that only soldiers and their families are here. *Puta madre*, what have I done?

'Yes Juan, it is a club like any other, people come to eat, drink, play the pokies. Don't look so worried love. It's okay. Let's go get some food.'

Maybe everyone who is here does not support the military. They come to eat, like Frances says. There are families with children. The people look very Australian. I cannot see the Lebanese or the Chinese that live in this *barrio* eating here. The Australians here must support the soldiers. This means they will be very patriotic. The patriotism that slices countries like mortadella, each slice falling from the machine ready to be eaten in war. They won't want the migrants in their club.

I follow Frances to the food buffet. She shows me where I get a tray to carry the food. I am back at the hostel, lining up for food in the cafeteria. The smell of boiled cabbage, overcooked meat. The lumpy mashed potato in the tray, like plaster. The *ollas popular* in Montevideo served better food. Carmen sometimes helped out at the one near the *Cerro*. They made *puchero*, with plenty of meat, vegetables, and *garbanzos* too. They fed a whole *barrio*.

Carmen and I ate everything at the hostel. We had to. Malena ate nothing except the ice-cream that was served on Sundays. Poor Carmen would have to cook for her in our room over a small camping stove. It was humiliating lining up for the food. I was the man, and this is where I had brought my family. Carmen never complained. We lived in a rounded, corrugated iron hut where the Australian government housed migrants. Rows and rows of huts, like the slums in Uruguay. The five of us, in one big room. A sofa bed that Carmen and I opened up to sleep in every night, a bunk bed and small single bed. I felt so much shame, but we were safe. The streets were quiet, a quiet like we had never heard before. At night there was nobody on the street and nothing open. These people had no curfew. What were they scared of? Carmen and I could not understand. Why did they not go outside at night?

'Juan do you like lamb? There is roast lamb,' Frances tells me.

I look at the roast lamb. Good, I like lamb. Carmen made a beautiful roast lamb. She made little cuts in it and put garlic and anchovies. Then covered it in chimichurri. Delicious.

I look at the trays of vegetables, peas, pumpkin, carrots, potatoes, broccoli, chips. Each one in its own little box.

There is also pasta. The one with the cream and the bacon. Lola made it once and it made me very sick. I was up all night going to the toilet.

'What are you having Juan?"

'I think I will have the lamb with some potatoes and pumpkin.' The other vegetables look like they have drowned when cooked.

'I'm having the *larson*.' She points to the lasagna.

'You mean the Lasagna

'You say *larson*. It's French.'

'Frances, the Italians would kill you. Lasagna is Italian, you say la – san – ya.' I say it very slowly.

'Anyway, that's what I'm having. I always thought it was French, with that name. It sounds French.'

I look at her. She is smiling. Her smile makes me smile. I pay for our food, and we walk to our table. Frances suggests we go and get some drinks at the bar. I ask for a bottle of red wine for us. Then Frances orders a glass of white wine.

'I already ask for red wine, a bottle for both of us.'

'You didn't ask me if I wanted red wine. I drink white wine.'

'With lasagna? You are crazy. Lasagna goes with red wine.'

'Is that an Italian thing too?'

'No, it's just what you do. You drink red wine with red meat and white wine with white meat.' This is what Malena's husband told me. He is an educated European man.

'Well, I'm not a conformist and I make my own decisions.' She takes he white wine and we walk back to the table.

'Okay, okay.'

Finally, we sit down to eat. I pour myself a glass of wine. It has a good earthy smell to it. Like you can almost smell the grapevine it came from. '*Salud*,' I say as I pick up my glass.

'Cheers, here's to us and great night,' Frances says as she clinks her glass against mine. Her wine smells strong, like an old woman's perfume. I will have to teach her about wine.

It is very busy. The club is big and noisy. Lots of people come to the RSL and not just old ones there are young people too, like Lola and Betty. They can't all support the military surely.

'Tell me Juan, how is Lola, is she better?'

'Yes, she looked better today.' I desperately hope for Lola to get better. To totally recover, not get better then sick again. My smart and beautiful daughter, broken and I cannot fix her.

'Poor love. There's no point in worrying, that's what life has taught me. Just gives you a bigger frown line and feeds the pain inside. Besides you can't change anything. These days I try and let go of worry. Life can be very tough. I had a bad time when my son got sick.'

'Frances, you never told me you had a son.' As I say this I can feel a piece of meat has stuck in my back molar. I cannot put off going to the dentist anymore.

'He died, nearly twenty years ago. Suicide.'

I almost drop the glass in my hand.

'Why, Frances, why did he do this?'

'He was very sick. He had bipolar. You know, sometimes he was manic. Up all night, going out at all hours, spending all his money. Then he would get depressed, very depressed, everything was dark. Didn't get out of bed. One day, he went in the bathroom and didn't come out. He drowned himself in the bath. His father found him.'

I look at Frances and I cannot imagine she had so much suffering. She is always so happy, laughing. She makes me feel happy. I look forward to seeing her in the park. Some days I get very nostalgic. I think about Uruguay when I was a young man. I cannot believe that I am this old and my life has passed so quickly, like a movie on fast forward and so many people have left this movie. Then I go to the park and meet Frances and I forget about all of that. I even forget that I am old.

'That is terrible. I cannot imagine the pain of losing your child.' The pain of watching Lola suffer was already so huge.

'It was worse for Malcolm, my husband. He blamed himself. He had been very strict with Steven; he said he should have showed him more love. It wasn't that. He was sick. It's a chemical imbalance in his brain and Steven didn't want to take his medication. He said it made him numb, he couldn't feel.'

I have stopped eating. My eyes are fixed on Frances.

'I'm okay,' she says as she cuts her food.

I watch her cut her food and put it in her mouth. She is an incredible woman. 'Tell me about your son, what was he like?'

'He was a beautiful child. Big green eyes, reddish brownish hair. That was from his Irish ancestors. He had darker skin, like me from my Aboriginal mother. When he was little Steven was happy and energetic. He and Mal played cricket in the backyard. In high school he changed, became solemn, didn't leave his room.'

I think of Alex, and of Lola too.

'Sometimes when I looked at him, I could see wildness and terror in his eyes.'

I reach out and take her hand. 'You have suffered too much Frances.'

'Malcolm rang me when it happened. By the time I got home, the ambulance was in the driveway and Steven was lying on a stretcher. A white sheet covered him. I pulled the sheet away and kissed him for the last time.'

I could see her eyes were moist. I didn't mean to make her sad.

'I'm sorry Frances, you don't need to say anymore.'

'It's alright Bub. I will always have Steven in my heart. His spirit comes to me sometimes.'

I look down at my food. The lamb is covered with a brown sauce. I smell it. It smells like the food Lola had in hospital when Alex was born. The sauce is thick. I scrape some with my knife. Even the pumpkin is covered with this sauce.

'Don't you like gravy?' Frances asks as she looks at my plate.

'Gravy is that what this sauce is called. It looks like a bad diarrhoea. Why do they put this on the food?' Frances is looking at me and she laughs.

'Do you want mine love?'

'What is in this sauce?' I am still scraping it off the lamb. It is thick.

'Try it; it's the juices from the meat with flour added to thicken it. I can't believe you've never had gravy. What do you put on your meat?'

'What do you mean what I put on my meat? I don't pour sauce like you pour cement. I have mustard, or mayonnaise or chimichurri.'

I realise she would not know what chimichurri is. I try to explain it to her.

'The chimichurri, is the best. We make it with parsley, oregano, garlic, olive oil.'

'I love how you say that; you pucker your lips. Oh, you're cute, say it again.'

I feel embarrassed like a teenage boy with the pimples.

'Come on Juan, say it.'

'Okay. Chimichurri'

We are both laughing. For the first time I notice her eyes. They are not green and they are not blue. Maybe a greeny blue, like the Atlantic Ocean of my youth.

'Chimi, chimi. It sounds like a dance. Cha cha cha. That's what we should do, go dancing. Can you dance Juan?'

'Of course, I can dance, what do you think I am a brute?'

I have not danced since Carmen died.

'Let's do it then. I used to go ballroom dancing years ago with Malcolm. Bless his soul. What do you like to dance?'

Dancing is like a marriage. Your partner is with you for the life of the dance. You build it together and support each other. It is an expression of love, how you carry your partner. You take her into the *rumba*, her feet and your feet moving together, that is your moment. We step into the tango, our feet, and our arms, our bodies knowing exactly where they have to be at every beat. As we salsa, our bodies move to and from each other and our feet seem to be enjoying their own perfect party. The music is contagious, and everyone is dancing. Carmen's brother Mario is there and her sister Gladys too. They are smiling as they dance. The whole room is moving to that beat, we are one with that salsa.

'Juan, you didn't answer. What do you like to dance? I bet you can tango.'

'A little.'

'Oh, let's do it Juan, let's go dancing. I haven't been dancing in years.'

I look at her eyes. They look greener. She is a like a little girl asking to go to the zoo.

'Yes, Frances, I will take you dancing.'

After we eat, Frances suggests we play the poker machines. This is new for me too. I watch her putting the coins in and pulling the lever. I think of what she told me, her mother was Aboriginal. I don't know any Aboriginal people, only Frances.

'Frances what was your mother's name?'

She turns to look at me, as she pulls the lever on the noisy machine.

'Her name was Doris. Why?'

Doris didn't sound like an Aboriginal name. Maybe she changed it. This happened in South America, Indigenous people given Spanish names. A way to dominate and annihilate, strip people of their name, their culture, their identity. It must have been the same in Australia.

'I'm curious. Did she have an Aboriginal name?'

Frances releases her hold on the lever of the machine. She turns to face me.

'She was taken from her family as a little girl. She was given a new name.'

'Where did they take her?'

'They took the children away and put them in homes and trained the girls to become servants for the whites.'

This remarkable woman has had so much suffering in her life. I want to take her in my arms and hold her close. I think of Frances' mother, she must have been so frightened. And for her mother to have her children stolen from her. Imperialism is the same all over the world. Carmen taught me about the *Salsipuedes* massacre in 1831 in Uruguay. *Charraus* were slaughtered like animals and women and children were taken to become servants for the Spanish.

'They can never take away your heritage Frances. Your incredible strength must come from your mother and your people.'

She takes my hand in hers. 'My mother was a survivor. She was very resilient, and she taught me so much.'

'I can see that in you Frances.'

'I am so lucky to have found you Juan.'

'No, I am the lucky one, that you are in my life Frances.'

She smiles at me and turns to pull the lever on the machine.

BETTY

Coffee Soap
Ingredients:
- Coconut oil
- Lye
- Liquid coffee
- Vanilla extract
- Cinnamon powder
- Coffee grounds

El Rincon is distant from my world. The ham and cheese sandwiches of my childhood greet me along with the *alfajores* I devoured at the South American events we went to. The sweet *dulce de leche* stuck between the crumbly biscuits. The smell of strong coffee piercing my nostrils. The possibility of coffee soap pops into my head. I watch Papá, relaxed and jovial as he greets Miguel, such a contrast to how he interacts with the English-speaking world. Here, he can be himself, I can see it in the way he straightens his shoulders, and moves confidently towards a table, leading the way, not waiting for me to navigate for both of us.

Before I go home today, I want to ask him where he went last night. Miguel comes over and takes our order. Papá asks for his usual short black and I order a *cedron* tea. I look over at the rows of *yerba* on the shelf. Papá rarely drinks *mate* these days. It was something they did together. Mum had the *mate* ready when Papá came home from work. I look at the *yerba* stand again, and I see the yellow and green Canarias packet, their favourite. Preparing *mate* is a ritual, I've seen Lola do it to when she drinks it with Leo. They put the *yerba* in the gourd, make a little hollow, then add warm water and let it sit for a while. The first *mate* is the worst, Mum would always have that one, as you get the dusty bits from the *yerba* that hasn't settled yet.

'Betty you are driving, you will fall asleep, have a coffee.'

'Papá, you know I don't drink coffee.'

'And I tell you coffee is not bad for you.'

'It's a drug, a stimulant.'

'Look at me; I have been drinking coffee for seventy years. Do I look like I take drugs?'

I can't contain my laughter. Papá looks at me as he takes a sip of his coffee and spurts it out of his mouth.

'Why are you laughing?'

'I imagined you shooting up coffee.'

He lets out a loud chuckle and we are both laughing so much, my stomach hurts.

I'll ask him now that he is relaxed. 'Where did you go yesterday when you said you couldn't come to Teresa Maldonado's house?'

He takes another sip of his coffee and adjusts his chair. He looks out the window, as he speaks.

'I went to meet someone.'

His eyes cannot meet mine and as I look out the window too, we both see a big woman with sunglasses and a red scarf around her neck waving madly at us as she walks towards the café.

'It's Maria.' I gesture to her to come.

'Not that gypsy again.'

'Please Papá, she's a good person.'

Maria makes her way around to the door and comes over to us. Her loud voice fills the whole café.

'*Mi amorcito*, Betty, how are you?'

She hugs and kisses me. Then turns to Papá. He reluctantly puts his cheek for Maria to kiss him. Instead, she takes him in a big hug, embracing him with her large tuckshop arms. Then she kisses him on the cheek, leaving a red lipstick mark on it. She pulls a chair over and sits down, taking off her green shawl and placing it on her lap.

'Oh, *Juancito*, so good to see you. Your daughters are so lucky to have you. You'll have to take poor Florencia in too now. I've seen her a couple of times since the funeral and the poor girl is a mess. Gladys was such a special woman.'

'She sure was. Maybe I should ask Flo to come and stay with us for a couple of weeks, just to get away from it all. It's such a beautiful time of year. The trees have such divine colours now.'

As I say it, I realise Flo hasn't been up to Mullum for years. The last time she visited she drove up with Tia Gladys.

'I'm sure she would love that. When do you go home *amor*?'

'Today. Papá and I were having our farewell breakfast.'

'Oh, I hope I'm not interrupting a father-daughter moment.'

'Of course not, Maria. It's always good to see you.'

Miguel comes over with a *cortado* for Maria, before she has ordered.

'Maria, why don't you do a small reading for Papá? He's going through something special.'

Papá glares at me as he shifts uncomfortably in his chair.

'Of course. Give me your hand Juan.'

'No, not today, thanks.'

'Oh Papá. go on.' I'm curious to hear what Maria will tell him.

'No, I don't want to. You know I don't believe this stuff.'

'Well then if you don't believe it, it won't matter. It will be fun. Just give Maria your ring. You can do it like that, can't you Maria?'

'Of course. Come on Juan. It won't hurt.'

'Please Papá.' He puts one hand over the other covering his wedding ring, as I put on my best pleading face. 'Do it for me.'

He twists his ring around and around with the fingers of his other hand. Maria puts out her hand. He slowly and reluctantly takes the ring off and places it in her hand.

Maria holds the ring in her hands and looks out the window. Her face solemn. She then turns to Papá.

'There's a woman. I can see a woman in your life.'

I look at Maria, waiting for her to speak.

'There is a lot of laughter and dancing too. She's good for you Juan. But the girls need to keep out. I can see a vast amount of water too, like an ocean.'

'We're fine with it, Maria. It was me who put the ad in the paper for him.'

'*Ay, viejo*. I can't believe you had it in you. Good for you.'

She gives Papá the ring back. He takes it as he looks down and quickly puts it on his finger.

'That's what you were doing yesterday, you were going to meet her. Papá, you could've told us.'

Maria is looking at Papá. She takes the last sip from her *cortado*. 'I have to go, I'm meeting my daughter.' She gets up and wraps her green shawl around her shoulders. Papá and I stand up to kiss her goodbye. She whispers in Papá's ear and although I can hear it, the Spanish is too fast for me to understand. I can only catch the words *buena mujer*.

'Who is this woman? I'm happy for you Papá. I'd love to meet her when I come down next. What's her name?'

'She is called Frances, Francesca. Yes, that's her name Francesca.'

It hits me, that was the name of the woman in the park, the dreadful Australian woman. If her name is Francesca, maybe she is Italian. But she spoke like an Aussie, maybe she is an Italian that was born here. That can't be right, Italians came after the war, or maybe her family came earlier for some reason. Whoever she was, she was not who I was imagining when I put up the ad. I stare at Papá, dumbfounded.

LOLA

18 April 2012

*Papá hasn't rung me for two days and he's acting very strange.
Something is going on and I need to find out what it is. Leo says it must
be a woman. But why doesn't he want to tell us? He was open about it
before. Tonight, at dinner I'll ask him. In the meantime, I have my own
dilemma to deal with – Nick.*

I quickly close the book and rush around getting ready for work. I
haven't seen Nick since that day in his car. I feel anxious. I know I should
resign but I'm worried about money.

When I get to work, I find out I'm needed in the deli section. I don't like
the deli. The last time I worked there I cut my finger slicing salami. There
is a rawness to it that I find uncomfortable. All the meat is out there, and
you need to pick it up, carry it, slice it. And the smells: strong, powerful,
pungent, invasive.

The cheeses too, heady, and forceful. I like food but I don't like it to
overpower me. I don't like any smell to overpower me, to take over so that
I'm lost in its essence. I need to detach from it. I find that with sex too, the
smells are consuming, piercing, I want to push them away. Maybe I am a
prude. Kerry's probably right and so is Leo. I didn't even want to swim
naked when we went to Betty's place. It just wasn't right, not in front
of our kids. And in front of each other. Leo and Betty totally exposed
themselves to each other. I don't want that intimacy with my children or
with my brother-in-law.

I can see Nick walking towards the deli. He stops to chat to one of the
staff stacking toiletries in aisle nine. Maybe I could run to the bathroom
before he gets here. I tell Marisa I'm going to the bathroom, and I'll be
back in five minutes.

As I'm leaving, he sees me and walks quickly towards me. I ignore him and keep walking.

'Lola, can I see you in my office?'

I keep walking, pretending not to hear.

'Lola, Lola, stop please. I need to talk to you.'

I stop and don't turn around. He comes towards me, and I feel his hand on my arm. My legs feel wobbly, and I feel like I'm going to faint.

'Please Lola, come to my office. I really need to talk to you.'

'We're really busy at the deli.' I answer without turning to look at him.

'I've sent Sue to replace you.'

We walk to his office. He walks close to me. Too close. I hate it and I like it.

When we are inside his office, he closes the door.

'I've been worried about you Lola. Are you okay?'

When I rang in sick, I didn't say why. I don't like to tell people. If you have a physical illness people understand, they know what to say. With a mental illness, no one knows what's the right thing to say. Sometimes you're made to feel like it's a weakness. Like you're not strong enough to control your own mind.

'I'm fine.' I'm shaking. I want him to hold me. I want to feel his skin.

He takes my hands in his. I am powerless. I feel like crying. He moves his head towards me and presses his lips on mine. They are warm and moist. He caresses my hair as his tongue slips inside my mouth. Our tongues meet and play with each other. I disappear, I no longer am.

He kisses my eyelids, my nose, my chin, my neck, my ear. I hold him tightly. I feel his hand on my back. Then on my bum. He caresses it softly, then pinches it hard. I am jelly. He puts his hand down my pants, unzips my trousers. I feel his firm fingers exploring me all over. They are inside me. He finds my clitoris. It is his. He pulls my pants down and he sits me on his bare lap. I feel the hairs of his legs on my buttocks. He is inside me. I am crying. It's been a long time since I've been here. He is holding me tight.

My mind suddenly comes back.

'A condom, do you have a condom?'

'Not in my office'.

I get up quickly. What the fuck am I doing? I pull my pants up.

'I can't Nick, I'm going home. I can't do this. I can't come back here.'

'Come to my place tonight.'

'I can't Nick. I can't, I can't and I can't work here anymore either. I'm sorry.' I'm shaking.

'I like you Lola, I do, I'm not playing with you. I want you, Lola.' He reaches for my hand, but I pull it away.

'It's not about that. I just can't do this. It's not me, it's not right.'

I can't get out of there fast enough. My bag, I need to get my bag. It is in my locker. I can't even look at anyone as I walk out. I feel ashamed, overwhelmed, distraught.

I take the first taxi that comes along. The bus would take forever. I want to run straight to my room and hide under the covers of my bed.

Luckily when I get home no one is there. Not even Alex. I jump in the shower and let the warm water run over me. I want to stand there until there is nothing left.

The phone rings. It's Leo.

'I've got a surprise. Is your father coming to dinner tonight?'

'I think so. He hasn't rung me.'

'Good. I gotta go we're in the middle of a rehearsal. Cook extra, I'm bringing friends. Lola are you okay, your voice sounds very soft?'

'I'm okay, just tired.' Not in the mood for Leo's friends.

'I just remembered, aren't you supposed to be at work?'

'I quit. I can't do it anymore Leo.'

'You did the right thing; you're too smart to be working there. Lola. I love you.'

'I know. I love you too.'

He must never know. The pain, the hurt it wouldn't be fair. He doesn't deserve it. He is so loving towards me. He cares for me more than anyone ever has. He knows me. After Daniel was born, the sadness was consuming, there was no room for anything else. I was sure he would leave.

I didn't quite come back from that. I couldn't. I had lost something. Maybe it was hope, maybe it was love. I can't define it, but something was lost.

Can I really leave him? The phone rings again. This time it is Betty.

'Lola, there is a woman. Her name is Francesca. That's all I know. Just before I left, we bumped into Maria, and she felt his ring and said it was a woman and that we shouldn't interfere. All Papá told me was her name.'

'He's supposed to come for dinner tonight. Oh my god, what if he brings her.'

'I doubt it, he was still secretive. But he's happy Lola. When I was there, he was distracted, the tomato plants were dying. When the phone rang, he rushed to it and walked away with it. Oh, and the other thing, he sings. He sings old tangos. I think he's in love with this Francesca.'

'Don't be ridiculous, he would never fall in love again.'

'You never know. Ring me if you find out more.'

'Okay. Bye Betty.' As I put the phone down, I realise I have been pacing while talking to her. I can't stop, sitting still seems impossible.

Dinner. I need to think of something for tonight. My mind keeps going back to this afternoon. I'm sitting on Nick. His hands. His soft white skin. He's what Daniel calls a 'whitie'. Skin so white it's ghostly.

My dark legs against his. His blue eyes. It was the first time I'd seen blue eyes from so close. Translucent. The iris, the pupil defined. Soft, tangible.

Brown eyes are not like that. They are strong, intense. You can't see inside them. They are guards at the gate. Brown eyes have been enslaved, invaded, murdered, tortured, robbed, persecuted. They've lived through war, dictatorships, invasions. The eyes of fear and displacement, yet resilient. They hold hunger and pain.

I am at home with brown eyes. That's why I married Leo, too. Blue eyes would have been a betrayal. My children have dark brown eyes and olive skin. I wonder if blue-eyed children would hold the fear and pain of the generations before them.

Maybe my grandchildren will let go of the trauma we carry. It's too soon for my children's generation. Even Betty's children have entered the world with brown eyes. Their father's blue eyes are not strong enough to soothe the pain of generations.

When I was younger, I never had crushes on boys with blue eyes. My first real crush was on Michael Zepetti. An Italian boy who played rugby and ate mortadella sandwiches. We all liked Michael. When he finally made his choice, we were devastated.

He chose Karen, a runner with long blonde hair and the longest legs in the school. We couldn't compete. They were beautiful together, the wog and the Aussie. She was nearly a head taller than him. When I went shopping with my mum, I used to see them outside Woollies, sharing a cigarette and holding hands. They were so cool.

My first real boyfriend was Ahmed. We were both in year eleven. He was Lebanese and gorgeous. His arms were dark and muscly. He was a basketball player and danced hip hop before it was popular. I taught him to salsa, and he danced like a Latino. The boy spoke with his body, he moved so freely; it was enticing to watch him.

He would come to my house to study. We would sit in the kitchen, our books spread over the kitchen table, our knees touching underneath. My mum fed him, and he drank short espressos with Papá. I wanted to marry him and have children that looked just like him.

At the end of year eleven he started smoking pot and I barely saw him all summer. He was hanging around a group of kids from a different school. When school started back, he didn't return. He went to live in Wollongong with his uncle and aunt and got an apprenticeship as an electrician at the Steelworks. I cried for weeks. In Chemistry I sat by myself at the science bench.

A couple of years later I found out that Ahmed had got married and had a child. Our child. For years I saw our child; his birth, his first day of school, Ahmed and I on either side of him, holding his hands. With Ahmed it was always a boy. The three of us cuddling together on the couch. Even after Alex was born, I still saw my child with Ahmed. He was about thirteen. He had a smile that fell slightly to one side. His thick black hair was combed back. He was smart. Ahmed and I clapped when he was awarded dux of his year. Over the years he faded. By the time Daniel was born, he was no longer there.

Lebanese. We'll have Lebanese for dinner. I won't cook. I'll get take away. Papá will say I'm lazy. I'll get it early and set it all out, so it's ready when they get here.

At about 7pm I hear the doorbell. I open the door and see Papá. He is radiant. He is smiling as he pinches my face and kisses my forehead. I can smell aftershave on him. That's new. Papá is holding a bottle in a brown paper bag. He hands it to me and I notice it is cold. He must have bought white wine. He rarely brings white wine. It's always red.

'Put it in the fridge, it's beer.'

'Beer? You don't drink beer.'

'I do now. It's refreshing. You should try it, Lola. The first sip is a little bitter but then it's like cool water, you can't get enough. Now where is my favourite grandson I need to ask him something.'

'In his room. Go and see him. Don't let Daniel hear you say that.'

I watch him walk towards Alex's room. He even seems to be walking faster. He looks younger. And what's with the beer?

He comes back with Alex.

'So, what did you want to ask Alex, Papá?'

'It's between Abuelo and grandchild.' He winks at Alex.

Alex isn't giving anything away.

Papá pours me a glass of beer and we sit at the kitchen table. He cuts the salami and cheese that he has brought. Alex sits at the table and eats some salami. 'This is good, Abuelo.'

'I know, it is *perfecto*, not too spicy and not too plain.'

We hear the front door open, and Leo comes in with Rafa and an elderly woman.

Rafa is the last person I want to see tonight. There is no way we are going to find out what is happening with Papá and this woman with Rafa here.

Leo introduces the woman as Rafa's mother. He winks at me. I know what he is thinking. The woman is short, with African features.

'Elvia, this is my wife, Lola.' Leo says, as he puts his arm around me.

Elvia kisses me lightly on the cheek. Like Rafa, her skin is dark, but not black. Africanness, washed out with generations of Spanish blood forced upon it.

Rafa grew up in a very poor family in the *ciudad vieja*, the old part of Montevideo, where the city meets the wharf. They lived in a slum with other Afro-Uruguayan families, descendants of the slaves brought to South America by the Spaniards. All they could bring with them was their culture, which they passed on to their children in their dances and music. Rafa grew up as part of the colourful *Candombe*, each year in February at *Carnaval* time; *candombe* groups beat out their rhythms and fill the city streets with their dances. Young girls in bikinis swing their hips with a vigour that I have not seen elsewhere. The *Mamá viejas* dance their way alongside hundreds of drummers. That night is their night. They are celebrated and loved as their mesmerising sounds own the streets. The rest of the year they are back in the poverty and hunger that only those who have lived it understand. For one day they forget they are the sugar-coated peanut sellers on the street, the washer women, the children scavenging through the city's bins.

Rafa smiles at me. His curly hair falling over one eye. I know that Leo loves him. He has known Rafa longer than he has known me. He's family.

When I first met Rafa he lived with Isabel. A beautiful Colombian woman. They had two little boys. Rafa already had a daughter with an Australian woman he had married previously. Isabel left him and went back to Colombia with their sons. Soon after he met Stephanie and had another child. Then Stephanie left and he went to live with Carla, a fresh-faced country girl from an Italian family in Griffith. He and Carla had a girl. Little Frankie. We babysat her a few times. I loved holding that little girl. I fantasised she was my daughter. I cuddled her and made her pikelets. About a year ago Rafa left Carla and went to Uruguay. I know Carla was heartbroken. I barely saw her after that. When he came back, he saw Frankie a few times, then Carla moved back to Griffith to be closer to her family.

So many mothers, so many children, scattered like leaves. I think it's wrong. Leo tells me he gave them life. I wonder if Elvia knows she has all these grandchildren that most likely she will never meet.

I look at the short woman with the wide hips. She laughs and I see she has teeth missing. She is telling Leo about her plane trip over here. It was the first time she had been in the air.

'It was more beautiful than any dream, to see the clouds so close, you could almost touch them. Then the whiteness of the Antarctic, the furthest part of the world and I saw it with my own eyes.'

Leo had told me that Rafa sent her a ticket to fly across the Antarctic. It's a direct flight, twelve hours from Buenos Aires.

'And me who has never left Montevideo, imagine, flying over the world.'

Papá was now listening.

'A beautiful city Buenos Aires. Carmen and I went there for our honeymoon.'

I could hear her telling him how she had to stay in a hotel for the night and about the wonderful breakfast they gave her.

'Yes,' Papá was saying, 'the best bakeries in the world are in Buenos Aires.'

Leo comes over to me, puts his arm around me and asks *'Estas bien?'*

'I'm fine.' I quickly move away and start getting dinner on the table. I don't want him to touch me. I can't bear the guilt and yet I want Nick's skin on mine. I'm still thinking about all the children Rafa has. If Leo had told me he had children before I met him, what would I have done? To have to see them and be reminded every time you saw them that his love had been with other bodies, held other hands. Daniel and Alex having to share their father with other children. I look over at Alex. He is talking to Elvia and Papá. They start laughing. I see that Papá has served Elvia a glass of red wine.

Rafa and Leo have got the congas out and their hands move quickly as the *candombe* beat fills the room. Daniel gets a maraca and joins them. Alex picks up the clapsticks.

This is my family. What the fuck am I doing?

JUAN

Tengo miedo del encuentro
I am frightened of the meeting
con el pasado que vuelve.
With the past that is returning
A enfrentarse con mi vida
To confront my life all over
      '*Volver*', Carlos Gardel y Alfredo Le Pera

Walking into *El Club Uruguayo* in Hinchinbrook, a whiff of *asado* catches in my memory, lodged between my youth and my life with Carmen. I look down at the familiar red and brown carpet. So many steps I have taken here with Carmen.

On the walls are the photos of the board and the founders of the club. Ramon Cruz and a very young Alfredo Santalucia look down at me. I see pride in their eyes. It had been a huge achievement to establish the club. Alfredo was homesick for years, like Carmen, he missed everything, and nothing could replace the loss. He, Ramon, Jorge, and some of the others in the community built this club, to create a little piece of what they had left behind.

When Carmen and I walked into the club we left Australia at the door.

I look up at the rows of photos of football players. Young men standing together in their *celeste*. Some of them have probably never been to Uruguay. They carry *la celeste* inside them. It has been handed down to them by their parents. Pictures of the Uruguayan national team from recent world cups also have their place in this hall of patriotism.

I am stepping into my past with Frances beside me. Am I crazy? I have to get out of here. What the hell was I thinking bringing Frances. She is holding my arm and smiling.

149

'Juan, your license?' Frances looks at me, as she takes out her license, from her purse, to show the man at the counter.

I cannot move. I have my hand in my pocket, holding my wallet tightly. I am looking at her, but I cannot speak. I feel a slap on my back.

'Juan, *viejo*, how are you?'

It's Alfredo. I have not seen him since Carmen died. I am shaken out of my frozen state.

'*Bien* Alfredo.'

He looks at Frances, waiting for an introduction.

'This is Frances, my neighbour.'

Frances stares at me as Alfredo kisses her on the cheek. I give her my license and she shows it to the young man at the counter.

'Come and sit with us, we have a section at the end of a table, near the back. Rosa is here and some friends too.'

Frances gives me my license and takes my arm in hers.

I look into the crowd of black and grey heads as we follow Alfredo to the table.

The band is playing. It's a *cha cha cha*. Frances moves to the beat. I want to become invisible.

I keep my eyes on Alfredo's back. He is a good man. In Uruguay he was an accountant. Here he worked at the tobacco factory for years while he learnt English. Finally, he got a job as a bookkeeper for a company and stayed there until he retired.

Reluctantly I make my way to Alfredo's table. Milton and his wife Beatriz greet me with tight embraces. I introduce Frances. Beatriz kisses her and Milton shakes her hand. They make room for us to sit down. Groups of friends occupy sections of each long table.

Alfredo's wife, Rosa, is sitting at the table talking to a fat woman I do not know. They both look at Frances and kiss her on the cheek as I introduce her. They smile at her. Smiles that talk.

'Juan, isn't that your son-in-law playing?' Rosa asks me.

I look over at the stage. It's Leo's band. I cannot believe it. Why today?

'Let's dance, Bub, come on,' Frances says as she takes my arm.

'Frances, we eat first. I'm hungry.'

'The gnocchi are delicious,' Rosa's fat friend tells me.

'We'll eat later, come on one dance. This music just makes me want to get up there,' Frances insists, as she tugs at my arm.

She is up and dancing around me. Alfredo and the women are looking at me, smiling awkwardly.

'No Frances. I eat first.'

'Well, I'm going to dance.'

I can't believe what she does next. She goes to the dance floor alone and starts dancing. It is a salsa, and she is dancing by herself looking ridiculous. Dancing all wrong, like a *gringa*.

'Juan, let's get a bottle of wine.' Alfredo can see my embarrassment.

He puts his arm around my shoulders, and we walk to the bar.

'So how have you been *viejo*? Who's the woman?'

'She's, my neighbour. Her husband died and I'm helping her.'

'Yeah, yeah, come on Juan, we all like a bit of warmth in our old winter.'

'Alfredo, my son-in-law is here and my family don't know about Frances. What should I do?'

'Juan, come on you're an old man. They'll be fine. They'll be happy that you're going out again. She's a wild one, look at her dance. *Viejo* she's going to kill you. You are a lucky man.'

By the time we get back to the table. Frances is sitting talking to Rosa and the fat woman. She is telling them how we met. She's describing how I fell over. They are all laughing.

I pour everyone a glass of wine. I drink mine too quickly. As I go to take a drink, I see my grandson with Kerry's daughter walking towards me. My hand trembles and I spill my wine over Frances.

'Go go go to the bathroom to clean yourself.' I'm shouting the words to her. I don't want my grandson to see her.

'Juan, what is wrong with you?'

I'm pushing her to go. 'Now now or it will stain.'

It's too late Daniel is beside me.

'Abuelo, what are you doing here? Daniel hugs me. He kisses Rosa, Alfredo, and the fat friend.

Frances is now standing, her skirt covered in red wine. Daniel looks at her.

'I'm Frances.' She looks at Daniel and Ella.

They look at her and then Daniel turns to me.

Frances murmurs under her breath and walks away.

151

'Mum is over there. Do you want to come and sit with us?'

'Your mother is here? Why? She never goes to see your father play?'

'She wanted Alex to come too. I think it's supposed to be a family thing and we like the food here.'

'My mum is here too', Ella chips in.

'Why is your mum here Ella?'

'To be with Lola. She had a fight with Dad and she said we had to come.'

From my table I can see Lola. She is talking to Kerry. She's not even looking at the band. I can see Leo on the stage with his guitar and Lisa singing in Spanish. She has a beautiful voice but very bad pronunciation. I like Lisa; she is very good to Leo.

'Well, Abuelo are you coming?'

'Where?'

'To sit with us?"

I see Frances coming out of the ladies room.

'Go, go, I will come later I need to talk to Alfredo.' I'm practically pushing Daniel away. I don't want him to see Frances again.

The children go. Daniel looks at me a bit confused.

'Bub, look at my skirt, I can't get the wine stain off.'

Frances is holding her skirt. The women at our table look at her and shake their head in sympathy.

'We can go home; you can't stay with that dirty skirt.'

'No, it's okay let's eat first. I'm starving. Besides I want to try the barbeque, it looks amazing.'

I know this. The *parilla* will be spread out with *asado, chorizos* and *morzillas*. Each piece of meat a mouthwatering sight.

'We can eat later, let's go.' I get up.

'No Juan, we can eat here, I'm fine.' Frances sits down and pulls my arm to sit.

'I want to go, woman.' By now I am getting angry.

'Well, I don't. I came to eat and dance. I have danced, now I will eat.'

'Juan, sit down, it's okay, relax.' Alfredo tells me.

'Alfredo, I don't need you to tell me what to do.'

'I'm going to order, want to come Juan?' Frances is up and she walks towards the bistro.

I follow her. I am angry but I am still a gentleman. While we are in the line for our food, the band stops and I see Leo walking towards the bistro, where we are standing.

I try and look the other way, but it is too late, he is waving at me.

He stops to talk to someone on the way. While he is there, I see Lola walking towards him. She stops and he puts his arm around her. They are talking to Roberto; he is a drummer with another Latin band. He and Leo use to play together at the Latin American Cultural Centre.

Lola has seen me, and she is waving. I give her a small wave back.

'Who are you waving at?'

'My daughter is here, Frances.'

I wish the floor would sink and take me with it.

The meeting between Lola and Frances is uncomfortable. There is no kiss or handshake, only a cold hello. Lola is very rude not to kiss Frances or shake her hand. Frances ignores this and is warm and friendly. Lola, I know, is examining Frances. She looks at her skirt, her face, her hair. Lola is very judging of people. She puts people in boxes, the political ones, the stupid ones, the plastic women, the ignorant ones, the *machista* men. I have an idea of what box Frances will go in and it won't be a good one. She wants to eat Frances alive.

'How long have you known my father?' Lola asks, moving her eyes from Frances' hair to her skirt.

'Not long, honey.' She doesn't give too much away. I know Frances is probably used to this; you have to be when you are a survivor. You learn to live in the shadows. 'It's good to see you out. Your father told me you have been having a hard time.'

Lola looks at me like she wants to kill me.

The meeting of daughter and woman is interrupted by the announcement of the raffle. Temporary relief. First prize is a holiday to the Gold Coast for two people.

'Fingers crossed Bub, I bought a ticket on the way to the Ladies.'

Lola stares at me as Frances calls me Bub. She rolls her eyes and I think she looks like she may be sick. She is very white. I don't want to upset her, especially now after the last weeks of the anxiety the poor girl had. The first prize is called out. It goes to a couple sitting at a table at the front. I don't know them.

I am so happy I did not win. Imagine if I had to walk out to the front so every person could see me with Frances.

Now for the second prize. I have lost interest. Frances is still with her fingers crossed.

A little girl pulls the ticket out of the bucket and gives it to the tall man with the microphone.

'The lucky winner is *Numero* 154, Frances Patterson.'

Before I realise what has happened, Frances is kissing me and jumping and shouting, 'We won the salsa classes Juan.'

'Come on,' she grabs my hand and pulls me to the front to collect the prize.

I find myself standing in front of a generation of Uruguayans I have grown old with in Australia. I am holding the hand of a crazy Australian woman with a skirt that is too short, covered in wine, who makes me feel alive.

BETTY

Rosemary Oil
Ingredients:
- 4 cups of rosemary
- 8 cups of almond oil

Directions:
Remove the rosemary leaves from the stem and measure out four cups. Place the rosemary evenly into the small jars and cover with the almond oil, sealing the top. Put the jars on a sunny windowsill and leave them for three to four weeks.

The pungent woody smell fills my nostrils. Inhaling rosemary oil can reduce stress. I think of Lola and her refusal to accept plant therapies as I look at bunches of rosemary hanging in the shed. They will have to wait until tomorrow. I have seedlings to plant this morning.

The calmness of home is a comfort after having been with Lola and Papá. With them there is never stillness. It is exhausting. The pace, the angst, the nervousness that Lola lives with. The anxiety eating away at her. She's always been anxious, but it was never debilitating like it became as she grew older. When we were kids, she was easily scared. She couldn't watch the news or horror movies. If she did, she couldn't sleep and she asked to come into my bed. I'd tell her everything was okay and sing to her until she finally fell asleep. Sometimes I'd tell her jokes and she laughed and forget she was scared.

One time Papá was in the living room watching the news and Lola and I were in the kitchen doing our homework. I think Lola must have been about twelve years old. We could see the television from where we were sitting. Lola got up and went to the bathroom. She sat down for a few seconds and then went to the bathroom again. This continued for the entire time the news was on. Mamá asked her if she was feeling sick. Lola said no. When I asked her why she was going to the bathroom so much, she said to wash her hands.

'But they're not dirty,' I told her.

'I wash away the thoughts.'

'What thoughts?'

'The bad ones from the news. I don't want them to stick to me and then something bad happen to us.'

To this day I still remember that conversation because it was so bizarre. I must have been about ten years old. I kept thinking how can you wash away thoughts? Mum was in the kitchen, but because we were speaking in English, she didn't know what Lola was saying. She continued making dinner, like it was normal that Lola washed away thoughts.

For the next few months Lola continued to wash away thoughts until her hands became red and raw. Mum bought her a cream. Every night before bed she would smother her hands in a lather of hand cream and put gloves on before she climbed into bed.

Nobody thought to take Lola to a doctor or a psychologist. It was fixed with a hand cream from the local chemist. One day Lola just stopped, and her hands were no longer red. No one mentioned it again.

When Lola started going out with Leo, she became anxious again. She was about twenty. I still lived at home. Lola and I no longer shared a room because Malena had moved out and I moved into her room. We were still close and she confided in me. She told me Leo made her feel nervous because he was so cool, a musician, and she was such a nerd.

'Why do you go out with him if he doesn't make you feel good?' I asked her.

'I like him.'

When they first went out Leo treated her badly. He'd tell her he was coming to pick her up to go out. Lola would get herself ready and he wouldn't turn up. Lola would stay up crying, hoping he'd still turn up. A few days later he would turn up full of Latin charm, bunch of flowers in one hand and take her out to dinner. She was happy again. This went on for months. Malena told her he was a jerk and to stop seeing him. I told her he was a dickhead. But Lola had made up her mind. She wanted Leo even if it destroyed her. So, I watched my beautiful intelligent sister turn into an anxious dependent mess. Lola who was studying science and seemed to have a rational brain, could not see what this relationship was doing to her mental health. She thought Leo could bring back the culture she had lost. The parts our parents couldn't give her. To her, he was Uruguay. He would make her complete.

I will never understand it. As the years went by, Leo changed his behaviour and Lola became everything for him. They moulded into a relationship. Two completely different people, with nothing in common except their birthplace, became a family.

Leo genuinely loves Lola. I know that. I can see it. She's his only family. He has his music and Lola. She understands his background. There's no explaining. It works. But Lola. She gave up her life.

When Lola and I were growing up and sharing a room we dreamed big. Lola was always going to be a scientist. We'd play that she had discovered a drug to reverse aging. I pretended to be an old woman, using the broom as my walking stick. She would give me the drug and I would throw the broom to one side and begin jumping up and down on the bed and dancing. Then I was a reporter interviewing her about how she had discovered this magic drug and asking her what she planned to discover next. Sometimes we were both anthropologists, lost in a remote jungle, on our way to report on an indigenous people no white person had ever seen. We would lie down in the backyard with toilet rolls made into binoculars and talk quietly about what we could see. We then went back into our room and wrote a report of what we had witnessed.

I smile to myself with the thought of Lola and I looking through the toilet roll binoculars. Lost in these thoughts, I then realise I have planted the cucumber seedlings in the wrong place. I pull most of them out and start again. The cucumber, tomato, lettuce, and rocket will be ready for winter salads. I'm pleased with my garden this year. The hours I have spent digging, preparing the beds, and mulching have paid off.

The garlic has grown well too, and I have enough to sell at the markets. I've never sold vegetables at the markets before. It's always been oils and soaps. Garlic might not be a good mix with the other products. It's better if Chris sells it at the nursery. We bought the nursery ten years ago, with our friends Renee and Brad. When we first bought it, we all worked there. It was hard work, but I loved it. When I was pregnant with Leif, I became very tired and found it hard to stand up all day. My back hurt. We had a hammock in the nursery, and I would lie in it every afternoon after lunch until it became too uncomfortable. By then I was eight months pregnant, and I stopped working at the nursery. After Leif was born, I stayed home looking after him and Skye. I loved motherhood. The long days without structure, not having to be anywhere at a certain time. Some days I would make a picnic lunch, pack the kids in the car and go over to the nursery to have lunch with Chris. Leif would run around until he was exhausted then he'd climb into the hammock, and I sang to him while I rocked him to sleep. The simplicity was joyful.

When Skye started school, I decided I didn't want to go back to work at the nursery. By then Renee had left as she was expecting her first child and Chris had hired an apprentice. He and Brad had extended the nursery and created an organic herb business. They were also growing a lot of lavender as they supplied a local woman with lavender to make potpourri for a small business she had. I began experimenting with the lavender to make oil. I would put the flowers in a jar with a carrier oil, leaving it to brew for different periods of time, to see if the longer I left it the stronger the oil. I tried different base oils, almond, avocado, apricot kernel, coconut. I found by mixing the oils and the brewing time I created various types of lavender essential oil.

Then I expanded to rosemary, rose petals, peppermint. I continued experimenting with different plants and found the process creative as well as meditative. The satisfaction of starting off with a plant and ending with an oil was immense. I named my oils according to the plant and the process. I bought beautiful, small brown and blue glass bottles to store them in. After a few months I had so many I began selling them. I had massage oils, aromatherapy oils. I expanded into soaps and Blissed Out was born. At first it was very small, markets once a month. Now I have a website and sell online. It still is relatively small as I don't have the time to expand further. Nor do I want to. The simplicity in my life would go and that is my priority.

Beep beep beep. The piercing sound cuts through my thoughts. The noise, an incision into the stillness and quiet. I look up and I think it is Papá's car. It is not like him to arrive without warning. Something must be wrong. As I walk towards the car, I see a woman getting out, holding a little dog in her arms. She looks familiar. As I get closer, I remember. Yes, the woman at the park. Francesca.

'Betty.' Papá stretches his arms out to hug me. Coco jumps out of the car and runs towards me.

The woman and I look at each other. 'Betty, lovely to see you again. We met at the park, the day you were going to your aunt's funeral.'

'Yes, I remember.'

She is dressed in a bright green dress, which falls just below her knees. She is wearing green matching sandals. Large hoop earrings frame her round face. Her hair is tied back with a purple scarf. Her skin looks weathered and, as she smiles, I think I can see a missing tooth.

She puts the little dog down and extends her arms out to hug me. Before I have time to take off my gardening gloves, she has gathered me in her arms, and I'm pressed against her breasts. I smell her strong perfume, a musky type of smell.

Her dog runs off barking and chasing the chooks. She runs after him, yelling, 'Churchill come back.'

I look at Papá. He can tell I am not happy. The dog has one of the chickens cornered. Fuck. I run over and pick up the terrified chicken. My chickens are highly sensitive as they are rescue chickens, having survived the trauma of factory farming or abandonment.

'Put your dog in the car now.' My voice is firm and loud and it surprises me as I rarely raise my voice.

'I'm so sorry. He hasn't seen chickens before.'

'Nor has he seen vegetables before. He has trampled the seedlings I just planted.'

'I'm so sorry honey.'

'We won't stay long Betty. We are on our way to Brisbane.' Papá tells me as he looks over at the trampled seedlings. 'I'll help you plant them again.'

The woman looks at me. 'That's right we just popped in to say hello. We're doing a road trip. Your father told me he has never been on a road trip before, and he hasn't been to Brisbane. So, I said let's do it. You only live once. Last night we stopped at Coffs Harbour. We found a caravan park that allowed dogs. It was lovely. We walked the dogs along the beach. Wasn't it fun Bub?'

She looks over at Papá and squeezes his hand as she says 'Bub'.

This is Francesca. She doesn't seem Italian. This doesn't make sense.

'Yes, it was. I love the beach. Betty, we had dinner at this lovely café on the beach. It reminded me of Uruguay.'

Papá loves the beach. As children on the rare occasion we drove to the beach, at our insistence and Mum's, Papá, after complaining it was far too hot and telling us we would all burn and get skin cancer, would set up the beach umbrella and sit under it reading the Spanish paper until it was time to go. He didn't go in the water. The ocean was too rough, not like the Atlantic Ocean of his youth. As we ran to the water he would shout, 'Don't go too far out.'

'Would you like a cup of tea?' I ask them. They are here now. I can't just send them away without a cuppa.

'Love one, honey.' Frances replies.

'Your name is Francesca, right?'

The woman laughs. 'Oh Betty, that is so exotic, but I'm afraid I'm plain old Frances.'

Papá is looking away, pretending not to hear. He walks behind as Frances and I walk towards the house.

'Oh my, this is so bohemian.' Frances looks around as she puts her handbag down. 'I love it.'

Papá is the quietest I have ever seen him. I put the kettle on.

'How do you have your tea, Frances?'

'Milk and two sugars, please.'

'I only have soy or almond milk.'

'I have never tried that. Which one do you suggest?'

'Try the soy. What about you Papá do you want tea?'

'I'll have coffee, you know I don't drink tea Betty.'

'I don't have coffee. Remember? I told you last time you were here.'

'Ok, just water for me.'

He stands up and looks out the window. He is uncomfortable. I'm sure it was Frances' idea to stop by. Why did he agree to it? It was an opportunity to see the kids and he couldn't say no to seeing his grandchildren.

'Are the children at school?' Frances asks.

'Yes, but they'll be home very soon.'

'I'd love to meet them.'

I look at Papá. This is not what I had in mind when I put the personal ad up for him and he knows it too.

'We have biscuits in the car. Juan can you please get them. Can't have a cuppa without biscuits.'

'Betty doesn't eat them, and we don't need to eat more biscuits, *Frances*.' Papá says her name in a Spanish accent.

'Oh, come on Bub.'

'It's fine Papá. Just put them away before the kids get home.'

He gets up and walks to the car. Frances sits at the kitchen table.

'How long have you known my father?'

'A few months. He is such a lovely man. So romantic and funny. I know you and your sisters may find this difficult, but I really care about your father, and he feels the same towards me. We are happy together. I never in my wildest dreams thought I would find love again.'

The words together and love unnerve me. I do want Papá to be happy. But this woman? She looks and sounds like the Australia I never wanted to be part of.

I hear laughing and look outside and see Papá and the kids playing with Coco. He is giving them biscuits. They run inside still eating the biscuits.

'Grandpa gave them to us,' Sunshine explains.

'It's ok, I know,' I tell her. The three of them suddenly see Frances and look at her with surprise.

'This is my friend, Frances,' Papá tells them.

'Frances, this is Sunshine, Skye and Leif.'

'Hello. You are all so beautiful. Like your mother.'

Sunshine giggles. Skye says, 'Thank you' and Leif says, 'Hi' and walks away.

'Now tell me Sunshine, honey, how old are you?'

'I'm seven.'

'What about you Skye? You all have such pretty names.'

'I'm thirteen.'

'I've never met any of Grandpa's friends, you're the first one,' says Sunshine.

Frances lets out a throaty laugh.

'Are you staying over?' Sunshine asks.

'No, Frances and I are going to Brisbane. And we need to go very soon, we don't want to drive at night.'

Papá stands up and looks at Frances. He puts his hand on her back, almost pushing her up.

'Can I go to Brisbane with them Mum?'

'No, Sunshine, you cannot. You are not invited, and you have school tomorrow.'

'We'd love to take her, wouldn't we Juan?'

'You heard her mother; she has school tomorrow.' Papá looks at Frances sternly as he replies.

'Next time Bub, we'll take all of you. Wouldn't that be nice, Juan, to take the grandchildren for a holiday and give the parents a break?'

Papá looks at me. He can read my silence.

'I'm going to take the dogs some water,' says Sunshine. We all look at her as she gets a bowl and fills it with water. When she walks out, we get up and follow her.

Papá kisses me on the cheek. He whispers, 'Thank you.'

Frances gives Sunshine and Skye a kiss and hug, leaving red lipstick on their cheeks.

We watch Coco climb into the back seat with Churchill.

Frances stretches her arms out to hug me. We embrace awkwardly. I can smell that heady musk scent on her again. I can't stand those perfumes full of chemicals.

Skye and Sunshine chase the car down the driveway as we wave goodbye.

LOLA

20 May 2012

A trip to Mullumbimby. I'm going to the heartland of hippiedom, anti-vaxxers, vegetarianism, non-evidence-based therapies. All the things my sister believes in, and I don't. She does vaccinate her children. That must be her nursing background.

My writing is messy as the train moves, shaking the little table on which my journal rests. I take a sip of water from the plastic bottle I bought from the train's kiosk.

Outside everything seems so green. Picturesque, like a story book. Rolling green hills. Every now and then I see a cluster of great big boulders, whizzing past the train window. It makes me wonder how it must have been for Aboriginal people before they were invaded. Existing in this vastness, connected to country, being part of the land. It's an amazing continent. Such a contrast to the small flat land that is Uruguay.

This is the first time I have left the boys since they were born. Leo insisted I should come. 'You need it,' he said. Did he mean I need it, or do they need to be away from me? I feel so ashamed. It will be good to be away from the city, and Betty and I seem to be getting on.

Even Papá has commented on how Betty seems changed. Papá is so preoccupied with his own life now. While it is a relief that he has things to do, I need to fill the holes in my life that Papá did. I'm scared that the thoughts and doubts will fill them.

Papá doesn't ring everyday anymore; he doesn't come over for coffee. He doesn't even complain about his arthritis or how the cat next door pees on his tomato plants. He has stopped complaining and started singing. He sings old tangos and eats steak sandwiches at the pub. When I told him, I was going to spend a couple of weeks at Betty's he even smiled and told me to have a good time. He didn't tell me that the boys need me, or that he has an appointment I need to take him to. He just said, go it will be good for you, and the boys will learn to appreciate you.

And who was that woman? The one he introduced to us at the Uruguayan club. And why was she all over him? How did he ever meet her? It bothered me how she touched him and called him Bub. I've slowly come around to the idea of Papá meeting someone through the ad, so why am I uncomfortable seeing him with a woman? It seems alright when I think about it, but to see it stirs something. Why did Mamá have to die? He's lost without her.

I'm such a hypocrite. I can't even look Leo in the eye. When I look at him, the image of Nick, me sitting on him with my undies around my ankles in his office takes over my mind. Why the fuck did I do that? And in his office, the thought of it makes my stomach turn. I am such a mess. Yet thinking of Nick excites me at the same time it torments me. His white skin, his blue eyes, the feel of his skin.

I do love Leo. He and the boys are my life. I can't begin to imagine a life without Leo. He has been there almost all my adult life. Yet sometimes I'm not there. Over the years it has become more noticeable. More and more often, I have nothing to say to Leo, besides the day-to-day domestic talk. I know that he adores me and that seems to be enough for him. Why can't I just accept that, but no I want more, that's my problem, I always want more. Leo says I'm needy. Am I needy or unsatisfied? I haven't had the experiences I imagined I would. I thought I would travel with my degree, work in South America or Europe. Do something important and useful. Sometimes I feel like I have outgrown Leo. When I met him, I was so in awe of his world, now that I know it intimately, it bores me. Years ago, Leo showed me a world that was new. An exciting bohemian world. But I wasn't really part of it, I never have been.

When I was younger, I made friends with some of the women at the Latin American Cultural Centre. I wanted to be part of that world, to fit in. We organised a Latin Women's Collective of women who needed to find a place for themselves in this country. It gave us an identity and a reason to hang out at the Centre. I didn't have to be there only to accompany Leo, I had my own reasons for going. I took the role of Coordinator for the Women's Collective. We applied for grants to put on a Latin film festival and a weekend of short plays. We were successful and put on a great event. Everyone wanted a bite of the glory that went with being part of the Cultural Centre. For many the terror they had been immersed in was now behind them. For some art and music filled the longing within them. The Cultural Centre launched musicians, poets and artists, who may never have arisen had they stayed behind. Bus drivers became poets, bankers turned into musicians, engineering students painters, cleaning women dance teachers.

I was getting off at Lismore and Betty would meet me. The train journey means more time to think and that is a bad idea. I want to close my mind off, I want the train to take me to a place outside my own head. I try to sleep but the seat is uncomfortable. If I lean against the window, my neck cramps.

The guilt is becoming unbearable. When I was at school, I used to envy the kids that went to scripture, because they had somewhere to put their guilt. I had to carry it around, like a big stone weighing me down. What was I even guilty about then? Sometimes I wish I had grown up with one of those families, where the parents ask you about your feelings and call you sweetie and honey and give you little cloud images for your worries to float away, like I read in parenting books. Instead, it was, 'Stop being stupid and think how lucky you are. Think of all the children that don't have enough to eat in this world, or don't even have an opportunity to go to school.' Maybe those children felt no guilt or worry, they had nothing.

After another two hours of wriggling and fighting my own thoughts, the train pulls into Lismore. As I look out the window, I see Betty, gorgeous as always, long flowing hair, white blouse, patterned tights. I wave.

'So good that you're here,' she says as she embraces me.

I start to cry. I don't know why, but I suddenly feel safe. I hug her tight. I remember the last time I hugged Mamá. Betty wipes my tears and strokes my hair.

'It's okay, Lola. It's all going to be fine.'

We drive to Betty's place listening to some Indian meditation music and talking about Papá. I tell her about the woman at the Uruguayan club.

'That's her, the woman he came up here with. Fuck, why her, of all the Latin American women he could meet.'

'They came here, to your place?'

'Yes, they were on some road trip. Lola, it was awful. I can't understand how Papá can be with that woman. They have nothing in common. He has to speak English with her, how can they even communicate?'

I don't want to tell Betty she is being patronising. We don't need to argue now. Papá's English is limited but he can communicate. I don't know about on an intimate level. The thought of that is nauseating.

'Maybe you should talk to him about it, find out what exactly is going on?'

'Why me?'

'Because you're his favourite, now that Malena's not here.'

'What do you mean, I'm his favourite. He doesn't have a favourite.' The smell of sandalwood floats up my nose. It must be coming from the little diffuser hanging on the rear-view mirror.

'Lola, are you blind? Of course, he has a favourite, he always has.'

'He's always loved us all the same. Why? Do you have a favourite with your kids? I don't.'

We've turned off into a country road and stopped for cows to cross. A group of black and white animals cross the road, one behind the other. My eyes rest on a calf, close behind its mother.

Betty turns to look at me. 'Lola, why do you think I was always going to Tia Gladys'? Yes, he loved us all, but he liked you and Malena better. You were easier to get on with. You didn't challenge him like I did. And no, I don't have a favourite with my kids, I'm aware of what it was like, and I wouldn't put my kids through that. Talking about kids how is Alex doing?'

'Same, still in his room, angry at me and Leo. I don't even know why; he won't talk to me.'

'You know that Leif wants to change school? He says he doesn't want to go to a hippie school. He thinks it's an embarrassment. He wants to go the local high school next year.'

As the last cow crosses the road, a man walking next to it waves at us. Betty starts the car and we keep driving.

'Let him change schools. Steiner schools are out of touch with the real world. And even though you may not like it, Leif will be living in the real world one day.'

'That's ridiculous, public schools are out of touch. They are totally insensitive to an individual's needs and creativity. They teach as if they are herding cattle, excuse the pun.'

I laugh as I think of the cows we just saw crossing the road, in a line, obediently. Betty laughs too.

'I was going to say that schools have changed since we went to school. Then I thought of the cows and how schools make kids line up and walk in a line.'

'Exactly my point. Alex doesn't seem that inspired by school.'

'Alex is not inspired by anything these days.'

I didn't want to talk about Alex, it upset me. He and I used to be so close and now he barely speaks to me.

'You know I spoke to Malena a couple of days ago and she said Matteo's being difficult too. He's given up swimming and has a girlfriend. Malena doesn't like her.'

By the time we get to Betty's house I felt exhausted and just want to sleep.

I love Betty's house. The stained-glass windows, the little nooks. It looks like a house out of a fairy tale. The Indian cushions on the sofa and the bigger ones in a corner with the books the kids are reading.

'Do you want a shower, or do you want to eat something first?'

'I really want to lie down and sleep.'

I want to shut my eyes and not think about Alex, or Papá and that woman, or the image of me sitting on Nick. I want to sleep until every painful thought and image is erased.

'Ok, while you sleep, I'll be out in the garden, I have a backlog of seeds that need planting. Chris and the kids will be back in about an hour, and we can have something to eat.'

As Betty closes the door to the room I am lying in, I look at her enviously. Why am I the one to carry the burden of everything?

JUAN

No te duermas mi querida
Don't fall asleep my darling
No te duermas mi adorada
Don't fall asleep my love
Que viene aclarando el día
The day is getting brighter
La madrugada
The early morning
      '*La madrugada*', Saul Salinas y Carlos Gardel

I cannot believe I am doing this. Carmen would be laughing at me. Well until she saw Frances, then she would not laugh anymore.

Me, Juan Ramon Sanchez, going to salsa class. Me, learning to dance. It is an insult. I am one of the best dancers in the whole of the Latin American community. I should be teaching the class not a student of the class.

I can hear the doorbell. It must be Frances. When I open the door, I feel like I will fall over. 'Francesita, what are you wearing? This is not Rio, we are not at the Carnival.'

'Do you like it? The skirt is an old one I had, and I added the frills. Look at how good it twirls.'

She spins around, with the green and purple frills flying about her. It is ridiculous. Her skinny old legs look like two broomsticks. But more ridiculous is the hat. My eyes land on the plastic banana on top of her head.

'The hat I found at Vinnies and added the fruit, isn't it great? I'm so excited.'

'Frances, you have it all wrong. We are going to dance salsa, not samba, you can't go dressed like Carmen Miranda.'

'Juan, it's the Latin look and feel, I'm getting into the mood.'

The woman looks ridiculous, but I don't want to upset her. Her enthusiasm takes me in its hold. She takes my hands and looks at me with that silly, I am helpless face, that only women can do. Come to think of it, Coco does it too. Then I feel helpless and give Frances a big kiss on her forehead and a hug.

'I will only go if you take the hat off.'

'I will do it just for you my Juan because you are so adorable when you are angry, your lovely accent gets stronger, and your forehead moves in that sexy way.'

'Ok, we go.' I take the hat off her head and throw it on the table then gently slap her bum.

'Ooh Juan, I think this is going to be a good night.'

When we get to the club, we have to walk past the bar to get to the room where the classes are. Alfredo and Gustavo are at the bar. They wave at me, Gustavo winks. I know what they are thinking. I think they would do the same if they could. It is a gift to feel like a teenager in this old man's body, being struck by bolts of joy.

Gustavo has been married to Olga, who is shaped like a refrigerator and probably eats as much as can fit in one, for more years than he likes to count. He has the face of a man past the use-by-date, like an old cheese.

Alfredo's wife, Rosa is very nice, and she is not fat, but I never see them laughing together or dancing. When they come to the club or to a barbeque they are always sitting. One next to the other.

That is one thing Carmen and I never lost, our romance. When we went out, we held hands. We used to watch television together in winter under the blanket, eating chocolates and laughing. On Sundays I would drink a little whisky and Carmen a lemonade, while she cooked lunch, and I cleaned the verandah or worked in the garden.

As we walk in, I look around the room. Most of the class look like *gringos*. There are only four men. One is very tall, and his girlfriend is very short. She is talking and laughing, and he is very quiet. I think she made him come.

The teacher introduces herself. Daniela, she tells us she is from Bolivia. I have never seen a Bolivian dancing salsa. This will be interesting. She asks everyone to introduce themselves.

There is a Portuguese man. He looks about thirty-five. He is Duarte.

Then there is a man named, Dimitri, I think he is Greek. The woman with him speaks Spanish, her name is Estela and she is very beautiful. The Greek is a lucky man.

The very tall man is Jason, the short girlfriend is Christine.

Then there is me. I am the oldest of all the people here.

Daniela, the teacher, asks us to get into a big circle. She puts on some salsa music and asks us to dance whatever we like. She explains this is a warming up exercise. It is important to move and not to think too much. After only a few seconds I know why these people come to classes. They are a disaster. The tall man is too still, like a telegraph pole. His short girlfriend moves like she is playing hopscotch, jumping all over the place.

The Greek man is trying hard, he looks at his beautiful girlfriend. She is a good dancer, moving her hips to the beat. The music stops and the men look relieved.

'Good, now you are warmed up we can start with some steps. First watch me and then I will get you to follow,' Daniela tells us.

I look at her dance. Not bad. She then asks us to stand in two lines. She tells us first we will work with our feet and not to worry about our arms.

She stands in front; we look and then she says, 'All together.'

I feel the beat of the music and fall into step. Frances stands next to me; her steps are too big. I say quietly to her 'Frances, you are dancing, not running from a fire, little steps.'

The Greek and the telegraph pole look at me.

Behind me I hear a woman counting. I feel like telling her to listen to the music, not to count. Then Daniela starts counting and telling everyone to shift their weight: right foot; left foot; right foot; left foot. One, two, three, four forward then back one, two, three, four, I think she is getting everyone confused. Between the counting and the shifting, not much dancing is happening. This is salsa not mathematics.

Salsa, you must feel it with your body. You let the music take you, you ride on the rhythm. If you get lost, listen to the *clave*, and it brings you back again. They are the sticks that mark the beat.

'Very good, well done everyone,' Daniela says. 'Did you notice that when you shift the weight from one foot to the other, you get movement in your hips?' Frances is the first one to say, oh yes. Her excitement, like a wave rising and rolling, then scattering its energy and gathering everyone in it.

'What about if we try partners, Frances you and Juan, come to the front and we can show the others.'

I take hold of Frances' waist.

'Juan let's try just holding hands first so the others can see your bodies move better,' the teacher tells me.

I am about to say this is not how we dance salsa traditionally, but I think better I keep my mouth shut. Daniela is the teacher, even if she is a *Boliviana*, she is the salsa teacher. Lola would be proud of me, doing what I'm told.

I take hold of Frances' hands. They are cold. Daniela turns the music on. I feel like I am dancing with a heavy sack, and I have to pull it this way and then the other way. Frances is looking at her feet. She goes back and forward, mixing up the steps. It is a mess, not a dance.

'Thank you. Frances, would you mind if I dance with Juan, just to show the others a bit faster?'

'He's all yours, but not too close,' Frances says to Daniela as she takes my hand. Daniela's hands are soft and warm. Immediately we fall into step with the rhythm. It is a joy to dance with a woman who knows how to move. I lead, she follows and as we are about to finish, I hold my arm up and Daniela twirls under it as she holds my hand. We finish perfectly on time, and everyone claps.

'Now with your partners, take hold of their hands and look into each other's eyes, don't look at your feet. Keep your eyes on each other.'

Again, I take hold of Frances' hands. She smiles.

'Listen to the music, Frances, let it take you, you are riding the rhythm, like if you are flying on a magic carpet, it takes you.'

'Let's do it Juan.' Her enthusiasm embraces me.

I smile at this passionate old woman, so full of life, who makes my heart feel happy.

We go home tired. Our old bodies dragging behind our youthful spirits.

We sit in Frances' lounge room, drinking a coffee. An instant coffee. I have to buy her a percolator. She tells me she grew up drinking tea. When the English robbed the Aboriginal people of their land and dignity, they used them to work for the whites and paid them in tea, flour, and tobacco. This is what Frances told me. I never liked the English, now I despise them.

I reach over and take Frances' hand. It is warm. I bring her hand up to my lips and kiss her hand softly. I reach over and kiss her neck. Our lips meet and I'm aroused as her warm mouth presses hard against mine. As we kiss, she leans into me until her body is on top of mine as we fall back on the couch. She begins to unzip my trousers. I have not felt this hard for years. Carmen and I did not have intimacy during her illness. The cancer ate cruelly at her body until there was barely any body left to hold. I was even afraid of hugging her too hard, for fear of breaking her bones.

I feel Frances' body against mine. The way our shapes connect is an unfamiliar fit compared to Carmen. Her breasts are soft against my chest, her thighs just right, wound around me as her feet lightly touch the back of my knees. Frances' legs are much thinner, and they don't hold the warmth of Carmen's thighs.

I push Frances gently off me and take her hand as we walk to the bedroom. It is dark and neither of us turns the light on. As we stand by the bed, I unzip her skirt and it falls to the ground. I slowly pull her blouse over her head; she takes off her bra as I kiss her breasts. Age has robbed their firmness. I hold them in my hands and continue kissing them. I take off my trousers and we lie on the bed. Frances pulls my shirt off. I gently caress her belly, making soft circles around her belly button. She giggles as my hand finds her pubic hair. I put my finger inside her and find her surprisingly wet. What pleasure at our age. She moans loudly as my finger explores her vagina. The thin walls are a reminder that this too has been ravaged by age. She looks at me, and without words guides my penis inside her. She wraps her thin legs around my body. She caresses my back as I enter her. I look at her face, it has softened. Then we are both heaving and moaning with pleasure. '*Te quiero* Frances.'

In our nakedness we find each other.

LOLA

26 May 2012

I wake up to Sunshine singing in the kitchen. I smile to myself. I've been here for nearly a week, and I feel so much better. Lighter. It's been good working with Betty in the garden each morning and going for long walks in the afternoon. She's even got me doing yoga with her. I've stopped drinking coffee. For the first couple of days, I had headaches and now I feel fine. I don't feel so irritable and anxious. I feel like everything has slowed down. Giving up coffee is like letting go of a lover, familiarity, and dependency.

Staying with Betty has brought me closer to her. We haven't spent so much time together since we shared a room as girls. I'd forgotten how much fun she can be. She has such a sense of joy when she plays with the girls. I haven't laughed so much in a very long time. Skye and Sunshine showing us how to run and spring into a cartwheel. Me falling over, not even been able to kick my legs in the air. Sunshine said I looked like a frog. It was good to laugh. To give in to the fun with all my being. My mind no longer fighting itself. I have escaped my head and returned to my body. Relief.

Sex used to be like that when I first met Leo. The wars in my head dissolved as my body succumbed to pure pleasure. The focus on every lick, every warm kiss. His skin touching mine. My wet, smooth vagina thick with longing, desperately hanging on for the ride to orgasm its state of total gratification and release. Through Leo, I found my body. But years later, my head refused to let go. Until Nick.

At Betty's it's becoming easier to find my body again. Maybe because everything requires physical work. Collecting wood for the fire, picking vegetables for dinner.

In the evenings we cook together, vegetable curries and chapattis, capsicums stuffed with rice and black beans, dhal and fried eggplant and even a vegan chocolate cake. We listen to old songs and sing as we prepare

175

dinner. Sunshine dances. Occasionally Leif joins in, playing to the tunes on his drums or guitar.

I now understand why she is a vegan. It's a commitment to living by her beliefs, it's not just about being healthy and stopping animal cruelty and exploitation or a privileged choice. It's about our earth and protecting the environment. I hadn't thought about it like that before Betty explained it. The huge amount of food needed to feed animals for meat production has effects on deforestation. Species lose their habitats and can become extinct. The worst, and when I tell Papá this he may start to understand too, is that eating meat can contribute to malnutrition because poor people in developing countries grow cash crops to feed animals instead of crops to feed themselves.

So, my sister is a political being. She may not be out there shouting and marching in the streets, but she contributes to slowing down global warming quietly, by living in the way she believes will make the world a better place and our planet safer.

Malena and I marched against the war in Iraq, Alex in the pram. We held placards outside Parliament house to protest cuts in education. Then we went home and continued to live like we always did. We cooked our barbeques, drank our lattes, bought Italian leather shoes. Our activism was a compartment, neat and tidy, we did do it and packed it away until the next rally.

We always criticised Betty for being selfish. How arrogant! Betty and Chris live their politics every day. Yesterday Chris told me they are looking into going fully off-grid. He and a neighbour are exploring getting windmills to share between their properties. When I tell Papá, he will think they are mad. He sees Betty and Chris' lives as going backwards, to how he and Mamá were brought up, choosing not to have the comforts that are available. Making things that are easy to buy like soap, not eating meat when it's cheap at the supermarket. Getting wood to get your oven going, instead of turning a switch. Using greywater for washing their clothes, when you can turn on the tap and it always comes out. Not like the old showers in Uruguay where you washed yourself under a trickle of water.

Today I'm helping Betty to make soaps. Betty tells me that by using the soap we are making today, eczema can be cured. She says it's better than any cream from a chemist. The sceptic in me wonders.

Betty turned away from her medical training and became interested in herbal medicine, aromatherapy, and homeopathy. When she first tried to talk to us about it, Papá told her that if smelling flowers and drinking concoctions of beaten leaves could cure anything there would be huge multinationals selling the stuff to every poor man in Asia and South America, like Nestles did with their baby formula. Betty didn't even attempt to argue. She just said, it works for me and never brought it up again.

Papá couldn't leave it alone and said that's because you're not sick. Mamá was alive then and unaware of the tumour growing inside her. She said her mother used to know the plants in her village and used some of them to cure headaches, stomach aches, rashes and bites. That's because they had no money for medicines, Papá cried out.

They worked, said Mamá. The old people had knowledge that we don't have anymore.

Papá retorted, Carmen, your mother was an ignorant *campesina*. She hadn't even been to the capital until she met your father. Remember the story Gladys tells? How she was kicked by a goat and your mother made you urinate into a cup then Gladys drink it to prevent internal injury. He told that story on numerous occasions. It was for his own benefit, to remind himself that the little education he had was more than some people in his country. By putting down the knowledge of country people, he was able to bury his shame.

After breakfast we drive the kids to school and go into town for a few things. The town is small and colourful, lined with a bakery, supermarket, a few cafés, a health food shop, fruit and vegetable co-op, and the Anglicare op shop. There is a music shop with a row of djembes drums in the window and I'm suddenly reminded of home. My stomach starts to cramp, and I feel like I might be sick.

Betty stops to talk to a few people as we wander around. Some of them are barefoot. When you're poor not having shoes is shameful. White privilege punches me in the face as I think of Papá and how he never had new shoes as a child, always someone's hand-me-downs, often with holes. He had to fill them with newspaper to keep the wet and cold away.

We stop at the health food shop as Betty wants to buy activated almonds. I try and explain to her that almonds are almonds, activation is a bullshit term for expensive nuts. She's not interested as she looks for the activated nuts. I walk behind her, trying to explain that soaking nuts does not break down any of the proteins or phytates. She turns around and looks at me.

'Activated almonds are easier to digest in my experience.'

'Let's do an experiment. You eat the activated almonds, which, by the way, you can make yourself by soaking for one week. The next week you eat the non-activated and see if there is a difference.'

She looks at me, her dark eyes fixed on mine.

'Lola, it works for me, I have eaten both in the past and activated is best okay.' She turns around and walks towards the nuts aisle, leaving me in the rows of vitamins and supplements. As I'm standing there a woman wearing a long skirt and a red and green head scarf wrapped around her long brunette crispy curly hair walks past me. She looks at me and smiles. The woman sees Betty and she and Betty scream in joy and hug and kiss. When they let go of each other, Betty says, 'Alicia, this is my sister, Lola.'

The woman takes me in a tight embrace.

'Lola, I'm so happy to finally meet you. You know Betty is like a sister to me. If you girls aren't busy, *vamos* to have a chai at Lulu's.'

My face feels hot and flushed from the grip of Alicia's embrace. I want to leave.

'I'd love a chai,' Betty answers.

Too late.

'Alicia gives the best massage, Lola. You could have one, it will be so good for you. Lola has been a bit stressed lately.'

Lately, she means for the last twenty years.

'I'd love to *amorcito*, I use your sister's oils. They are very therapeutic and uplifting.'

I've never had a massage and the thought of Alicia touching me naked unnerves me. I find out that Alicia was born in Columbia and came to Australia on her own when she was seventeen, to study English and live with an uncle in Melbourne. The uncle turned out to be abusive, so she left and found herself in Byron Bay. There she met a Dutch backpacker and became pregnant. Two years later, a single mother, she landed in Mullumbimby.

'Imagine my delight when I met Betty, another Latina, here. Your sister made me feel part of her family. She was the one that suggested I do the massage course and a new world opened.'

Slowly I was warming to Alicia. It must have been hard, a young woman in a foreign country on her own. We drink warm, milky sweet chai as they talk about how they came to find what they loved. We are sitting outside in the sun on colourful cushions. The sun warms my bare arms and the light breeze touches my cheeks. The pleasantness of it takes me by surprise.

'And you Lola, what about you?'

'I'm sort of between jobs.'

I was. I no longer worked at the supermarket, and I had to find another job. We couldn't live on Leo's income.

'Lola is having a bit of a holiday, some time out from everything.'

'Oh, you should do the Vipassana meditation then. It helped me so much when I was searching and dissatisfied with everything,' Alicia tells me as she looks at me and puts her hand on mine.

'I've been doing some meditation with Betty.'

'Then you would love this. It's a bit tough at first, but then magnificent. Everything falls into place. Better than ten years of therapy.'

'Do you do that style of meditation?' I ask Betty.

'No Lola, Vipassana takes a lot of practice. You go to the centre and stay there for about ten days to learn the method.'

'Yes, and you don't talk. You meditate and observe silence. You really learn so much about yourself. I shed layers of *mierda* during that time. When it was over, I felt almost like a newborn,' adds Alicia.

To sit in my head for ten days without speaking or distractions would drive me to either a panic attack or psychosis. I don't want to tell Alicia this.

When we go, Alicia takes me into another tight embrace.

'Let me know if you want to do the meditation. I can drive you there to talk to them first.'

Suddenly I feel like I'm choking on my own breath. When we get home, Betty suggests we make soaps.

'I think you'll enjoy it.'

We go outside to the shed, where there is a large workbench with all the oils and equipment. I feel like I'm back at school in the science lab.

I use the lye calculator to measure out the right amount of sodium hydroxide.

'What oils are we using Betty?'

'Almond, coconut and avocado. Do you want to measure them out?'

'Well of course, I am the scientist.'

Betty smiles at me.

'It's nice to see you happy again.'

I smile, as I measure the oils.

'I'll measure the water,' Betty says.

'Alicia is a good person. She didn't mean to upset you.'

'I know.'

'Have you ever thought of moving out of the city Lola? I think you might enjoy it.'

'Can you imagine Leo, in the country? And Alex, he would hate it.'

'What about you Lols, what do you want?'

'The almond oil, please, can you pass it to me. I don't know. I've lived for so many years coping, trying to stay well, making sure the boys and Papá are okay.' I could feel a lump in my throat.

'You're actually stronger than you think.'

Do I tell her about Nick? If anyone, Betty would understand. I blurt it out. 'I had sex with someone and I'm thinking of leaving Leo.'

Betty drops the bottle of oil in her hand.

JUAN

Qué importa el sueño, que a mis pupilas roban,
What does it matter, the stolen sleep
las mentidas horas de bailar sin calma
the deceptive hours of dancing without resting.
'*Porteño y bailarin*', Carlos Di Sarli y Héctor Marcó

I'm laughing to myself thinking about the salsa class. With Frances I have fun, a fun I didn't think possible in Australia. I want my daughters to understand Frances makes me feel alive. I'm finding parts of myself that have been missing since I was a young man in Uruguay. She has opened places in me and places in Australia. On the road trip we stopped at parks and beautiful beaches. Beaches with big coastlines and white soft sand. We took our shoes off and walked along them, the dogs running in front of us. The waves came in and wet our feet. It felt good and free. At the parks we stopped, she told me the names of the different gum trees and the birds, the rosellas, and the cockatoos. Now when I look up and see a bird, I want to know what this bird is. Before it was bird or tree. Now it is black cockatoo or scribbly gum. My world is bigger with Frances. This is what I want my daughters to know. They look at Frances and see an old uneducated woman with skin that has lived for too long under the Australian sun. They can't see the beauty that hides under this. Like me she too had a childhood without comfort, made to feel shame. Frances even had to pretend she was Italian and not Aboriginal. Her mother was scared they would take her children away, like she had been taken from her mother. That type of pain lives inside you. She wanted to save Frances and her brother from this. They had to be cleaner than the white people, everything had to be spotless, their house, their clothes. Clean meant white and respectful. The cruelty of the English, stealing children, destroying families.

In Uruguay the military destroyed families too. Taking away those that wanted to bring change, torturing them, then killing them. Pregnant women too. They stole their children and killed the mothers. The babies were given to military families or supporters of the regime.

I saw people numb the pain with alcohol, the more drink, the duller the pain. Carmen buried her pain very deep and kept the hope that her brother would turn up one day, alive. Carmen's parents' grief was so huge it killed them. Don Manuel died a year after Mario went missing and Carmen's mother two years later.

That is what I find so incredible about Frances, how she has so much love and joy to give when she has lived through tragedy. I don't understand how grief and trauma destroys some people and not others. Maybe if I did, I could help Lola. What I do know is that you need to take the morsels of happiness life throws at you and hold on to them because they are precious, it's what we live for. I am not a religious man. I do not believe there is a greater power looking out for us. Life is just what happens, a series of circumstances and we have little control. When you have that small chance to steer your life towards happiness you do it.

The trip with Frances brought me closer to her, seeing where she spent her childhood. On the way home from Brisbane, we drove inland. I wanted to see where Frances grew up. We drove to Dubbo and went to the house where Frances lived with her parents and brother. It is on the edge of the town. A fibro house, still standing. Aboriginal children were playing in the yard. They waved at us.

Frances told me the house looked the same, except for a broken window that had been covered with a piece of plywood. The lemon tree her mother planted in a corner of the front garden is much bigger and heavy with lemons. Around the tree are fallen lemons, left to rot.

We went to the pub for lunch. The same one Frances went to with her family on special occasions. It was expensive to eat out. I told her I never ate out until I was a young man with a job.

Dubbo is big for a country town. It reminded me of Mercedes in Uruguay, the closest city to the village where Carmen grew up before her family moved to Montevideo. The first time I visited Mercedes I felt at home. It stood strong on the banks of *el Rio Negro*, the plaza with its palm trees, brushing against the *platanos*. We ate *chivitos* at Café del Sol, then walked along the rambla by the river. Uruguay is contained, you can drive from one side of the country to the other in one day.

Australia is a very big country. We drove for hours inland from the coast. Towns with few houses, a pub, maybe a post office, the highway splitting them in half. Dust and isolation. Kilometres of grasslands, sheep, cattle, crops. Vastness and open skies.

Frances suggested we visit Moree, where there are hot springs that would be good for our arthritis. There was a melancholy about it, like it was mourning a loss. The streets were empty, waiting for life to begin.

We went to the hot pools and found ourselves in a nursing home on water. Grey heads lined every pool. It was quiet, except for the soft voices of the old people sitting like ducks in water. In a waiting room, wishing for new life not death. We sat in thirty-eight-degree water until I could take it no longer, sweat was pouring down my face. Hopefully the minerals did the job. Unlike the movie, *Cocoon*, however, we didn't skip out of there feeling twenty years younger.

It was here that I learned about the Freedom Riders, people who travelled in a bus across Australia to protest racism. They came to Moree because Aboriginal people were not allowed in the local pool. I am shocked when Frances tells me this. This is their country, and they are told where they can and where they can't go by some white imbeciles.

BETTY

Lemongrass Soap
Ingredients:
- Lemongrass oil
- Coconut oil
- Avocado oil
- Olive oil
- Distilled water
- Optional – dried lemongrass

Lola went home today. I'm going to miss her for the first time in years. It was good to see her relax and open. I know she's in there somewhere, she just gets lost in all the worry, fear, and insecurity. Poor Lola, it must be exhausting having so much shit in your head constantly. While she was here, she was able to laugh and let go bit. Then she told me she's thinking of leaving Leo and had an affair. I didn't see that coming.

'Mum, phone for you,' Leif shouts out.

Why isn't he at school?

I pick up the phone and talk to Kate from the Conservation group. They need people to help paint banners for the anti-logging protest on the weekend.

I walk down the hallway to Leif's room and knock on the door. He answers and I walk in. He's lying on the bed reading a book.

'Why aren't you at school? I thought Dad dropped you off.'

He looks up from his book. 'Mum, I couldn't do it today. You know what they are doing all day? Practising for that stupid play about the rainforest. I'm in the crowd, I don't even have a proper part.'

I look at my son, his tousled brown hair, almost covering his left eye, his long lanky body stretched out on the bed. He is leaving boyhood.

I sit on his bed. 'What are you reading?'

He looks up from the book. *The Book Thief.*

'What's it about?'

'A girl in Nazi Germany, during the war. The narrator is not the girl, it's death.'

'That's different.' I pat his thigh. 'Tomorrow you are going back to school. I'm going out to make some soaps. When I get back, I want a cup of tea and to hear about the book.'

Leif smiles at me.

Before I go into the shed, I give the lavender and rosemary oils sitting on the sunny shelf a good shake.

In the shed I measure out the oils. I replace the castor oil with avocado oil. I know it's not the same, but I don't like castor oil. My soaps don't make a fluffy lather like supermarket soaps, because I've removed the castor oil, however they smell amazing. The lemongrass oil I'm using today, I made last year, from lemongrass I grew. It has a delicious, earthy lemony aroma I want to fall into.

I measure the lye carefully and add it to the distilled water. The fumes are unpleasant, but it's over quickly. The shed door and window are open.

Then it's time to heat the oils over the little camp stove. Once heated the glossy mixture of oils is mixed with the lye and I stir and watch it thicken. It reminds me of *crema pastelera*, which Mum made for desserts on special occasions. Lola and I licked the spoons and left the bowl spotless. It was sugary and delicious. As I open the bottle with the lemongrass oil, the sweet and citrusy aroma is released. I pour thirty drops into the soap mixture, stirring it well so that the fragrance is mixed in evenly. I pour the mix into the moulds and sprinkle dried lemongrass over the top. Gently I cover them with a towel. They'll be ready for the markets in a few weeks.

I walk back to the house, the lemongrass scent lingering.

LOLA

30 June 2012

Today I will tell Leo. I'm so fucking scared. I won't tell him about Nick, why more pain. I've walked away from safety and now I can't go back. Part of me wants to crawl back in and hide, but another part of me is pushing me out. I'm restless and I'm scared. I'm scared of the future but I'm more scared to let go of the past. I need to tell Leo today. I can't keep living this life anymore. I'll move out, find another job. While I was at Betty's I looked at jobs. I haven't been inside a laboratory for fifteen years. The entry level one would be good, I could ease my way back. It's on the south coast, not too far, but far enough for a new start. The boys will like it near the beach. I can't imagine leaving them.

As I put my journal down, I'm thinking that of course the boys will want to come with me. Or will they? For the first time I think that leaving Leo could mean leaving the boys, what if they want to stay with him? No, this is not going to happen. I don't think I could do it without the boys.

Being away from the city and Leo, staying with Betty, I felt stronger. I enjoyed making the soaps. It gave me confidence. It brought back what it felt like to work in the lab, analysing blood and tissue. Looking through the microscope, being able to differentiate between healthy and unhealthy tissue. Finding answers, asking questions, talking to colleagues.

This will be a good. It will be good for all of us. Leo will be devastated.

Last night Alex told me he wants to go to South America as an exchange student. He wants to improve his Spanish, find out about his background. Maybe it's about forgetting Alison too, although he would never say that. I still don't know what happened between them. The loss of first love, a pain so deep you think you can't breathe. Alex held it all in.

Apparently, he met a boy from Brazil at school who is here as an exchange student. He is from São Paulo. The boy told him Australia was very quiet. While it was good for sleeping and studying, he missed home. He said he had chosen Australia because it was so far away and not many people lived here. He wanted something completely different to where he came from. He told Alex to visit South America, the girls will go crazy for a *gatinho* from Australia. Alex explained that meant you were hot. He said it with a half-smile, trying to hide his pleasure at being told he was attractive to girls. This is the most Alex has ever talked to me about girls. Did he have sex with Alison? When I asked Leo to talk to Alex about sex, he replied, 'The boy will know what to do, we all did. He doesn't want to hear it from his father. Make sure he has condoms.'

I tried to talk to Alex about safe sex and to tell him that girls might not be ready even if they say they are, as I remembered my first awkward fumbling with Ahmed. Alex was embarrassed. He told me it was all good and walked away.

We discussed what country in South America he would like to go to. His Brazilian friend suggested Argentina. It's got a great city in Buenos Aires, plenty to do. I feel Uruguay would be best. He can meet relatives and it's a small and safe country. I suggested a country town, maybe near where his grandmother was born. Alex said he would only agree on Uruguay if he went to the capital. The capital is like a big country town. He doesn't know that.

I told Papá. He was delighted and said it would do the boy a lot of good. He even offered to help pay for it. He knows Leo and I can't afford it for more than a couple of months. Papá said send him for six months or one year. That way he can practice his Spanish and 'make his world bigger'. I know he was thinking it would be good for Alex to be away from Leo, although he didn't say that. Papá doesn't say a lot about Leo, but I know he is disappointed.

It will be good for Alex. To be a teenager in Uruguay, how I would have loved that. Except for me it would have been under a military dictatorship. An adolescence lived in repression, being squashed during a time of growth. School, an education of patriotic lies and denied critical thinking. Teachers who strayed from this were removed and blacklisted. Tio Mario was a history teacher. He was removed from his classroom in front of his students. Two *milicos* came and took him away, one on either side, holding him by each arm. Apparently as he was escorted out, the students beat their hands on the desks. Besides the noise of many hands against the old desks, no sound was made. He was never seen again. He was loved by his students, known for his generosity and warmth. His wife, my Tia Laura, was blacklisted from teaching too. She was a Spanish teacher and luckily, she was able to work as a private tutor during those years. That's how she supported her family; my two cousins and her mother. The *milicos* went to their house to scare Tia Laura too. She was hit across the head, and left bleeding, her mother stood in shock as she saw her daughter beaten. The next day they left Montevideo and went to live with Tia Laura's brother in Salto. Papá went to the house to pick up some of Tio Mario's things.

Tio Mario is one of the *desaparecidos*, murdered by the military. Disappeared, because their bodies were never found. Maybe it provides some hope that one day the person will reappear, that they got away and were hiding in a little town in some far away country. Mamá knew her brother would never reappear, yet she never said that. She couldn't let him go.

While Uruguay still lives with the wounds of the dictatorship years, with time some families divided by allegiances and fear may start to speak to each other. It's happened in my family, to Mamá's cousins, two brothers on opposite sides. One in the military, the other with the *Frente*. I can't imagine Daniel and Alex in that situation, on conflicting sides. Her older cousin became a general in the military. Mamá did not speak of him. Once when I asked her, she said he was dead to her. She killed the relative that lived and gave life to the dead one.

When my uncle, the general, became sick and old, his youngest brother, Sergio, went to see him. They had not talked for twenty-five years. Mamá was shocked and could not believe it. I remember her telling Papá, how can Sergio forgive a murderer?

Sergio and the General started to see each other regularly. Somehow, they became brothers again. Mamá was furious. She was too far away to understand.

As the years pass some wounds may close. Others cannot. While grandmothers are still searching for the grandchildren the dictatorship stole from the daughters it murdered, wounds are raw. It may take generations to ensure this terror never happens again. Maybe it is the conversations of brothers like my uncles that need to take place.

Alex will get to see Uruguay through young eyes and experience the Latin spirit and how people interact. After I left Uruguay, I only returned twice. I would have liked to have gone back when my parents did, but they did not ask me, and I didn't suggest it. Besides I wouldn't have wanted to leave Leo's side. We weren't living together then, but I felt if I left, I could have lost him. There were so many young Latin women around the Cultural Centre, many more attractive and confident than I was. A lot of them could sing and play music. I was insecure.

Leo never wanted to go back to Uruguay, and I was afraid to go without him. Now I need to step into that fear otherwise I will never know freedom, nor myself.

I wish Malena was here. I know she would help me through this. I'll give her a quick ring before I talk to Leo. As a teenager, I grew closer to Malena. She understands feeling afraid and insecure and that sometimes you need someone to listen, unlike Betty who offers solutions to get over it and move on.

I pick up the phone and put in the number. It rings for ages before she answers. She sounds sleepy.

'Hi Malena, how are you?'

'I'm sorry I didn't realise that was the time.'

'No, no everything is fine.'

'Yes, he's good.'

I want to tell her about Papá and Frances, but the words stick in my throat.

'I'm just a bit on edge, that's all.'

'Of course I'm taking medication,' I tell her when she asks.

Is this the time to tell her I'm thinking of moving out? I can hardly say it myself.

'Malena, I'll ring you later.'

'No go back to sleep.'

'Love you too.'

I hang up and start pacing up and down our small living room. The bongo drums sit in a corner, a couple of books on top of them. There are dirty cups and glasses on the coffee table. Why am I the only person in the house capable of carrying dishes to the sink?

Alex and Daniel are at school. Now is a good time to talk to Leo. I put on the water to start a round of *mate*.

My hands are shaking as I put the *yerba* in the gourd and I spill *yerba* on the benchtop. Fuck! I fill the thermos with hot water and walk out the back. Leo is sitting in the sun, on a milk crate, strumming his guitar.

He smiles at me. I hold out a *mate* for him. He puts the guitar down and takes the *mate*.

'I want to talk to you about something Leo.'

He looks up at me as he sips on the *bombilla*. It's a beautiful silver one that used to belong to Tia Gladys. Betty gave it to me when she came back from helping Flo pack up Tia's house. Flo wanted me to have it as I'm the only one in our generation who drinks *mate*.

'I've been thinking about something that is going to change everything.'

'That sounds like a song.'

'I'm serious Leo.'

'Okay what is it, tell me.'

I stand up and walk up and down the small patio. Once I say the words, we will no longer be the same. The words I have to say will change all our lives. How the fuck do I start? Leo is looking at me.

'Lola, come on you're making me nervous now.'

'I think we need to separate.' I say it quickly while I'm standing, looking over the fence. I continue to walk up and down.

'Where is this coming from? Don't tell me, Betty put this idea in your head. She was here for a few days, and she wants to fix your life too.'

I look at him. 'Leo, it was my idea.'

'Lola, *que carajo*, are you saying? You met someone, tell me.'

'No, I just need to do this.'

'What about Alex and Danny?'

'They can come with me, I'll move out.'

'No, no, no. You're not taking my children anywhere. If you want to go, you go but not Alex *y* Danny.'

The tears are now so many I can't stop them. I look at Leo. He gets up and takes his guitar and walks inside. At the door he turns around and says, 'Go Lola, there's no more to say. You want to go, then go.'

I'm left standing with the *mate*. I throw it against the fence, so hard that it smashes and the *bombilla* falls among the basil.

JUAN

Si me perdonas
If you forgive me
el tiempo viejo otra ves vendra
The old times will be back
la primavera de nuestras vidas
The spring of our lives
veras que todo nos sonreira
You will see that everything will smile at us
    '*Volvio Una Noche*', Alfredo Le Pera y Carlos Gardel

We are having dinner at the bowling club and I'm waiting for Frances to get our drinks. She insisted. This is another discovery for me. Carmen and I would walk past this club and look at the old people, dressed in white, playing bowling. We didn't know anyone could come to this club. You can come here and eat and not play the bowling. It's like the RSL, you can go there too and not support the military. The food here is quite good. I'm having the roast beef with potatoes, pumpkin, and carrots. And the gravy of course. After you try it a few times, it is not so bad. Of course, the chimichurri is superior, but I now like the gravy too. You can buy it in a packet at the supermarket. Frances showed me. Now when I cook myself a steak, sometimes I have gravy. Every day I become a little more Australian, the tastes of this country become more familiar. I like it. I no longer live on the edge of Australia, now I can walk in it. Frances is making this possible. I think I love this woman. This wonderful woman, who comes from a world so different to mine, has made me feel whole again. Like I felt before I left Uruguay when I still had a whole life in front of me.

Frances puts a bottle of champagne on the table.

'Champagne, ooh la la. What are we celebrating?'

She puts her hand on mine.

'Brisbane was so much fun. Stopping at different places along the coast on the way, having barbeques. That lovely caravan park we stayed in just out of Brisbane. And Byron Bay, well that was just so beautiful. That beach, to think you can't go further east.'

'Yes, it was a fantastic trip, Frances. I enjoy it very much. You are a very special woman.'

'We had fun, didn't we?'

'Of course, we have fun. I just say it was a fantastic trip. Plus, we slept like babies, after the fun we had in the bed.'

I can't believe I have this much sex in my old age. I pinch myself to check it is real. I take Frances' hands in mine. Her long fingers feel familiar. They have touched me everywhere.

'Ooh you naughty man. We get on well, we laugh. I think we make each other happy.'

'Frances, I have not been this happy in a very long time. You have changed my life. Is this what we are celebrating?'

I pop the cork and pour us both a glass of champagne. I take her arm and intertwine it with mine as we take the first drink.

'I have something even more wonderful for us than the road trip.'

Now I am thinking she is going to ask me to marry her. I am getting nervous. I love her, but marriage? What will I say without upsetting her?

She takes her hand away, picks up her handbag and puts her hand in the bag. She pulls out a piece of paper and places it in front of me.

'What is this?'

She smiles at me. I look at the paper. There is a picture of a big ship in the background. At the front is a photo of a beautiful young woman with long dark hair and a young man. They are in position, ready to dance. He has one arm around her waist and with his other hand he holds the woman's hand, ready to spin her around. I read the words underneath the picture. 'Salsa Sailing'.

'Well, what do you think?' Frances asks me.

'It is a lovely photo of two beautiful people dancing.'

'No silly, what do you think about us going on this cruise?'

A cruise. Sailing on the ocean. To me this is for rich people, a life of luxury, drinking wine and looking at the sea, with nothing to do. Now the woman has gone completely mad.

'Well?' She looks at me, almost pleading, desperation in her eyes.

'Frances, this is not for people like us. How can I pay for this?'

'You don't need to Bub'.

'Now you are going to tell me you have won the lottery.'

She laughs. 'Juan, you are so cute. Just tell me you want to go.'

'But Frances, this is ridiculous.'

She puts her hand in her bag and pulls out an envelope. She gives me the envelope.

'Open it.'

I open the envelope and there are two tickets. They look like plane tickets. I read it. One has my name on it and the other her name. My hand is shaking as I read where we are going. 'Mexico City'.

I look at Frances. 'Please Frances, tell me, what have you done?'

'Now love, don't worry. It is all sorted. We fly to Mexico and from there we take the ship to cruise the Caribbean. We even get off in Cuba. You know how you told me you always wanted to visit Cuba, how you admired that they told the Americans to piss off. Please tell me you're excited.'

I look at her. She is like a schoolgirl, smiling nervously. So happy with what she has done. But to me this is a shock. 'Frances, I can't accept this.'

'Juan, listen to me first. I had some money that I was putting away, plus Malcolm's superannuation. My plan was to use it for a holiday. A proper holiday, overseas, maybe to Paris or Italy. After I met you, I don't want that anymore. I prefer to do something special with you. Imagine a cruise, how fancy. The two of us drinking cocktails, sunbaking by the pool, dancing in the evenings. Oooh, it will be so romantic. Please say yes, Juan. Besides it's too late, what would I do with your ticket?'

I look at her. I look down at the table. I look at the tickets in front of me.

Cuba. Yes, I always wanted to go. But not like this, dancing on a ship to Fidel's door. Frances is looking at me. I cannot explain this to her. It is who I am. My life with Carmen.

I look at the champagne bottle on the table, and our two glasses together. My food, practically untouched.

'Let's go home Frances.'

I get up and put my jacket on. I want to leave as fast as possible. Frances gets up. I can see tears in her eyes.

'Juan, I didn't mean to offend you. I had the money. I want to use it with you. Juan please stop.'

I can't stop. I am walking and walking out of that club, out of that world. Frances is behind me.

'Please Juan stop. You're being ridiculous. This is something special for us.'

I stop and turn to face Frances. 'Frances, it's not the money. Yes, I don't think it is right that you pay for me. But it is bigger.'

It is my family, my life, what we have lived through.

'I will drive you home.' I'm practically running to the car. I don't even know how my old legs can take me so fast. Frances is walking behind me, talking but I cannot hear anymore.

BETTY

Winter has settled into the Steiner school, the maple trees have shed their leaves, spreading a carpet of browns and reds across the ground. Sunshine's class is out in the garden, weeding. From the school's kitchen, I can see her swinging plaits, as she jumps up and down.

Kara and I are making spinach pies and vegetable soup. We picked the spinach this morning and the borlotti beans for the soup were soaked overnight. Parents cook lunch every day at the school. We have a roster. I do every second Tuesday. In summer and spring, we make salads and sandwiches from seasonal vegetables that the kids have grown or that parents bring from their gardens. The kids bake the bread, delicious chewy sourdough with a crispy crust. This is followed by fruit from the little orchard the school has. Apricots, so sweet they taste like jam, oranges, juicy and sweet, yet tart. The sweetness of peaches that lingers in your mouth.

'Leif doesn't want to be a vegan.' I blurt out to Kara. 'He told me he has the right to eat what he wants.' It feels like a confession, full of shame.

Kara looks up from the huge pot she is stirring.

I cannot understand it. He knows why we choose to be vegan. He knows the damage that eating animals has on the environment and on our bodies.

'Well let him. Don't cook for him, make him cook his own dead animals.'

'You think?'

'It's normal Betty. He's a teenager, he needs to rebel about something. Let him get it out of his system.' Maybe Kara is right.

Leif wants to swap healthy food for stuff that has been sitting on shelves for longer than I want to think about, made by people in factories where they don't want to be. The way Mum filled moulds in the biscuit factory, where it was no longer food, but the sweat of someone's labour with a mix of chemicals.

When I get home, I wash up the breakfast dishes that were left in the sink this morning.

'Hey honey, what you thinking about?' Chris asks as he comes up to me and pecks me on the cheek.

I'm staring out the window, my hands in the sink.

'You're home early.'

'I came by to pick up some seeds.'

'Chris, I'm thinking about Leif, and I'm worried about him. I don't want him to eat meat or leave Steiner.' I couldn't bring myself to tell Kara this morning that Leif also wants to change schools.

Chris laughs.

'Why do you think it's funny?' I turn around to look at Chris and as I take my hands out of the sink soapy water goes on the floor.

'I'm thinking it's so innocent. I don't want him to become a caveman either, but we need to choose our battles. Let him make some choices, it's part of growing up and these choices are harmless.'

'Not really, eating meat is not harmless and you know that.'

'Betts, what I'm trying to say is that if this is his rebellion, it's fine. At least he's not asking to smoke pot.'

'So, do we enrol him in the public high school for next year? There'll be plenty of pot there.'

'There's pot everywhere, you know that. That's not what this is about. He's searching for his identity, it's normal.'

'Mm, it just doesn't feel right.' Chris is sensible and level-headed, and we are a team. I want to believe he is right.

He takes me in a big hug, and I rub his head with my soapy hands.

'You know he might want to leave one day, move to the big smoke, just like you left being a Westie and came up here.'

'That's it, now you're asking for it.' I break free from his embrace, take the wet dishrag and throw it at him. I run outside and he chases me.

'And who was a surfie boy?' I taunt him as I run.

Chris grew up on the northern beaches in Sydney, very white and very mainstream as he describes it. Life came in a package of surfing, hot chips, boiled vegetables, bonfires on the beach and beer. Ethnic food was pizza. When he finished school, he had a gap year and went backpacking in South America. He said he was looking for something as far away and as different as possible to what he had grown up with.

He catches me and we fall on the grass outside, laughing.

'I want Leif to be able to tell us anything, even if he knows we won't agree.' I say this as we lie on the grass, looking up at the sky. I think of my own adolescence, where I didn't share anything with my parents. The time I borrowed the car to drive to a party and when I got there, I drank so much cheap cider it was impossible to drive home. I rang Papá to tell him I wanted to stay the night at the party host's house. He said absolutely not and to drive home now. I didn't tell him I was drunk. Was I protecting him or was I protecting myself? I rang Lola in my drunken state and told her Papá said I had to drive home. She asked her friend, Debbie, to drive her to pick me up. When they got there, they cleaned me up, made me an instant coffee and Lola drove the station wagon home. When we got home, Papá and Mum were watching television. They heard us come in and Mum shouted out, 'How was the party, Betty?'

I managed to shout back 'good', as I ran to the bedroom. Poor Lola had to go back out quietly and clean my vomit off the car seat and floor.

Malena and Lola did a lot of protecting our parents, shielding them from the 'Australian world' they would never understand. I think they believed our parents already had so much pain they couldn't add to it. We looked after each other. Malena made sure I knew about birth control at least a year before I had sex. Mum never talked about it, nor did we ask her to. Malena had to explain periods to us too. When Lola and I got our periods, we told Mum, and she celebrated that now we were young women, and she gave us money to go and buy pads. They were expensive and we weren't allowed to use them at night. Mum sewed pads out of old flannelette sheets, which we used at home and during the night. I was so embarrassed, especially when we hung them out to dry, like a white Tibetan prayer flag on the Hills Hoist for everyone to see.

I want my children to feel comfortable to tell me anything. If respecting Leif's choice to eat animals is the way to keep the trust and communication open, I will do it, as much as it pains me to see dead animals being cooked and eaten in my house.

'I don't know about the public school, I'm scared there will be fights, like at my school.'

I think of Fairfield High. The fights. On the oval at lunchtime or out the back of the school. Any conflict was sorted with a fist fight. It wasn't only the boys. The Aussie girls were always ready for a punch up over a stolen boyfriend or a look they didn't like. They particularly disliked the Vietnamese girls. They made fun of their accents. There were Laotian and Khmer students too, but the Aussies called them all dirty chinks. There were Timorese and Lebanese. The Lebs stood their ground. All of us were trying to fit in, in a world that didn't really want us. I don't think any of the parents knew what went on at school, most of them were busy working and didn't speak English. They had their world and we had ours, they had to find their place in the factories, and we had to fight for ours in school. I just wanted to get out of there as soon as I could. We were the wogs and would always be, if we stayed.

'I went to a public school Betts, it was fine.'

'Yes, but in a good area. Here you get all types.'

'Someone's being a tad snobby. That's going to cost you. At least ten wheelbarrows of compost down to the bottom garden.'

I get up and go into a downward dog.

'I don't think so, or else someone will have to cook dinner tonight. I know there can be bullies at any school. We need to make sure he can stand up for himself.'

'He's a strong kid, he'll be fine.'

I come out of my downward dog and go into an extended child's pose.

'You know my school was a battlefield and you had to find your tribe to survive. I was in a group of the popular South American girls, I still remember them; Graciela, whom everyone called Grace, Beatriz, and Carolina. We held our own. We had the advantage that we smoked, how that was an advantage now sounds crazy, but that meant we congregated in the toilets or out in the back field, as far away as possible without leaving the school. Smoking meant we found ourselves with the Aussie smokers, sometimes sharing lighters in the toilet and often together in detention, another thing hidden from Papá and Mum, thanks to Lola again. That gave us something in common and we became more accepted and less targeted.'

I think of the teachers, powerless to stop the slurs and the fights. It was bigger than the classroom or the school. We were all sitting ducks. No one talked.

I rise from child's pose and join Chris, who is sitting cross-legged, playing with a twig.

'You survived, look at the amazing life we have. Leif doesn't have a quarter of the disadvantages you had. He'll be right. Plus, he's good at sports, that always helps.'

I think of Lola running with her long skinny legs. She was fast, often came first and went to regional athletic carnivals. That bought her protection.

I played on the school volleyball team. When we played against other schools, we had to show them we were the top dog, that meant we had to be united, and the racism and nastiness was directed outward and not at each other.

Chris gets up. 'It will be okay, and we'll keep talking to him. He knows what our values are. He's a good kid.'

'I love you. I better go organise some food before the kids get home.'

I get up and kiss him, standing on my tippy toes. He lifts me and swings me around.

'Love you too, Betts,' he says as he places me back down on the grass.

I still don't feel totally convinced. Education needs to be gentle; children need to be safe to learn and that is what Leif will lose if he changes school. At Steiner, the parents and teachers share similar values and that helps maintain the equilibrium. In a public school you don't have that, there's no shared values among the parents, and the classroom and the playground will reflect that. That was my experience at high school, students fighting to survive, values and beliefs expressed by fists. We didn't have words and we came from countries destroyed by wars and brutal governments. The Aussie kids were angry, poor or both. They suddenly found themselves surrounded by new languages, foreign cultures and kids carrying traumas they could not speak nor begin to understand. This mess was dumped among the kids, a tip of complicated emotions with no one to help sort them.

Malena went inside herself, the deeper she buried herself, the darker it was. Lola found a group of friends where she could hide to survive. They were a front, and this made it harder to break. I pushed my bravest face forward and took up the tough behaviours needed to keep the bullying at bay.

My children have been shielded from the ugliness of Australia. I don't want Leif to step into it.

LOLA

10 July 2012

I look at the paintings in the waiting room. They are Monet prints. Waterlilies, fields of colourful flowers, bridges, and well-dressed women of another era. I know they are meant to be calming, but instead I feel angry. I'm angry at Leo, I'm angry at Alex for wanting to stay with Leo and I fucking hate these paintings. They're not peasants working in fields or children in factories. More middle-class shit. The sweet façade of middle Australia is everywhere. In the media, in Parliament, in schools, universities, in offices, in the labs I used to work in. White middle Australia wants to annihilate the stories they trampled on to get where they are today. They get in your head too, so that you believe you'll never be as good as they are. Then there's the shame.

I can't stop my right leg from bouncing up and down. I want to, but any message from my brain is being rejected.

Simone opens the door to her room. 'Hello Lola, please come in.'

I sit on the blue armchair. It's big and I feel like Alice in a house where life is too large to fit into. Simone sits opposite me in a similar looking chair. She has her notebook on her lap. She is a little on the *gorda* side and the chair is a comfortable fit.

'It's been a while, Lola. What brings you here?'

I haven't seen her for over two years. The last time I sat in this chair was when I changed my medication, and the new one still had not kicked in. The in-between stage sent me down a tunnel of irrational thoughts and anxiety I couldn't fight on my own. The doctor suggested to go back and see my psychologist.

'I've decided to leave my husband and my eldest son wants to stay with him. I feel so angry about it.' The words spill out, before I even have a chance to sort them in my head.

'That's big Lola, it's natural to have strong emotions. Do you feel angry about both leaving your husband and at your son for wanting to stay with him?'

'I'm mostly angry at my son for not coming with me.'

Simone writes in her notes. The she looks up.

'Why do you think that is?'

If I knew that I wouldn't be here, you idiot I want to say.

'I don't know.'

'Did you ask him where he wanted to live?'

Of course, I didn't ask him, I told him we would be moving. I'm his mother. Besides it's not good for him to stay with Leo.

'No?'

Simone looks at me, waiting for me to speak.

'No, I don't think it's good for him to stay with his father.'

'Why is that, Lola?'

I explain that Alex is not communicating with either Leo or myself and I know Leo would leave him alone, he wouldn't try to find out what Alex is thinking or what he does for so many hours in his room.

'Maybe Alex needs his space, and he knows Leo will respect that.'

And I won't? That's what she's saying.

'Alex has broken up with his girlfriend and I'm worried about him spending so much time alone.' I don't tell her that he does go out with his friends sometimes.

As I look down, I notice the colour of the carpet. It's a cream colour. The carpet is not too thick or plush.

'Is there anything else you're concerned about, besides him spending too much time in his room?'

He doesn't talk to me as much as he used to. I don't even know why he broke up with Alison. But, I say, no. Simone then explains how it's normal for adolescent boys to move away from their parents and spend more time with their peers. She even suggests that while I don't know what Alex is doing in his room, he could be communicating with his friends online. She tells me the important thing is to be there for when he does need Leo and me. That's basically the same thing Leo said, and his advice was free.

I don't want to spend all my time talking about Alex. I know it won't be helpful. It won't make Alex come and live with me. Leo was smug when

Alex said he was staying with him. We both know it's because he's aware that Leo will leave him alone and not expect anything from him. What will be helpful will be organising for him to go on exchange to Uruguay. I came here to process my decision about leaving Leo. That's the problem with seeing a therapist, you need to be careful how you start the session and get to the point you want to talk about, so that the session isn't wasted on backstory, or you go off on a tangent.

Simone must really like Monet. There are more prints on the walls in here too.

'I sort of had an affair.'

I look at my feet when I say this. I'm drowning in shame. I can't look at Simone. She doesn't say anything. I'm familiar with this approach. She waits, in silence, to see what else I might say.

'But I'm not leaving Leo for him, it's not like that.'

I look up at Simone, as she scribbles in her notebook. Fuck, she will have a file, saying I had an affair. It's on paper. The fact that it's on paper and not only in my head unnerves me. I want her to tear it up. Instead, I say, 'Leo doesn't know, and I won't tell him.'

Finally, she says something. 'It is your choice whether you tell him or not.'

I know that. State the bloody obvious Simone. Why am I even paying for this?

The print of the bridge over the waterlilies is above Simone's head.

'Do you want to talk about how you're feeling about leaving Leo?'

I do and I don't want to talk about it. But I know I need to because it will help me understand it.

'It's hard to put into words. I feel I need to separate, or somehow, I'll cease to exist, it's weird when I try to explain it.'

'They're very strong feelings, ceasing to exist. Can you talk a bit more about this?'

I imagine myself walking along the bridge in the picture, holding a parasol.

'With Leo, as much as I love him, I've started to feel like I'm not whole. I'm a version of myself that fits with him, and there's more of me, hiding inside myself. Like who would I have been if I hadn't met him? Would my journey have been so damaged by anxiety if I'd had a different life? Maybe I would have completed my masters degree and worked overseas? Who knows, I have all these questions about what my life would have been had it taken a different trajectory. I need to know if I can stand on my own two feet, without having Leo to fall back on. I'm terrified, but there's a part of me pushing me to do it. It's all a big mess.'

My eyes are moist, and the tears start streaming gently down my cheeks. Simone passes me the tissue box.

'While it feels like a mess, it sounds like there is some clarity in the mess, you have made a choice, and that's a start. You can also see that you're not your authentic self and you want to tap into that authenticity. That's wonderful Lola.'

If it's so wonderful, why do I feel like my insides are being wrung. What's this authenticity shit? If I'm so authentic I should be able to tell Leo, I had sex with Nick. I'm an authentic liar. I want to go. I look up at the clock. We still have twenty minutes. Simone is looking at me, waiting for me to speak. She has put her notebook down and smooths her skirt with both hands.

I've fallen among the waterlilies.

'Lola, what you are going through is incredibly difficult, you need to be kind to yourself, show yourself compassion, like you would a friend.'

By that she means, lock your inner bully up, the fascist that wants to be boss. I'm familiar with this guy.

The tears turn into sobs, those big heaving sobs. The tissue box is now in my lap and I'm ripping tissue after tissue out.

Simone lets me cry for the next ten minutes. When the sobs subside, she asks, 'Will you be okay to drive home? You're welcome to sit in the waiting room for as long as you need to. Please be gentle with yourself when you go home. Do you have a teddy bear or something similar you can hold?'

What, no, of course I don't have a teddy bear. I'm a grown woman. I look up at her without moving.

She walks over to a shelf and takes a brown knitted bear with a purple cap and bowtie and gives it to me. 'Take Bobby, you can bring him back at our next session.' She hands me the bear and I take it and hold it with my hand. I've never had a teddy bear, so I'm not sure what to do with it.

'These emotions are very raw, very deep, they can go back a long way, maybe to when you were a child. Look after yourself, like you would your own children. You can hold Bobby, like if you were a little girl, needing comfort and safety. Let's make an appointment for next week. If you need to talk before then, ring me, okay.'

We make the appointment while I'm cuddling Bobby. I nod to whatever else Simone says. I feel like I'm seven years old again.

Then it's time to pay and I'm reminded that this is a transaction.

On the way home I go through McDonalds drive-through in Stanmore and buy a hot chocolate. I need something warming and comforting. I stop the car in the McDonalds parking lot and drink my hot chocolate. Life is so fucking complicated and hard.

In my family we don't inherit money. We inherit diseases. Cancer, arthritis, diabetes, depression, anxiety. I guess I'm working through my inheritance once again.

JUAN

Yo quisiera mujer que comprendas
I wish woman that you understand
El cariño tan leal que te tengo
The loyal affection I have for you
Que me paso las horas pensando
That I spend hours thinking
Y es esa la causa que yo ya ni duermo
And for that reason, I can't even sleep
    '*Tu vieja Ventana*', G.D Barberi, Carlos Gardel y José Ricardo

The bathroom window frames a red sunset. Not even this makes me smile today. I close the door on the sunset and go back to my music in the lounge room. Coco at my feet as Horacio Casares sings a tango.

Frances has rung me many times. I do not answer. I know this is wrong. It is not nice for her. But I do not know what to say. How can I explain she stepped into the world I shared with Carmen? I know she did not mean any harm to me and how could she see what she was doing?

Poor Frances. I like her very much. I think I love her too. I smile to myself as I think of her in that ridiculous hat with the banana on the top. She makes me laugh and feel light-hearted. But Cuba? This is not for Frances and me.

In 1959, Fidel Castro came to Montevideo. Carmen and I were there, with thousands of other Uruguayans. He was our hero. He was the one who took away from the rich and made the country belong to every Cubano. It was one of those grey Montevideo winter days. The cold wind was blowing from *las pampas Argentinas*, slicing our faces. We all stood at *Plaza Independencia*, waiting for Fidel, in our big coats. Carmen was wearing a blue scarf. I still remember it. Her image is like a photo in my memory. She looked so beautiful, in her winter coat and blue scarf. She had a bit of lipstick. Carmen never wore a lot of make-up. She didn't have to; she was a natural beauty. Elegant.

I had my old Pentax camera, ready to get a shot of Fidel. The excitement in the crowd was building. People chanted, *'Fidel, Fidel a los yankees dale duro.'* There were people holding placards of Che Guevara, and *'El pueblo esta con Cuba'*.

We waited for three hours until Fidel came out on the platform that had been put up for him. For the next three hours we listened to this man speak. He was a captivating speaker. You could not take your eyes off him. He stood strong, in his commander's suit and hat, the clothes he would wear for the next forty years. His trademark. I had my arm around Carmen. We were mesmerised.

Coco runs to the door barking. Someone is knocking. What do I do if it is Frances? I get up from the couch, put my slippers on and walk slowly to the door. I put my hand on the handle. My heart is beating fast. My hand on the door handle is sweaty. I very slowly turn the handle and open the door.

It is Lola. She is crying. I look at her. She looks terrible. Her long dark hair an unbrushed mess. Her big bag hanging over her shoulder, making her look lopsided. She looks more skinny than usual.

'Lola, what happened?' She comes inside and hugs me so tight; I can barely move my arms out of her grasp to hold her. She cries and sniffles onto my chest.

'*Mija*, please tell me what is wrong?'

'I'm going to leave Leo.'

As she says this she cries even louder. Coco whimpers in solidarity.

'What has he done to you?'

'Nothing Papá. That is just it. He has not done anything. I mean he has done nothing to hurt me, so why am I leaving him?'

How do I tell her what we have all seen for the past twenty years and she did not see? Suddenly she breaks free from our hug and looks at me.

'It will be okay *mija*. Come in and sit down.'

Lola follows me to the kitchen and sits down.

'I make you a hot chocolate.'

She looks very small sitting on the chair, hunched over and crying. Coco has his head on her lap. I knew this day would come eventually.

'Drink this, it's Mexican hot chocolate. Miguel sells it in his shop now.'
I watch her as she takes a sip.

'Good, aah? *Mija* it took you a long time. Everything will be okay.'

'What do you mean, it took a long time. For what?'

'Lola because a man doesn't hit you or is faithful does not necessarily mean he is a good husband.'

My poor Lola. Always good at school but so bad at life.

'He's always there for me Papá. He looks after me when I'm sick.'

The girl really has no idea. How did Carmen and I not teach her this? The other two could do it, why not Lola?

The life he gave you made you sick, I want to say to her. This would be too strong; I cannot tell her this. Instead, I bring the Tim Tams. She takes a chocolate biscuit and puts it in her mouth. I look at her. This wonderful daughter of mine. She is intelligent and can be so funny when she is well. Life was there for her to take. Lola could have done anything, travelled anywhere. Carmen and I dreamed big for all our daughters. Somehow, she got stuck. Planted roots in the wrong garden, one that did not grow, and every day the roots got deeper and deeper so she could not move. Now it has become a monster to move, she will need a crane of strength. I hope she has that in her.

I stroke her head as she drinks her chocolate. She is beautiful, like her mother.

She is eating all the Tim Tams. She must be feeling very terrible. Lola normally never eats when she is feeling bad.

'This will be alright Lola. At first it will be hard, but with time life will be good. It is good Alex is thinking of going to Uruguay. What about Daniel, have you told him?'

'Yes. He is upset of course. He will come with me. I said we might move near the beach, and he liked the idea. The weird thing is, I'm still trying to understand why I have decided this. I just feel it. How do you explain a feeling? It's not that I don't love him anymore but there is something inside pushing me in a different direction. There is no specific reason.'

'Lola, the reason is in your heart, it is deep within yourself. I will tell you something. When I decided to come to Australia, all I knew was that I had to get my family out. I didn't know exactly what would happen if we stayed or how long the dictatorship would last for. And I knew nothing about Australia. Do you think I wasn't scared? I was terrified. I asked myself many times was this the right thing to do, to take my family to the other side of the world, where we knew nobody. Sometimes you need to jump into the unknown to save yourself. I had to do it for all of us.'

I feel tears in my eyes. I don't want Lola to see this. She has stopped eating Tim Tams and crying.

'I don't know if I am as brave as you Papá.'

'Of course, you are. This will be good Lola, and for the boys too. Do you want to move here? While Alex is away you and Daniel can have a room each.'

Lola looks up at me. 'I want to do this on my own. I need to.'

'If you want to stay here for a while until you know what you want to do that is okay too. You don't need to decide now.'

I want to protect her, to hold her and tell her this is a good thing. It will be like letting go of a brake that has been in place for too long. Slowly, movement will take place again and she will be able to reclaim her life.

As she blows her nose, she looks up at me.

'Papá, tell me about the woman who was with you at the Uruguayan club, you've never told me who she was or why you were with her. Betty said you went to her place with her. She wasn't from the ad, was she?'

Now I think I need the Tim Tams. 'Lola I too have something to tell you.'

I get up and put the jug on. I don't know why.

'She is not one of the women from the ad. Since I met her, I have forgotten all about the ad. Her name is Frances, and she is a very special woman. She is strong and funny, and she has made me laugh and dance again.'

The words come out faster than my thoughts.

'So, she was with you at the Club, you didn't meet her there?'

The tone in Lola's voice is one of disapproval. I don't want to make Lola more upset than she is. But as I talk about Frances, I feel warmth in my chest, and I think of how much I like being with her and how she has changed my life.

'Papá, where did you meet her?'

'At the park, Lola. We met at the park, walking our dogs. She has a little dog named Churchill.'

I smile as I think of how we met and that silly yappy dog which I have grown to love.

'Coco really likes Churchill too. They play together. We throw the ball to them, and they run to get it. Coco gets it most of the time of course. When we watch television, the dogs lie together. It's good for Coco to have some dog company.'

'It sounds like it's good for you too Papá. You really like this lady. I can see it, as you talk about her. Your face lights up.'

'No one will ever replace your Mamá. This is not what this is about. Please understand this.' I rub my hands together and look at the jug that has now boiled.

'I know Papá. I want you to be happy and I want to meet her properly. I was quick to judge when I saw her, and I know that's not fair. It's just she looked so well, different.'

I look at Lola and cannot believe she is saying this. Maybe it is not too late.

'I have a little problem. The last time I saw Frances, we went out to dinner, and she had a surprise for me. Well, when she told me the surprise, I was shocked. I didn't react very well. I took her home and have not spoken to her since that night.'

'Why what happened? Do you want me to *preparar el mate?*'

'*Bueno mija.*'

Do I tell Lola? She is looking at me, waiting. She doesn't speak. She gets up and empties the *yerba* from the *mate*, rinses it and fills it again.

'It is very hard for me to say this. What happened was very unexpected. Frances is a very generous woman. Her life has been hard. Her son killed himself, her husband died, and she can still find joy in life. She has not let pain eat at her. She is an optimist, living life as best she can.' As I talk about Frances, my heart beats faster and my stomach is whirling inside.

Lola quietly fills the *termo* and comes back to sit at the table.

'She has been very good for me Lola. Frances thought what she did was a good idea. She did it from her kind heart. We were having dinner, and she bought a bottle of champagne. I ask her what we are celebrating, and she takes an envelope out of her bag.'

I look at Lola. Her arms are crossed as she listens to me, waiting for me to continue. She pours a *mate* and hands it to me.

'In the envelope there were two tickets to Mexico with a cruise in the Caribbean. We even go to Cuba.' I can barely say Cuba out loud.

'She paid for them. So, she has money? And you were offended that she paid for this?'

I look at Lola. Maybe she does not understand.

'It's not only the money *mija*.'

'I know. She didn't ask you first. I don't think paying for you is the problem if she has the money. It's okay for a woman to pay Papá. But why didn't she ask you? You're right to be upset. These are decisions that people make together. You can't start a relationship springing surprises on people. What are you going to do?'

This is strange coming from Lola. When did she and Leo make decisions together? I pass her the *mate* back.

That is the problem. I don't know what to do. Lola is looking at me, waiting for my answer. She pours herself a *mate* and sips it noisily.

'I always wanted to go to Cuba with your Mamá, we talked about how one day we would go. I didn't give her that.'

'If Mamá hadn't become sick with cancer, you would have gone. You can't punish yourself Papá.'

'I know, but it's like I bring Frances into my life with Carmen if I go.'

My dreams with Carmen cannot be in my new life with Frances.

'First, I think you need to talk to Frances and tell her how you feel. The way you talk about her I can see you really like this woman. I can see it in your body, the way you seem animated.'

I cannot believe this is coming from Lola. Maybe she is right. I must talk to Frances and explain myself, otherwise I will lose her.

'Then I want to meet her. Properly I mean, not like at the *Club Uruguayo*.'

'Thank you, Lola. I know you will like her.'

Maybe this is the beginning of merging my worlds of family and Frances and a little more of Australia each day.

Lola takes another Tim Tam and before she puts it in her mouth asks me. 'Why is her dog called Churchill?'

'Her husband named the dog, *mija*, why?'

'You know Churchill was the English Prime Minister during the war. He was a conservative.'

Lola knows my education is very little. I did not even go to high school. I have a primary school education in Uruguay in the 1940s.

Even then, Uruguay was a progressive country. We did not learn about the history of England.

Lola is waiting for my answer. 'Of course, I know that, what English man is not conservative? They still have a queen, in this modern day.'

'So, why does she name her dog after a right-wing politician? It's like if you named your dog John Howard.'

We both look at Coco and laugh.

Frances is not a right-wing person, I know this. We talk about Kevin Rudd and Julia Gillard, and she supports the Labor party. Maybe her husband was conservative.

'Does she come from a right-wing family?'

I look at Coco, lying at Lola's feet.

'Frances is like us; she believes in social justice and equality for everyone. Maybe she agreed to the name, Churchill because one of her relatives was named Churchill too, after he was stolen.'

I don't want Lola to ask me anymore questions. If Frances' mother was stolen and given an English name, this could have happened to other relatives too.

'Stolen, how were they stolen?' The girl does not know when to stop. This is what she does to her children, that is why they don't want to talk. You can only dig so far; you need to know when to stop before you crash into people's heart.

'Her mother was Aboriginal, and the English stole her from her family. This is what they did *mija*, they were very cruel. They did this so the culture could not be passed to the next generation. The children were servants too.'

My heart is beating faster and faster as I talk about this. My hands are fists and I want to hit the table. Lola is looking at me, without moving. I think she is surprised I am teaching her about Australian history.

'They did not teach you this at school, did they *mija*? Every country has its dirty secrets they don't want you to know.'

'Frances is Aboriginal then?'

'Yes Lola, Frances is Aboriginal. She is a very strong woman, she had to survive with all the *mierda* the English put her people through.'

'I can't wait to meet her Papá and Churchill too.'

I smile at my daughter. New beginnings for both of us.

BETTY

Native Hibiscus Soap

Ingredients:

- Distilled water
- Sodium hydroxide
- Coconut oil and olive oil
- Almond oil
- Shea butter
- Native hibiscus flowers and Betty's native hibiscus essential oil

The warmth from the sun caresses my back as I bend down and pull out the purple flowers from an overgrown pocket down by the back creek. We hardly have time to get down here and the pretty purple flowers are everywhere. Blue billy goat is a weed, introduced from another country and it's stopping the native plants from growing and thriving. In some way we are like weeds, imported here and spreading everywhere, taking over the land of the traditional owners, so that they need to fight like the native plants for their land. When we are left with our own people, we plant ghettoes of weeds, like the one I was raised in.

I break off the purple flowers from the fury stems and put them down on one side and the fury stems in my weed bucket. Next week I will mulch and plant natives to keep the weeds away.

As I pull out the last of the weeds, I stand up and stretch. I look over at the bush. I am so lucky to live here. I may be an imported weed but I'm doing my best to nurture this land and reduce my carbon footprint. As I walk back to the house, my mind is on Lola. Yesterday we spoke on the phone. She told me she and Daniel are moving to the South Coast and she is leaving Leo and Sydney. I never thought this day would come. My sister will finally get a chance to find herself and follow her own dreams. I'm excited for her and proud of her too. I know she is upset about Alex wanting to stay with Leo. She needs to let him do this, like I need to let Leif change his diet and schools. As much as she wants to shout at Alex and drag him away, it's better to leave him. Apparently, Papá said, tell Alex he goes with Lola or with him. He's a child, it's not his decision.

The purple weeds look pretty in the vase I've chosen for them, a dark green ceramic. I put the vase on the little bookshelf in the family room, the purple contrasts with the green leaves of the banksia outside the window.

A piece of sourdough, spread thick with avocado in hand, I sit at the computer. This is the part of the business I'm not so keen on. Making the soaps and oils is pleasurable, it gives me a sense of completeness. Going through the orders and getting them ready to send off, not so much. First, I check the emails. There's one from Lola.

Hey Betty,

Thanks for the chat yesterday and sharing your issues with Leif. You and Chris are great parents. After talking to you I feel better about Alex staying with Leo. I know what you mean about asserting our need for identity separate from family. I didn't really understand this before as it was not something I had done. Unlike you, I needed familiarity, the unknown was threatening. I've always been the one that feared everything – the dark, girls at school who could bash you, going away on a camp without you guys, rollercoasters, big waves at the beach, smoking dope, being alone. Remember Papá used to say Malena cried about everything and I was frightened of everything. You told me about the book you read from the school library that said, 'the smarter you are the more things can scare you.' You told me I should think about that when I was scared. I felt good when you told me that. You do that now with your kids, you validate their feelings. At home I felt my feelings were wrong. I was the weird one for being scared. After that I couldn't trust my own feelings.

Letting Alex make his own decision will show that I trust him and respect him. You're right.

I spoke to Malena. Did you know she's getting an au pair? How bougee is that? She's forgetting her roots. Papá still hasn't told her about Frances. Daniel and I are going with Papá to have dinner at her house tomorrow.

I'll ring to tell you how it went. We need to give her a chance, for Papá's sake. He really likes her. They might even go on a cruise together!!!

Talk soon, love you my gorgeous sister. xxx

Lola.

I stare at the words on the screen. Lola is reaching out to me for the first time in over a decade. This next stage of her life will be hard and I want to be there for her. There's a shift in her, a loosening, like when you take a deep breath and let it out with your whole body. A return to our essence, like the native plants returning to the earth when the weeds have gone.

JUAN

Toma esa rosa encarnada
Take that red rose
Y abrila que esta en capullo
And open it, it's in bud
Y veras mi corazon
And you will see my heart
Abrazado con el tuyo
Embraced with yours
   '*Una rosa para mi rosa*', Saul Salinas y Carlos Gardel

We stop outside Frances' red brick house. 'This is it,' I announce to Lola and my grandson. I'm grateful to Lola for helping me to see past my pain and reach out to Frances. Frances' house is small but practical. It is one of those project houses built in the 1970s. She and her husband bought it new. They both worked hard to pay for a roof over their heads. Like Carmen and me. We bought our house new too. I had never lived in a new house before. We were the first to use everything, the stove, the shower, the toilet. Maybe the builders used the toilet. I felt very proud walking into our new house. It was all clean and shiny. We spent all our working life paying for that house and then after it was all paid, Carmen died.

I ring the doorbell. It makes the sound of a little bird, a canary.

Frances opens the door. She looks happy. She is wearing a white and blue dress, light and flowing, like a curtain. She has pearl earrings and a multi-coloured scarf in her hair.

'Welcome all, come in. Are these for me?' she asks looking at the flowers I have in my hand.

'No, they are for Churchill.'

She laughs, that loud, contagious laugh of hers that makes me want to laugh too. She kisses me and I introduce her to Lola and Daniel. She

221

kisses Lola on the cheek and gives Daniel a hug. No one mentions the Uruguayan club. We all pretend this is the first time they meet.

'I'm so pleased to meet you both properly and that you are here for dinner.'

I go to put the green shopping bag on the dining table, but I notice the table has a tablecloth today with dinner plates. I put the bag on the kitchen bench and take out the wine.

'Ladies, wine?'

'Ooh, yes please, love. I have coke for you Danny.' Frances looks over at him and smiles.

'Frances we also bring the entrance.'

'The entrance to what Bub?'

'The meal of course.'

'Papá, it's entrée. You brought the entrée.' Lola corrects me and looks very serious. She is standing by the dining table, unsure whether to sit down or not. Daniel is beside her.

Frances laughs. She laughs very loud again and keeps laughing. This makes me laugh. Then Lola and Daniel laugh too.

'So, what is the entrance, Juan?' She winks at Daniel.

I take out the little white box that I bought from the Uruguayan cake shop and open it, displaying the delicacies for them all to see.

'*Saladitos*,' says Lola.

'I love *saladitos*,' says Daniel.

'What are *salitos*?' asks Frances in a horrible accent.

'You say *sal-a-di-tos*. Here try one.'

I hold out a little puff pastry filled with ham and cheese, with sugar sprinkled on top, for her to take a bite. Lola is looking at me as I feed Frances the *saladito*. I know she is watching everything, like a detective, gathering the information.

I dreamt of these little sweet and savoury pastries when I was a boy. I would walk into the *confiteria* and see the rows and rows of them alongside little rolls of cheese and ham, pastries with fish and olives, mini croissants, and little brioches with sweet cream cheese. If I was lucky and I had a few coins, I would buy one. Sometimes the woman in the shop was kind and gave me an extra one. I would go outside and sit at the *Plaza del Entrevero* on 18 de Julio Avenue and eat them very slowly so that I could taste each bite. I felt like a king.

'*Sal-ay-dito*,' Frances repeats slowly, and she laughs.

'Your accent is improving Frances.'

She looks at me. 'Patience Juan, patience. I'll get there.'

'They are canapes, in English.' Lola explains.

We all sit down and eat the wonderful *saladitos*. Daniel is beaming as he drinks the coca cola Frances gave him. Lola doesn't buy it because she doesn't want him to get holes in his teeth or get fat.

'This is nice,' says Frances as she drinks her wine.

I look over at Lola across the table. While she sips on her wine, her eyes are looking at the photos on the wall. They land on Frances' son. He is a boy in school uniform. Frances told me the photo was taken when he was twelve. He is standing tall with a cheeky grin. He looks like Frances, the same shape face and olive skin. He is a handsome boy.

Lola puts her wine glass down. As she opens her mouth, I jump in quick. I don't want her to ask about the photo.

'Daniel plays in the school band Frances. I went last week to see him. He is very good.'

'What instrument do you play Daniel?'

Daniel's mouth is full. He has been eating *saladitos* non-stop. He swallows before he answers.

'I play bass. Three of us play bass. Tom, Rohan, and me. We even have a solo. You should come with Abuelo next time we play.'

Lola glares at Daniel.

'I'd love that Bub. I used to play a bit of guitar myself you know.'

The woman is full of surprises.

'Did you play in a band?' Daniel asks, as he holds a *saladito* in one hand and a glass of coca cola in the other.

Frances laughs. 'No, I played for fun with some friends. Old country songs.'

'What about you Lola, do you play?'

'No, two musicians in the family are enough,' she says this softly as she looks down, fidgeting with a serviette.

'Your Dad tells me you work in a supermarket. I know those jobs can be hard. I worked in a hospital serving food to patients for 27 years. On your feet all day.'

I look at Lola. I know she is trying.

'Yes, it is tiresome, but at least you get to go home and not think about work. But a hospital, you would see a lot of sadness.'

'Yes, but you also see a lot of hope and joy too when people recover. And the babies, new life, it always makes you happy. You do see some cranky old bastards. There was one I could never forget. He'd been a General in the army. Bitter as an old lemon he was. Poor man, had been used to giving orders and here he was having to ask for help to piss in a bed pan.'

She smiles. 'But when his grandson came to visit, his face totally changed. He was softer, he smiled. The little boy sat next to him on the bed, and he held him while they watched television. I would bring in extra dessert if I saw his grandson was visiting.'

'What happened to him?' Lola asked.

'He died. Poor bugger had pancreatic cancer. It's quick, you know.'

Lola, always taking the conversation to the sad places.

'More wine, ladies?' I hold up the wine bottle.

'Not for me, Papá.'

'I'll bring the meal, shall I?' Frances stands up and walks over to the stove.

I'll help you Frances,' Lola says as she gets up.

'No thanks honey, it's all done.'

She comes back with an enormous dish of mashed potatoes. I look at Lola. I know what she will be thinking. Daniel, Lola, and I are looking at the mashed potatoes in front of us. No one dares to speak. Frances turns around and goes back into the kitchen. She comes back with a big bowl of salad. I look at the salad. It has many colours. I don't want to think what is in it.

'Dig in. Don't be shy.'

Frances spoons out the mashed potatoes and I can see there is meat underneath. She puts some on my plate.

'Just a small serving for me, says Lola.'

'I hope you like shepherd's pie.'

This makes me laugh. I imagine the poor boys with their sheep or goats on a mountain eating this pie. 'Why is this called shepherd's pie? Shepherds didn't eat pies.'

Daniel laughs. Then Frances laughs too. Even Lola smiles.

'Juan, you are funny. This is an English recipe. I grew up with this. My mum would make it. Except we couldn't always afford cheese. See this one has golden melted cheese on top.'

'It's nothing to do with the shepherds? Did you know about this dish?' I ask Lola.

Frances is laughing so hard; she can barely talk. Finally, she says, 'It's just the name.'

'I had it once at the hospital when Daniel was born,' Lola says, as she picks up a piece of the pie with her fork. I do the same.

'Anyway, it is very nice Frances. More salt would make it better, but it is good, right Daniel?'

'Yes, very good,' Daniel says, putting an enormous amount into his mouth.

Lola is silent. Again, she looks at the photo of Frances' son.

'Have some salad, Lola.' Frances pushes the salad towards Lola.

Lola takes it and serves it onto her plate.

I look at the salad on Lola's plate. It has pineapple and olives.

'Frances, you added olives, very Mediterranean.'

Frances smiles. 'Actually, they are grapes.' She is pleased with herself.

'Frances, this is not a fruit salad. You have pineapple and grapes with lettuce and tomato.'

Lola has picked up a grape with her fork and is putting it into her mouth.

'It's exotic, Bub, nouvelle cuisine.' She smiles at me and reaches out with her hand to touch mine.

Daniel looks at her hand on mine and quickly looks away.

'Now you are going to tell me we are having vegetables for dessert.'

'No, I have a surprise.' She serves herself some salad and puts some on my plate too.

'What do you do with yourself now that you don't work Frances?' Lola asks.

'Churchill keeps me active. I have my garden and my water aerobics. Plus, I don't have so much time now that I have your father to keep me busy.'

She looks at me, tenderly.

'Did he tell you about our trip to Brisbane? We had so much fun. It felt like we were young again. Stopping when we felt like it, walking along the beach. We did stop at the Big Banana. Have you been there, Bub?'

Frances is looking at Daniel. He shakes his head.

'You'll have to come with us next time we go. You know you can walk through the banana. There's a water park too. You would love it. Of course, we had banana ice creams. You know your father, he insisted on having a coffee too.'

'Yes, but the coffee was bad'.

An image of Frances and me eating ice-creams in front of the big banana comes to mind. A young woman offered to take a photo of us and Frances gave her the camera.

'I can't imagine they would serve decent coffee at a place like that,' says Lola.

'There were a lot of tourists too. Lots of Chinese. So many Chinese coming to Australia now. When you go into the city, too, it is full of Chinese, and I don't mean Chinatown. Juan and I went to see a film in George Street last week and you were lucky if you could see an Aussie.'

'What do you mean, lucky if you could see an Aussie?' Lola asks, looking annoyed.

'It's just an expression. I mean not many like us. Lots of Asian people in the city.'

'Does that surprise you given how close we are to Asia?' Lola asks, her voice pitched, ready to take on anyone who might not share our politics.

'Bub, I'm not being racist; it was an observation. I love how multicultural Australia is. I wouldn't have met your father if Australia wasn't multicultural. I love multicultural people.'

I look at Lola. She has the face that says, I'm running out of patience for stupid people. She needs to understand that Frances is like me, a simple person. We don't have university education.

'Frances, I don't mean to be rude, but people are not multicultural. The society is multicultural.'

Lola likes to correct people.

'I disagree Lola, we are all multicultural. We all have many cultures in us. Take me, I have Irish, Aboriginal, Welsh and who knows what else.'

'Frances is right Lola. We too have Spanish, Charrua, Italian.'

Lola is staring at Frances. 'You are Aboriginal?' she asks.

'Yes, my mother is Aboriginal.' Frances starts picking up the empty plates.

'Frances tell Lola how you had to pretend you weren't Aboriginal.' I think of Frances' mother and the pain inflicted on her.

'When we were growing up, Mum told us to say we were Italian, because we were dark.'

Daniel looks up at Frances. 'Why?'

'Aboriginal children were taken from their parents and put with white families or in institutions. Mum was scared we'd be taken. She was protecting us.'

'Was your mother taken?' Lola asks, as she screws up another serviette into her fist.

I do not know why Lola keeps asking questions that are taking the conversation to depressing places.

'Yes, she was. She was taken as a little girl, put in a home far away from her family. She wasn't allowed to speak her language.'

'Did she ever find her family?'

'Lola, I don't think Frances wants to talk about this.'

'It's okay Bub. She never did find her family. She knew she was born in Dubbo. She was a Wiradjuri woman. That's why I was born there too, she wanted to go back to her country.'

'What about you Frances, did you ever look for relatives?' Lola has put the serviette down and is looking intensely at Frances.

'I didn't, but my brother Rob did. He got very involved with the Aboriginal community. He knows many of our mob.' She puts both her hands on the table. 'Now, what about dessert. Who likes pavlova?'

'Yes, please I love pavlova.' Daniel is now interested.

'Did you ever meet any of your family?' Lola is still looking at Frances.

'Lola, that's enough,' I say this and get up.

'Sorry Frances,' says Lola as she looks down at her food.

'It's okay.' Frances is too kind. 'I met my Aunty Marie once. I went to see my brother and he said he had a surprise for me, and we drove to her house. It was very emotional to meet her. She looked like my mother, the same brown eyes, the same smile.'

I can't believe what happens next. Lola gets up and she hugs Frances. Both their eyes are watery. Lola manages to do this every time, she takes people to the sad spaces in their heart, where grief is buried. The girl needs to lighten up. She goes through life in storms of tears.

'Better get that pavlova.' Frances gets up and wipes her eyes on the sleeve of the curtain dress.

She comes back with an enormous meringue cake, full of cream, strawberries, and kiwi fruits. It looks incredible.

Lola is looking at Frances. Her defences have fallen; her face has softened. I smile to myself. Today is a good day despite the tears.

Frances cuts a slice of the pavlova and hands it to a waiting Daniel. He immediately starts eating.

'Yum,' he exclaims after the first bite. She hands Lola a piece and then one to me. With the spoon I cut through the cream and meringue and place it in my mouth. As I bite into it, I am reminded of a *postre chaja*, the combination of the crunchy meringue and soft cream transports me to the *confiterias* in Montevideo where I ate sweet pastries with Carmen.

'Frances this cake is delicious. I give you a Juan star, because I can't give you the Michelle one.'

Lola bursts into laughter as she looks at me. 'Yes, it's the best pavlova I have tasted. By the way, it's a Michelin star Papá.'

Daniel is stuffing so much meringue into his mouth, that Lola tells him to slow down. 'I love it,' he says.

We drive home in silence, except for the sound of Piazzola's tango.

I stop the car outside my house. As we are about to get out, Lola turns to me and says, 'I have a new job. It is in a lab on the South Coast.'

I look at my daughter and stretch across the car seat to hug her tightly.

'This is good Lola. This is very good *mija*.'

I feel my eyes are moist.

'Papá, I am happy for you. Frances is a good woman. She may not be who Betty or I imagined you would find, but you are happy when you are with her. You laugh and you smile. She adores you. I can see it, in the way she talks to you, how she looks at you. I want you to be happy and if being happy is being with Frances then I want that for you, and we will make her feel welcome in our family.'

The tears are now rolling down my old cheeks. I hug Lola tighter.

Daniel is looking at us. 'Am I the only one not crying today?'

The three of us laugh loudly.

'Lolita. I love you so much. I know this will be a new start for both of us.'

LOLA

15 August 2012

Day 27 of leaving Leo. It still feels like a dream, like any day it will end and I will be back in the kitchen in Lewisham, hearing Leo's guitar. I stamp my feet hard on the wooden floor and rub my hands together. It is real.

I look out the window at the garden. Broccoli, cabbage, parsley, oregano. It is small, but it is a beginning. I created it. My very own garden. The purple cabbage, its colour fills the garden bed. *Brassica oleracea*. Latin names from botany books I read. The sound rolls off my tongue smoothly. I liked reading the botanical names of plants. *Dimorphotheca aurantica*, it felt so good to say. *Helianthus* turned into sunflower, a wild carrot is a *Daucus carota*. I used to test myself. I would try and remember ten names at time and then write them down. Usually, I would get most of them right. It kept my mind in check and stopped it from wandering into dark crevices.

Before planting seedlings here, I turned the soil, it was clay and a bit grainy, but I liked the feel of it on my hands. A Betty moment, I connected to the earth in some way. I let it run through my fingers onto the ground. The satisfaction of my hands working the earth, the physicality of it, of being in the moment. I bring the soil up to my nose and smell it. A heady organic smell. I add water to it and smear it on my hands. A memory of plasticine is dislodged and floods my senses. I am five years old. I hear a loud voice speak in Spanish. There are children sitting at small desks. A little girl looks at me, eyes lost in fear. There is darkness and I feel my throat closing. I want to scream but when I open my mouth no sound comes out. I look at my shaking hands. What the fuck was that?

When the garden bed was ready, I planted the seedlings and watered them. Every day they grow a little more. Like my new life, everyday it gets bigger and further away from my old life. Papá will like the garden when he sees it. He will be impressed. His daughter's life a quiet life, but her own life. Papá. I smile to myself as I think of him. Soon he'll be salsa sailing with Frances on that ridiculous cruise. Cruising the Caribbean, dancing at every port: Havana, Mexico, the Bahamas. The crassness of it. Mamá would never believe it. Her Juan, on a *gringo* cruise dancing salsa all the way to Cuba. But Papá is happy. I've seen a side to him that I have not seen before. He seems sprightlier, freer. He's forgotten about his arthritis and the knee pain. The burdens he has carried are slipping away. The toll of the dictatorship, migration, providing for a family, caring for a sick wife, is slowly dwindling. He seems to have stopped worrying about me as much too.

A flock of silver gulls fly past, a flurry of white and grey feathers filling the sky. They fly in a V formation. I wonder who takes the lead and how their power dynamics work.

When I told Papá I was leaving Leo, he said it was the best decision I had made, and it had taken me a very long time to see that Leo wasn't right for me. I hadn't expected that. I knew he saw Leo as irresponsible, a boy in a man's body. Leo has never really grown up. Growing up meant responsibilities and that frightened Leo.

It has been hard. I still miss Leo, his silly chuckle, like he is choking on air. Even now I can see him making me laugh with his stupid jokes. He always made me laugh. But that was Leo, have a laugh, live in the moment and everything will be alright. But it hadn't. I lived a life I stumbled into. At times I lived incapacitated for months, years, consumed by an anxiety that took over every thought. I became a prisoner of my own mind. I don't know why it happened or if it will keep happening. All I know is that I feel a freedom I have never felt before, a release.

I'm slowly disentangling Leo from my life. Like an octopus that has been tightly wound around me; I dislodge tentacle by tentacle, each tentacle separating a little more of our life together. As I emerge, I find little parts of myself and I remember what it was like to breathe, to breathe and feel whole again.

I look out to the sea. The waves, crash against the rocks. The escarpment is magnificent. This must be one of the most striking coastlines in the world. How ironic, Coalcliff. Coal, something so destructive to the planet in such a beautiful place.

The cottage is old. It is one of the miner's cottages, built from weatherboard in the early nineteen hundreds. It's draughty but it has a charm about it that I love. The landlady, a friend of Kerry's, had it as a holiday rental. Kerry kindly convinced her to rent it out to me for a year. Each morning before work I walk along the beach. Watching the waves as they roll in and back out again relaxes me.

The sea change has brought Daniel happiness too. He likes the local high school and is even learning to surf. It has been good for him. He's maturing. Maybe he feels a little protective of me, as it's only the two of us. He checks in on me before he goes to bed each night.

Alex remains with Leo. I tried really hard to get him to come but he refused. He is still angry with me. I'm hoping the exchange in Uruguay will give him time to reflect and experience other ways of relating and living. Leo is still angry with me, too. He needs to stay angry, otherwise his life will unravel. He cannot forgive. He could not forgive his father. He will not forgive me. I will become another room in his mind where he closes the door and never enters it again.

Tomorrow, I may see him at the airport when we go to see Papá and Alex fly out to Mexico. I didn't want to go from sharing a life together to nothing. I imagined a friendship, shared parenting, some family meals. I didn't set out to destroy a family but to stay was to destroy myself. I fooled myself into thinking I could shape myself into the mould of Lola, partner of Leo the musician, and mother of Alex and Daniel. A happy family of four. I morphed and wriggled and tried so hard to fit into the mould, but it broke me. I was slowly dying. This was not the mother my children needed. You can't know and love others until you know and love yourself. I may have jumped into the unknown and it will be uncomfortable for a while, maybe a long while. But can one stay in a comfort that leaves you gasping for air? Surely that is not comfort. Comfort is transitory. An illusion. It may be in uncomfortableness that I come to know myself.

BETTY

Peppermint Essential Oil
Ingredients:
- Crushed peppermint leaves
- Olive oil or grapeseed oil

Peppermint oil produces a cooling effect, the refreshing menthol it contains can relieve frustration and anger. It stimulates receptors sensitive to cold in the skin and mucous membranes, creating a sensation of coolness and freshness. As I unscrew the lid of the little bottle, the mintyness soars up into my nose. I breathe it in, take a little oil and rub it on my temples.

Today is the first day Leif is cooking his own dinner. Chris and I agreed that Leif can choose to be carnivorous, but we won't be cooking meat, nor buying it. I give him money and he goes to the butcher or the supermarket and brings his own dead animals home. I wonder if he will feel the way Jack did when he killed the pig in *Lord of the Flies*. Imposing his will on it and taking away its life, the satisfaction of power bigger than the satisfaction of providing food. Leif choosing his own path may give him that.

I cook our meal first and then Leif cooks his. He is frying lamb chops. The kitchen window is open and the fan on the rangehood is on, but the smell is still overpowering. I go out into the garden. It reminds me of when Mum cooked us steak. This would be accompanied by mashed potato, a fried egg and a salad made up of raw onion, lettuce, and tomato. The challenge was getting it all ready and on the plate at the same time. Lola often mashed the potato to give Mum an extra hand. When Lola made it, the potato was creamy and smooth. Mum's was always lumpy as she had too many things to do at the same time. Mum would be shouting at her to hurry up as Lola mashed the potatoes, adding plenty of butter and milk to make it creamy.

Malena was always in her room doing homework. She would be in there for hours slogging away. She collected marks, the way some people collect stamps or coins. She was dux every year, to prove she was the smartest and better than the other kids at the school. Mum and Papá's cheering squad didn't help. I think she felt if she didn't collect marks and awards, she wouldn't be valued or loved.

'I'm still eating the salad you made and the pie,' Leif shouts out to me through the kitchen window.

The stink of rebellion whiffs through the window and out into the garden. Sunshine comes running out.

'Mum, Leif is cooking meat, and it stinks.'

'I know Sunny, he's wants to try eating meat for a little while.'

'But an animal had to die and now he's frying up parts of the body.'

I feel my throat tighten.

'I know, it's horrible, but now that he is older, he wants to try different things.'

'Is he going to have sex too?' She looks up at me as I find myself searching for an answer.

'Not now, he's too young for that. Eating meat is different, it's a choice about what you put in your body. It's his body and we are letting him try it.'

'What about if he wants to put drugs in his body?' She picks up a stick and is waving it like a wand.

The smell of meat is stuck in my throat. I guess we are having this conversation now.

'That's very different and he won't be doing that, besides that's illegal, eating animals is not.'

She stops waving the stick around and looks at me. 'I'm never going to eat animals.'

I look at her little round face and rosy cheeks. Her innocence is beautiful. Her brown eyes full of wonder. She is always curious, wanting to learn new things, full of questions.

'Is Grandpa going to marry Frances? If he is, I want to be a flower girl.'

This one hits me in the chest like an unexpected punch. Sunshine is looking up at me, waiting for my response.

'I don't think so, Sunshine.' I bloody well hope not. Surely that is not going to happen.

LOLA

25 August 2012

Daniel told me that elephant seals can breathe under water for two hours. His science teacher told him. They were talking about marine mammals in class, listing them all. Daniel remembered some old photos of mine, from when I visited la Isla de Lobos, *in* Punta del Este *in Uruguay. He told the class there are sea wolves in Uruguay. The other students had not heard of this animal. The teacher corrected him and explained they are called sea lions. Daniel was embarrassed that he said sea wolves, the translation from the Spanish. It reminded me of when in home economics in high school I referred to the soup ladle as the 'big soup spoon'. I knew it was the* cucharon *but I had never heard the English word for it.*

I read this out to Simone.

The gaps. The gaps in the English language, each word a reminder that you are defective. In university the gaps widened, they were huge class gaps, chasms, I could never jump across. At times I attempted to string words across them like a tightrope, balancing each word carefully. A funambulist I was not. Words didn't flow and I kept falling. I watched the blonde ponytails speak empty sentences with confidence. The private school boys paragraphed bullshit articulately.

I'm sitting in Simone's armchair. She is looking at me, pen in her hand and folder balancing on her lap. She brushes her hair back with her other hand.

'My lack of confidence is a class thing. I don't think it's totally a defect in my personality.'

Simone looks at me, waiting for me to say more. I don't think I ever discussed class politics in therapy before.

235

'When you're on the margins, your confidence is chipped away.'

That's why it was safe with Leo. It was home. But I needed to get out there again.

'Lola, what do you mean you are on the margins, why do you identify in this way?'

Am I really starting with the ABC of class politics? I want to say because I grew up with migrant parents, who didn't speak the language, I didn't have access to all the education and privileges you had.

'I grew up in a suburb with one of the highest migrant and refugee populations in Australia. My parents only mixed with other South Americans. We didn't know Australia or have the privileges that middle-class white Australia has. When I went to university, I felt that alienation. There I realised there was a whole other world that we had missed out on.'

Simone, nods as my words and emotions pour out onto her armchair.

'How did that make you feel?'

Fucking angry and that I wasn't good enough and that I shouldn't be there.

'I felt out of place, it wasn't my world, and they didn't want me in it.'

'Why did you think you weren't accepted there?'

I don't think she understands, she was probably a blonde ponytail too.

'Because I didn't speak like they did, I didn't look like they did or think like they did.'

Saying this stuff made me feel better. That's what therapy is supposed to do. Understanding is supposed to bring relief. The more you work through your emotional shit you begin to understand it, but you're never rid of it. You just stir and stir in that wound until it's not as raw.

'When I first started university, the lecturer corrected my pronunciation.'

Simone looks at me, waiting for me to say something else.

'She did it in the lecture room too. I asked a question and then in front of everyone, before she answered the question, she said, 'In this university we pronounce it like this,' and she spoke the name slowly.' I can't bring myself to tell Simone how I pronounced Jung's name. I still feel stupid.

'You were made to feel less educated? Naturally that is going to affect your confidence.'

Hallelujah now we're talking. I nod and feel the tears coming.

'Yes, I was humiliated in front of my peers.'

That is what white privilege does, it makes others feel inferior.

'How did you respond Lola?'

'I didn't go back to that class, I changed subject.' After it happened, I went home, slipped into bed, and hid under the blanket for the next two days. I told Malena what happened. She said it was a type of discrimination and I could report it. I didn't have the strength to. We had an argument over whether you can argue class discrimination. Her law brain kicked in and she was pushing for it. I wanted to forget it happened. Besides what could they do? The lecturer wasn't going to lose her job over that. Malena went with me to the faculty and I changed subjects. I never heard of Jung again, until I found myself in Jungian dream journal therapy, where I wrote every crazy dream I had, talked to the characters from those dreams and played with toys in a sandbox.

I want to talk about Frances and Papá too and half the session is over. Simone has been nodding so much I'm sure her neck will be needing physio. I want to give Frances a chance. She's been good for Papá. Betty is being a snob about it. So what, Frances is not who we imagined for Papá. There's no bullshit about her. I like that. Betty has been living among those middle-class hippies and now she sounds like one. She thinks it's important that Aboriginal people go to the Steiner school and share their art and language, but she doesn't know any Aboriginal people.

'My father has met someone, a woman and she's not the sort of person we thought he would ever be friends with, let alone in a relationship with.'

Simone nods again, waiting to see if I say anything else before she poses one of her therapy questions.

'She's not South-American, she's Aboriginal.'

When I told Betty Frances was Aboriginal, and what Frances had told us about her childhood, Betty said, 'She doesn't identify as Aboriginal, really does she? Like she didn't grow up Aboriginal.' Those exact racist words came out of her mouth. In that moment she reminded me of the blonde ponytails in psychology tutorials discussing why children should be removed from women who refused to leave violent husbands. No fucking idea.

'How do you feel about your father's relationship with this woman?'

'He's happy.'

'I'm not sure what you are trying to say. He's happy so does that make you happy about this too?'

I am happy for him, but it still doesn't feel quite right. It's not familiar.

'He's different. He does things he's never done before, like going to pubs and he acts happier than he was when my mother was alive. He sings. I can't remember him ever singing.'

Parents are like backrests in the background. They stand there, you don't expect them to change and move. If you need to fall back, you can lean on them. That must be what Alex is feeling too. I removed a comfortable backrest.

'What are you concerned about, Lola?'

I look down at my shoes, the same old black sandals I've worn for the last three years.

'I don't know. Maybe I'm afraid he won't need me as much.'

Papá filled my day, without him ringing and coming over so often it has meant I have more spaces, there's more cracks to navigate.

'What does that mean for you?'

'When others need me, I focus less on myself, I don't overthink my own problems as much. I get a break from all the shit in my head.'

'I understand what you are saying Lola, but this could also be a good time to find out what you like to do. We talked about authenticity at our last session. What would you say to a friend in your situation?'

Here we go, the compassionate friend shit. I'm not my fucking friend. The problem with doing therapy for a long time is you learn all the techniques. At times it feels like I'm that person who finishes their partner's sentences. Some of my replies are overused, like old clothes that have been put through the washing machine too many times.

I look down at the cream-coloured carpet. I wonder if Simone chose the colour.

'I would tell her to take herself out and do things she has always wanted to do but hasn't been able to because she was too scared or too sick.'

That's not a bad idea. Where did that come from? I could take a book, cross over to Manly on the ferry and sit on the beach. I forgot, I'm living on the coast now. I can take a train to Kiama and watch the Blowhole. Eat fish and chips on the beach. Walk in the Minnamurra rainforest.

'I can take day trips on the weekend to places I've never been to or know I will enjoy. Maybe I could learn to swim.'

Neither Malena nor I can swim. We didn't go to swimming lessons and in Fairfield we were too far from the coast. Swimming lessons were expensive, it was one of those things that middle class kids do, along with piano lessons and tennis. Chris taught Betty to swim. It's weird to think we live on a great big island, and we can't swim.

'That's a great idea Lola and the exercise will be good for your mental health too. Is there anything else before we wrap up?'

Wrap up means put all your emotions away, like you put your purse back in your handbag or toys back in the toy box. It isn't always easy to stuff them back in, however today it seems okay. I actually feel alright. I smile at Simone.

JUAN

The airport is the waiting room, waiting to go from one culture to another. It excites me and makes me nervous. I get nostalgic but afraid of what I might find different when I arrive.

The last time I was here I stood with Carmen. It was her last trip. She was very thin; life was quickly leaving her body. I was afraid of taking her back. I thought the trip would kill her. She insisted. She told me; Juan I don't want to die without saying goodbye. I need to go home.

Everywhere I look I see Carmen. The café where we sat, drank a coffee and ate a sandwich while we waited for our flight, the shop where she bought a magazine. The *Weekly Woman*. It was her favourite. She could hardly read English, but she liked the pictures. The recipes were her favourite. She showed me the Christmas one. It had lots of pictures of turkeys and those Australian Christmas cakes that weigh as much as a baby. The turkey was good. One year Carmen injected the turkey with whiskey. She said it was for the flavour. This one she didn't see in the woman magazine, her friend Antonia told her. Six hours that turkey was in the oven, making the house very hot. It was not food for summer. The next year we did an *asado* outside and everyone was cool and happy.

This airport was where we first stepped on Australian land. Carmen and I with three little girls, dressed in our best clothes; suede skirts, a suit jacket, stockings with a pearl necklace and shoes that were new and uncomfortable. With two trolleys full of suitcases, we pushed our life into Australia.

'Here Bub, I bought you a coffee.' Frances hands me a cardboard cup. I look at her and smile.

'Are you okay Juan? This is the first time you have been back here without her, isn't it?'

I look at Frances and nod.

'It's my first time leaving Australia. First times are always hard and to tell you the truth I'm a little nervous.'

'You, Mrs Adventure, nervous, no.'

I put my arm around her. 'Frances, it is because of you that my life is no longer stuck. It is because of you that I can get on a plane again. Thank you.'

I see Lola hurrying towards us, Daniel behind her.

'Where's Alex?', she asks me nervously. I know what she is thinking.

'He will be here, don't worry. Danny, come and give your old Abuelo a hug.' I hold him tight. 'Look after your mother,' I whisper into his ear.

We let go of each other and he goes over to Frances and gives her a hug.

I smile at Frances, and she winks at me.

'Have you got everything Papá? Passport?'

'Lola, it's okay.' I know she is nervous, but my nerves are settling like feet in new shoes.

I see Alex walking over with a huge backpack on his back. Leo is behind him.

'My God, the boy will fall over with that weight.'

We all look over at Alex as he walks towards us.

'Alex, have you got half a supermarket in there? We are not going to some village in the middle of the jungle. There will be plenty of shops.'

He smiles at me.

'Better to be prepared,' he tells me. He looks serious and older than his sixteen years. I know it's uncomfortable being here with both Lola and Leo.

Leo shakes my hand; he gives Daniel a hug and puts out his hand for Frances to shake. He doesn't look at Lola. To him she is not there. He is in pain, and he cannot see past his pain. I want to shake him and tell him to grow up. I want to tell him to be a man. I say nothing. This is not the place. He has always been selfish. He never gave my daughter the life she deserved. She always lived in the shadows, when she should have been in the light living her life. I need my daughter and grandchildren to be alright.

Alex puts the massive pack down. He looks like a Peruvian carrying the *gringos*' bags for them on the way to Machu Pichu. He goes over to Lola and hugs her. She looks like she is about to cry.

'I'll get a coffee while you check in,' Lola says.

'I have to go.' Leo hugs Alex. 'Take everything in,' he tells him.

It is good that Alex is coming with us. He will spend three days in Mexico with us, then fly to Buenos Aires, then Montevideo. Lola has found a good family for him to stay with. It is close to where I grew up. He will stay for six months. It will be good for him to be away while Lola gets her life organised and Leo deals with what is happening. I don't think Leo will ever understand why Lola had to go. I am so proud of Lola, and she has been very understanding of me. It was she who told me to go on this crazy trip. She knows Frances is a good woman.

I expected Betty to be the most accepting of all my daughters. She does not like Frances. She only sees through her 'hippy eyes'. Sometimes you need to look with other eyes to understand and love people. Frances has taught me this. She does not judge people; she accepts them for who they are. Betty has built a world for herself, and her family that is in a bubble. When the children grow up, she may get a big surprise. They may become stockbrokers and live in a big city, eating meat every day. Lola told me Leif now eats meat and doesn't want to go to the hippy school. It's starting.

And Malena. My beautiful Malena. I wrote her a long letter to tell her about Frances and my trip. She rang me a few days after she received the letter. She said she read it many times. She told me she was very surprised and then she talked about the children. Maybe she will come to Australia next year. She did not ask me anything about Frances.

We show our children a path and we walk together, holding their hands. One day we come to an intersection, and they begin to walk alone. We still feel their hand in ours. They choose their road. We may not agree with the road they have chosen. We want to shout, no, not that one, turn into the other one, but we don't. It is their journey we cannot walk it for them, we only hope they don't fall too much. When they fall, we cannot be there with a seat under their bum to catch them every time. We hope that the strength we gave them will help them to get back up and keep walking and maybe change direction.

Life is a long and complicated road. Many times, I must look deep inside myself to pull something out to keep going strong. But I have also found many beautiful things on this road. I am a lucky man.

'Papá, they are calling your flight. It's time to go.'

Lola looks at me and Frances. She smiles.

Frances picks up her bag. The bag is green with big pink flowers on it.

We won't be losing it. She hugs Lola and Daniel.

'I'll look after him, don't you worry, Lola.'

'Well look who's talking, I'll have to make sure you are on good behaviour on this trip.' Frances looks at me and grins as I say this.

I hug Daniel. Thank you, God, that Leo left.

Lola hugs me so hard I think I may need oxygen.

'I love you, Papá. Have a wonderful trip.'

'Thank you, Lolita. You be strong. I know you will be okay.'

I can feel her tears on my cheek.

Daniel and Alex hug and give each other a strange handshake with fists and claps. Alex hugs Lola and her tears turn into sobs.

We wave as we go through the departure gate. I feel a lump in my throat.

Mexico here we come.

BETTY

Orange Essential Oil

Ingredients:
- Orange peels
- Alcohol

Pied currawongs sing as they land in the front garden. A splash of black plumage covering the grass, like a glossy bedspread. My eyes follow two of them as they chase each other. I sit on my favourite chair on the porch to drink a cup of peppermint tea.

It has been five days since Papá flew to Mexico with Frances. He hasn't rung me. Only Lola has been in contact with him. She laughed as she told me about the phone calls with him. The trip to the Frida Kahlo Museum. It was Frances who wanted to go. She had seen a movie about Frida. They took the metro and went on their own. Papá told Lola it was too expensive to take a tour. The metro was two dollars, and the tour was about forty dollars. He said, 'I'm not a *gringo* in Latin America, these Mexicans are not going to rob me.' So off they went on the metro. He said he and Frances were squashed like sardines, but they got there okay. The museum was full of old Spaniards on a tour. They tagged along and listened to the guide explain about the *casa azul* and the paintings. He had to keep translating so Frances could understand.

Apparently, he keeps telling Frances to be quiet, 'If you speak English, they will charge you double.'

Everywhere they go they have to say no chilli. He told Lola 'These Mexicans must have holes in their stomachs from so much chilli. Even chilli in their eggs for breakfast.'

He also reported that the beer is good. Frances thinks it's better than Australian beer. Frances, I can hardly bring myself to say her name. That woman who is so removed from everything my father believes in, what he's lived through. I still don't understand how it happened. We wanted a companion for him, a nice Latin American woman, with whom he could go out to the movies or dinner. But Frances. When he comes back from that ludicrous cruise it will all be over. The novelty will have worn off. Spending every single day with that woman for six weeks will make him see how unfitting it is. They're two worlds with nothing in common.

Why does Lola encourage Papá? She's the one who's usually so quick to judge, the one who clings to security. So much so that she married her own Uruguay and trapped herself in a safe bubble, her anxiety clawing at it until it burst. This is the Lola that tells me Frances is a good person and it's wonderful to see Papá happy.

Maybe because she's finally free she can see something I can't. Or this new freedom has made her delusional. Like when you first fall in love, and you see everything with your love-sick eyes and the world, and everyone in it, is glorious and just how it should be.

You know that my dad drinks beer now, I tell Chris as we enjoy the sunrise from the veranda. The pink light flitting through the trees.

He takes a sip from his cup of tea and smiles at me.

'Is that a statement or a judgement?'

It's neither, it's just weird. That woman, Frances, has put him onto it.'

'That's what it is. It's not that he drinks beer, it's her you don't like.'

I look over at the purple beans in the front vegetable garden. I'll pick some tonight for dinner. They taste incredible, lightly steamed, with a little olive oil drizzled over them.

'I didn't imagine someone like that for my dad. They have nothing in common.'

'Maybe that's the attraction, they are learning about each other's worlds.'

The day was swallowing the night as thin streaks of orange appeared.

'Chris, it's not a nice world she's showing him. It's the crass mainstream I despise. They go to the pub, the RSL. He no longer grows tomatoes. He doesn't complain about his bad knee. I don't know if he remembers he has a bad knee.'

'That's not a bad thing, the knee I mean.' Chris reaches over at takes my hand in his.

'We need to look at the positive in this Betts. Your father has someone to spend time with, he's giving your sister space and he's trying new things.

By the way, Sunshine liked her. That day they stopped here, Sunshine told me Grandpa's friend was going to take them on holidays and she had a cute little dog.'

The light of the stars now tucked away. Last night it was very clear and when I looked up, I saw *las tres marias*, in Orion's belt. Mum first pointed them out to me when we moved to Australia. She said we are still under the same sky and maybe that just brought us closer to home.

I know Chris is right, but it doesn't sit well for me.

'That's not going to be happening. Can you imagine, they would be fed sugar and white bread and biscuits.'

'Maybe you're stereotyping, you don't know that.'

I knew it. She was the mother of the Aussie girls at school, the woman who ran the school canteen, the supervisor at Kmart where I worked as a teenager. She was that woman. The women who served Australia in jobs where English was required. They smoked, ate white sliced bread and drank cups of tea with too much sugar. They kept the bland, ugly, soulless machine going.

'Apparently she's Aboriginal, that's what Lola said.'

'And that makes you feel bad you don't like her?' Chris was standing now looking down at me. He threw the bit of tea left in his cup over the veranda onto the garden.

'It's getting to you because if she's Aboriginal you think you need to feel different towards her, but you can't.'

'I'm not racist, this isn't about that, surely you understand Chris.'

'Then it's irrelevant if she's Aboriginal. Betts, you either like someone or you don't.'

Chris is right but the fact that she seems so removed from her Aboriginal culture makes me want to feel different. Maybe she too was robbed of her culture, like Lola claims to be, and made to adopt the worst of the English. When people are colonised, the psyche is invaded too. I don't know this woman and I can't be assuming things about her.

'I always wanted my parents to assimilate, to blend in. But not like this. My dad is letting in the parts of Australia I ran away from.'

'You are overthinking Betts, you've spent too much time with your sister lately.' He smiles at me, bends over, and kisses the top of my head. 'I'm going in to see if the kids are up.'

Maybe I am. I know how much I had to leave that world, how when I came to these lush valleys and rainforests, places of growth and beauty, I could erase the ugliness of what society does to people and places. Where there is no connection to the earth. Where there are malls and suburbs that all look the same. Where there's food that no longer looks like food, it's so removed from its origins. No one can think anymore because they are constantly fed entertainment, connected to society's crap, like a drip feeding you in a hospital.

I fear for my children too. I know one day they will want to move away and explore the world. I hope Chris and I have given them a solid grounding that will keep them independent, strong and able to find real happiness.

Happiness is such a strange thing. Am I happy? I believe I am. I have created the life I want for myself. A family I adore. I live in a beautiful part of the world. When I wake up in the morning, I look forward to the day ahead. Life makes me smile. I want that for Papá and Lola too. I need to give them time. Time to find themselves and what makes them happy. You can't find happiness in other people, only you can make yourself happy.

If I'm honest it doesn't matter whether I like Frances or not, she has helped Papá to move on, he will no longer be a backrest for Lola to fall onto and that will help Lola to find her own way.

LOLA

15 September 2012

Malena, Betty, Papá, Alex and I are all on different points across the earth. I don't think we have ever been spread out this much before. It's like the spaces that separate the way we view the world, which for many reasons can never quite come together.

I'm now living in what must be one of the most glorious places on the planet. I thought water views were for the rich but here I am a single parent with an ocean view. Of course, I thank Kerry for this. Every morning, I make my coffee and sit in the little sunroom, with the wooden window framing the ocean view like a painting. If it weren't for the movement in the water, I would think I'm looking at a painting.

I hear a car coming up the driveway and put my pen down. Kerry and Ella must be here. I go outside to meet them.

'Hey Lols,' Kerry shouts out as she closes the car door.

I look at my best friend and beam. 'Hi Kerry, hey Ella.'

Kerry takes me in an embrace. 'You look good Lola, more relaxed.'

'I'm hungry,' Ella tells me.

'That's my fault,' Kerry chips in. 'I refused to stop for food. I thought we could all go out for lunch.'

I look over at Ella. Her freckly face looks tired and flushed.

'Let's go inside and I'll make some sandwiches, we can go out later for a coffee and a walk on the beach. Ella go and get Daniel, he's in his room.'

Kerry and I walk up the driveway into the house, arm in arm.

'How is Daniel?' Kerry asks.

Daniel has settled well into life by the sea. He has new friends, and he goes to a lovely high school that's not too big like his previous school. It's a very white school. Rarely do I hear a language besides English on the streets here. What I've learned about this city is that the further you move away from the Steelworks, the whiter the suburbs become.

'He's good. He hasn't gone up to see Leo. They talk on the phone but that's about it.'

Kerry puts her bag down in the lounge room.

'Wow, this is so lovely, you've made it yours Lola. I can see you in every nook.'

I smile at her. 'Come let's go out the back and we can pick some basil for the bruschettas.'

I've never had such a big basil plant, and we smell its sweet minty fragrance before we see it.

As I pick the basil leaves, Kerry walks around the garden. She stops in front of the sunflowers. 'Did you plant these too?'

'Yep, aren't they amazing.'

'You've really blossomed here, Lola, pardon the pun.'

Leaving Leo has been so tough and painful. I felt like my insides were being ripped out. I could feel the pain in my body. At times it felt like when I first left Uruguay and Abuela was left behind and we screamed her name as we saw her wave us off and we were mustered onto the plane. We had to leave Uruguay to be free. And I had to leave Leo to be free.

'I'm getting there. I do feel vulnerable and it's still difficult, but I also feel stronger.'

'I can see it.'

'What about you Kerry? Everything okay with Gary?'

'Yeah, same, same. He's always working too much.'

We walk inside and I place the basil on the kitchen table and take out the tomatoes from the fridge. The ham is on the top shelf, and I take that out too. I know Daniel will want ham and tomato sandwiches.

Kerry takes off her sweater and sits at the table.

'Any news from Alex?'

I pick up a garlic head and rip two cloves of garlic to chop. 'He's doing well, settling into high school in Montevideo. The host family is great. I spoke to the mother when Alex rang. He spoke to me all in Spanish. I was impressed.'

I think of Alex and his need to go back to where it all started, to find his story and his reflection among those that look like him.

I cut the tomatoes into small pieces and add the basil and olive oil.

'What about your Dad and Frances, how are they going?' asks Kerry as she pops a piece of tomato, that's on the chopping board, into her mouth.

'They're good. The last I heard they had docked at the Bahamas.'

'I'd love to see Juan dancing on that boat.'

'Yeah, he's probably telling everyone they're doing it all wrong and he can show them how to dance.'

I grind salt into the tomatoes and basil mixture. 'You know what, Kerry, I'm happy for him and Frances. She's a good woman. Both her and my Dad have been through so much. They're survivors and they deserve happiness. Plus, they have fun together.'

We hear laughter coming from the lounge room followed by, 'Is lunch ready yet? We're hungry.'

'Kerry, can you butter the bread please.' I hand her the loaf and a knife.

'Five minutes guys,' I shout out.

'What about your job, are you liking it?'

I look at Kerry as she slathers butter on each slice of bread. Way more butter than I would use.

'I'm enjoying it more than I thought I would. It's a good team. The pathologist is friendly and patient. He took me to help him with a post-mortem last week.'

Kerry picks up a slice of ham and puts it on a slice of bread.

'That would have been confronting.'

'The weird thing is it wasn't. I didn't mind it. I actually liked it.'

She adds a slice of tomato over the ham and a slice of bread on top.

'Ella, Daniel, lunch,' I shout out.

The kids come in and sit at the kitchen table and take a sandwich each. I hand the bruschetta I just made to Kerry and finish adding the tomato mixture to mine.

'Do you want a bruschetta too Ella?'

'No, I'm okay with this. Daniel told me he is learning to surf. Can I learn too Mum?'

Before Kerry replies I say, 'You can come and stay in the holidays and do surf camp. What do you think Kerry?'

'Yeah, that sounds good.' She takes a bite into her bruschetta. 'Mmm, this is good.'

'Leif could come and stay too', Daniel adds. 'He's changing school, and he eats meat,' he tells Kerry and Ella.

'How does Betty feel about that?' Kerry asks.

'It's been difficult for Betty to accept but she can't keep them in her bubble forever.'

I think how funny it is that Betty feels we grew up with a black and white view of the world and she's become kind of a hippy fundamentalist. Of course, I would never say that to her, especially now that we've grown closer.

I look at Daniel, eating his sandwich.

'It's hard for teenage boys. Finding themselves amidst so much pressure about what they do, what they say, what they look like.'

I think of Simone's authenticity, while it sounds like psychologist babble, it means being true to yourself, knowing who you are, what your passion is.

'Your boys will grow into good men, Lola.'

Ella looks at Kerry and then me. 'It's hard being a girl too.'

Kerry smiles at her. 'Of course, it is, El, but Lola and I understand that more, because we were girls once too.'

'Can we go to the beach now?' Daniel asks as he stands up, chewing the last of his sandwich.

At the beach Kerry and I find a tree to sit under as we watch the kids in the water. It's hot for September, but I know the water will be cold. Coalcliff beach is one of the smaller beaches on this coastline, nestled between rocks and cliffs. Today the water is clear turquoise.

'This is such a beautiful part of the world,' Kerry says as she looks out at the ocean.

'Kerry, I need to tell you about something. I had sex with someone while I was with Leo. I can't even believe it myself. It sort of just happened.' I say it quickly as I look down at my feet.

I know that's what all people who cheat say. Cheat, I hate that word. I wasn't cheating, I was running. Running from a life I felt trapped in, running from my problems, running from myself and I didn't know where to go. He was there and he wanted me. It made me feel special. The thrill of kissing someone for the first time gave me a high and it shrouded all the dreadful feelings of anxiety, of loss, of grief. For that short time, I felt good. I forgot everything.

I can't look at Kerry's face.

'Lola, you know I wouldn't judge you. Life is complicated. You don't need to feel shame. Fuck women are always made to feel bad. I bet you men don't feel shame like that.'

Anxiety has stolen so much of my life and I need to reclaim some of it back. But I know what I did was wrong.

'You know what Lols, think of it as an exit strategy. It gave you the kick up the bum you needed to get your life back on track.'

'I love you Kerry.' I reach over and hug my old friend.

Then I stand up and take my t-shirt off.

Kerry looks at me. 'What are you doing?'

I pull my jeans off.

'I'm going in for swim.' I've been doing swimming lessons, and now I feel more confident in the water.

As I run out to the sea I shout out to Kerry, 'Last one in is a dirty rascal.'

Daniel comes up to me with the boogie board. 'Want to have a go Mum?'

He hands me the board.

I lie flat on the board and catch a wave, it lifts and pushes me forward, the cool water sprays my face. When I reach the shore I stand up and look over at Kerry, Daniel and Ella splashing in the sea. My feet are planted in the wet sand. I no longer feel afraid of the vastness before me.

ACKNOWLEDGEMENTS

This work has been a long time coming and there are many people and opportunities that made it possible.

I would like to thank the Newcastle Writers Festival for the Fresh Ink prize, which enabled me to continue writing this book. The support and work of Rosemarie Milsom to provide opportunities for new voices.

Thank you, Ed Wright, publisher at Puncher and Wattmann, for your valuable feedback and editing, and for making it possible for this story to be read and available in Australian bookshops.

My best friend and sister Gabi Martinez, who listened, read and provided feedback and who is always there for me.

Anne Hurni for taking the time to read a draft and provide feedback and conversation over many coffees.

Create NSW funding and Varuna, the beautiful writers house in the Blue Mountains. Both allowed me the space to focus on my writing, without thinking about work, cleaning and everything that needs fixing around my house.

Rita, who got me to pull out the beginning of the manuscript after it had been filed away in my computer for a few years.

Judi Morrison, for the cultural sensitivity report and generous feedback.

Abigail Nathan and Bernadette Foley, for their feedback in strengthening the story.

My children, always supportive of my creative work and willing to listen to me read out my work to them. My parents who migrated from the other side of the world, with no English and a primary school education. They encouraged my sister and I to get tertiary education and taught us about social justice.

A number of cafés, especially Double Ristretto and Bakers Wife in Springwood, where I sat to write, caffeinated and happy.

Thank you to Muurrbay for making the following dictionary accessible online. I used it to find a couple of words in language.

https://bundjalung.dalang.com.au/language/dictionary

www.ingramcontent.com/pod-product-compliance
Lightning Source LLC
Chambersburg PA
CBHW060347030726
47497CB00003B/633